SHRIMP & GRIT

SHRIMP & GRIT

A Tami Vaduva Novel

V.J. FITZ-HOWARD

Shrimp & Grit © 2020 by V.J. Fitz-Howard.

All rights reserved.

Published by Bloodwilde Press

No part of this book may be used, reproduced or transmitted in any form or by any means, electronic or mechanical, or by an information storage and retrieval system without permission in writing from the publisher.

This is a work of fiction. Names, characters, places, and incidents are either a product of the author's imagination or are used fictitiously, and any resemblance to actual persons, living or dead, business establishments, events or locales is entirely coincidental.

Published in the United States of America

ISBN (Paperback): 978-1-7342234-5-3
ISBN (Hardcover): 978-1-955039-03-1
ISBN (E-Book): 978-1-7342234-4-6

1.

"Where do you want me to put the U-joints, Mrs. Bland?" one of the Crabtree boys asked.

"On the top shelf, next to the powertrain assemblies."

"Yes, ma'am." He lifted the box overhead and slid it in the slot.

I heard beeps at the dock; his identical twin brother was backing up the forklift. He zipped around the corner. "Last load, ma'am. Where do you want it?"

I pointed.

"Yes, ma'am, Mrs. Bland," he said.

Honorably discharged from the United States Army only weeks prior, the boys—Dalton and Dustin Crabtree, whom I could not distinguish from each other—insisted on calling me "ma'am," or "Mrs. Bland," despite my invitation to address me in a more familiar manner.

After the last box of brake lubricant was loaded on the shelf, the twin operating the forklift slicked back his perspiration-soaked hair and said, "All done, ma'am."

I looked at my watch: zero-nine-thirty-six hours: twenty-four minutes to opening. "I am obliged to inform you gentlemen that under the provisions of the West Virginia Labor Code, section 21, subsections 3-10a, that during the course of a workday of six or more hours, all employers—*that means me*—shall make available for each of their employees—*that means you two*—at least two twenty-minute breaks."

The twin operating the forklift glanced over at his brother, whose thick red lips parted. "We was thinkin,' Mrs. Bland, that maybe we could have one of them ice cream socials, like yesterday."

I raised a skeptical eyebrow at the boys.

"Oh?"

The other twin smiled mischievously.

With my thumbnail, I scraped some grime lodged beneath the fingernail of my wedding ring-finger. When I was satisfied that they were sufficiently antsy for my reply, I looked up and said, "Single or double scoop?"

The first twin said, "Two scoops is always better than one, ma'am."

I directed Twin No. 1 to the corner of the stockroom, where broken-down cardboard boxes were scattered. Next, I instructed Twin No. 2 to go to the break room and fetch the Mountaineers blanket. Upon his return, he spread the blanket across the cardboard.

"Get out of those shirts, fellas."

Two robust "Yes, ma'ams!" followed. The boys peeled off their AutoMotives polo shirts.

Walking towards the corner, I pulled my polo over my head, unfastened and removed my bra, then laid down flat on my back, breasts jutting upward.

Each boy went to work on his respective "scoop."

Five minutes later, it was the twins' turn to be flat on their backs. I instructed them to lay side by side, but in opposite directions, like sardines in a tin. From face to beltline, neither brother had a mole, scar nor birthmark to differentiate him from his twin. If there was a weight differential between the two, it wasn't more than a pound.

I wedged myself between them and sat back, lowering myself slowly until my bottom rested on the heels of my sneakers. With each hand I unfastened belt buckles. When their skivvies were bunched up at the knees, I could finally tell them apart: as Dustin's veered right whereas Dalton's veered left.

I went to work on the fellas, hands pumping in opposite directions, like an oil derrick.

The Crabtree brothers—both of them with their hands folded behind their heads—grinned ear to ear. Handsome boys they were, too. But not *too* handsome. The blows they absorbed in service—when they boxed competitively on behalf of their regiment—knocked all the baby out of their faces.

I worked the boys with gusto. Presently Dalton looked up at me admiringly. "Ma'am, you're like a ragin' black stallion. That coal-black hair whipping back and forth like a horse's tail."

"And them big, black eyes," added Dustin. "Thoroughbred. Wild and Wonderful West Virginia through and through."

I told the boys they'd never believe it, but a few years before I'd been a blonde. "Ash-blonde," I said. "To be precise."

"Damn!" said Ricky.

"Even down there?" wondered Dalton, pointing at the crotch of my jeans.

"Even down there," I assured him. "Now you boys shut up."

I modulated my pace: fast-fast-fast, then slow-slow-slow, then fast-slow-fast, then slow-fast-slow.

A few minutes later, *"Oooooooooh,"* moaned Dustin.

"Ugggggggh," grunted Dalton two seconds after that.

"Now that I have paid you handsome young fellas the courtesy of lightening your loads," I explained. "I expect fifteen minutes' endurance from y'all."

The boys said they'd try their best.

We traded places on the mat again.

Just as we were about to start our go, Dustin looked up like a hound on point that just heard rustling leaves in a treetop. "Sounds like a CH-47 Chinook."

The boys looked skeptically at each other. Dustin furrowed his thick eyebrow. "A military transport chopper? At AutoMotives?"

"You're breaking my concentration, boys."

"Probably state troopers chasing some meth-head down the interstate, or an airlift to the hospital," Dustin surmised as his brother wadded up my panties and tossed them aside.

Dalton traced his finger over my pelvis. "It's a lie that blondes have more fun."

"Don't I know it, fellas."

"Roll over, ma'am," said Dustin.

I complied.

"M-m-m. Hard as concrete," Dalton said about my bottom.

I looked at my watch. "Fourteen minutes, boys."

Dustin asked if I could twist myself into that yoga pose from the day before.

I planted my palms and heels flat on the mat. The boys went to their spots and we had our go. Then the boys traded places and we had another go. The boys were in the process of trading again, for a third go, when Kandi's voice blasted over the P.A. system: "Mrs. Bland, come to the checkout. A man's here. Says it's urgent."

I jumped up and dressed.

"Dang it!" growled Dustin. "I was fixin' to—"

"—there'll be more breaks again tomorrow, boys. Meantime, you two get back to work."

2.

I zipped up, smoothed my hair and exited the storeroom.

When I saw the matching white helmets—them gigantic letters MP covering the men's foreheads—I froze. Then I smiled and approached casually. "May I help you gentlemen?"

The taller military policeman said, "Master Sergeant Luludja Vaduva, aka Tami Vaduva, D.O.D. identification number 1406711298, I'm serving a federal warrant for your arrest—for being absent without leave from your post. You will be held temporarily in a local jail until you are transferred to a military jail, where you will remain until you have a military court date, where you will be tried for desertion."

The short one reached for the handcuffs on his belt.

I raised hands, baring empty palms for inspection. "You've made a mistake, gentlemen. I'm not the woman you're looking for. My name is Tamsin Venables Bland. Let me show you my I.D." I reached around to my back pocket for my wallet.

"Don't move, ma'am!" the tall one said.

"But I can prove I'm who I say I am."

"We're taking you into custody, ma'am," the short one said.

Kandi the cashier went white. "Are you in trouble, Tamsin?"

"Everything's okay, Kandi. Just a misunderstanding. Take ten dollars out of the drawer and go fetch me a kale salad from

Panera." Her hands shaking, she pulled a ten-dollar bill out of the drawer. After she exited, I sharpened my tone with the MPs: "I'm Tamsin Venables Bland, widow of Colonel Cletus Esmond Bland III. I'm not absent from any Army post."

"We don't want trouble, ma'am," the short one said as both MPs lowered their hands to their holsters. "And don't think we weren't warned that you might make cause it. But we're prepared to give it to you. We've got backup out on the lot."

One of the Crabtree boys appeared. "Everything okay, Mrs. Bland?"

"This is a United States Army matter," the tall one said.

"I'm former Unites States Army, and Mrs. Bland is my employer, so I reckon it's a matter that concerns me, too."

"If you're ex-military, then you know 'whoever harbors, conceals, protects, or assists any such person who may have deserted from such service, knowing him to have deserted therefrom, or refuses to give up and deliver such person on the demand of any officer authorized to receive him, shall be fined or imprisoned not more than three years, or both.'"

The Crabtree boy looked at me curiously. "You're military, Mrs. Bland?"

I waved the Crabtree boy away. "Go back to the stockroom. Assemble that new shelving stacked along the east wall."

"You're sure?"

"*Git!*"

"Yes, ma'am!"

Two additional MPs appeared outside the front door.

The tall one took his handcuffs off his belt. "Present your wrists, ma'am. Or the four of us will haul you out. If this is the mistake you claim it is, you'll get a fair hearing before a military court."

The two in front of me I could have taken out. The two outside would have then come in, weapons drawn. They wouldn't have shot me. But then what? The mad dash to the stockroom, then jump off the loading dock and make a run for it? Where? Up in the hills? Back to Charlottesville? And what about my son? I couldn't figure out which would be a worse outcome for him: to become a ward of the state or get put under the supervision of my mother, who wasn't exactly the read-Dr. Seuss-to-your-grandchild or warm-cookies-and-milk sort of grandmother. After war-gaming my many bad options, I decided I'd go with them—and figure out an escape route later. The four MPs escorted me to the chopper without incident.

⌒

We landed on the parking lot of the Southern Regional Jail, located in Fayette County, West Virginia. It was a long, low-slung, gray cinderblock facility—like somebody squished a Walmart supercenter into a Big Lots into a Dollar Store.

While I was processed by the local jailer, the tall MP asked, did I have a lawyer?

"Cameron Smallwood. In Charlottesville. I want to talk to him now."

"We'll track him down for you."

The four MPs, along with the jailer, formed a protective ring around me—like they had just brought one of the 9/11 perpetrators into custody—and gang-escorted me to my cell.

"Under the law, I'm the one who makes the call."

"We'll make the call, master sergeant."

"I'm not 'master sergeant.' I'm Tamsin Vena—"

"—Turn right, just after that water fountain," the jailer said.

We walked down a long corridor. At the end was a big holding cell. Three women were already inside. Two African-American teenage girls who reeked of pot and a middle-aged Caucasian woman who reeked of pee.

"I want my lawyer!"

The guard placed the palm of his hand between my shoulder blades and nudged me into the cell. The door clinked shut behind me. "We'll be back shortly, ma'am."

I took a second look at my fellow cellmates, who were putting on attitude, like on all those gals-in-jail T.V. shows. I was gearing up for a fight. Which was the alpha-female who'd start calling me the c-word and try to make me vacate my seat or yank my hair?

But the girls ignored me.

We all sat there, on concrete benches, gazing in opposite directions. At first, my mind raced. *How did they find me? When would Cameron Smallwood arrive? What would happen to my son? My business?*

In time, though, I put these thoughts out of my mind. My training had taught me you don't fret over what you can't control in the future; you focus on the moment.

Which I did. Until there was no more on-the-moment-focusing to be done.

My mind next took me back to my military tours. To shootouts in Kandahar City and Karz. The six weeks' mountain warfare training I did in the Pamir Mountains—in the Gorno-Badakhshan province of Tajikistan. My surveillance work in Al-Karkh. The time I was hooked up to a car battery with jumper cables, after I was captured by ISIS.

. . . And the time I spent with Colonel Bland—on parade grounds, in combat, and, later, in his bunk, where our son was conceived.

After those topics were exhausted, I got so bored I started playing an imaginary game of checkers on the tiled wall.

Finally, one of the black girls, the one with glasses, spoke. "What you in for?"

"Nothing. Case of mistaken identity."

The girl grinned. "Me too."

"Same with me," said her friend.

"Just M.M.O.B," said the third inmate, the white woman with the stringy black hair and tattooed eyes.

Gruff laughter from all three.

"'M.M.O.B.'?" I asked.

"Minding my own business. There I was, just minding my own business," the white woman said. "Next thing I realize, I'm cuffed, sitting in back of a police cruiser."

"Always happen that way," one of the black girls said.

The gals laughed amongst themselves yet another time.

"What about you ladies?" I asked the black girls.

"Shoplifting," the black girl in glasses said.

"Trying on ain't the same as stealing," said her friend.

"But wearing it out of the store is," the white woman mumbled.

I looked at her. I reckoned she was my mother's age. "What about you?" I asked.

"Hillbilly heroin."

After sustaining injuries during combat, I was on more than one occasion offered OxyContin. I always refused.

It went quiet again, for about ten minutes, until the white gal said, "What'd you do?"

"Like I said, I'm innocent."

She rolled her eyes.

Two hours passed. The white woman, who was reclined on a bench of her own, chewing her nails, kept stealing glances at me. She looked at me, spat a sliver of fingernail at the floor, and said, "I know you."

"I don't think so."

"What's your name?"

"Tamsin Venables Bland."

"No, it ain't."

I shrugged and stared out through the bars. "If you say so."

About five minutes passed, at which time she said, "You went to Fayette High."

"I wasn't educated here. I'm actually new to town."

"Bullshit." Her glassy eyes, encircled by a constellation of miniature blue-black star tattoos, blinked heavily, like she was struggling to bring my face into focus. "Don't pretend you don't know what I'm talking about. I was a year behind you at Fayette. I dated Scooter Skinner one summer. I know you were friends with him—and that even bigger idiot, Ricky Ray Jeeter. You drove that El Camino."

I ignored her.

She started gnawing on her pinkie. "Ain't you gonna ask me my name?"

I stared hard at her, pretending we were strangers. Good Lord, was that really her? Last time I saw her she was young and juicy, like over-ripe fruit. Now she looked like a beggar in Helmand Province, Afghanistan. "Sorry, forgive my manners. What's your name?"

"Donna-Lynn Deneen. But you already know that."

"I'm quite certain we've never met." I felt like Judas Iscariot, denying I knew her. But I couldn't afford to blow my cover by being sympathetic to my former classmate. I put on the blank, fake smile I was taught to display when I lived in Charlottesville. *Come, Cameron, come now! Get me out of here.*

"Stuck up bitch," she mumbled.

"If you say so."

I turned my head, pretending a speck of dust just landed in my eye. I licked my index finger and rolled it across my eyeball. From the corner of my opposite eye I watched her slump on to her side and drift into sleep.

Another hour passed.

A loud buzzer sounded. The four MPs, along with the jailer, appeared at the cell door. "You," said the tall MP, pointing at me.

3.

The guard escorted me into an interrogation room with a two-way-mirrored-wall. "Wait here." He locked the door from the outside.

It was hot as blazes in there. They must have turned up the heat to enhance the discomfort. I sat there, tapping my fingers on the steel table, regretting that my fingernails were neither long nor painted turquoise or coral.

It wasn't a minute before the door clicked open.

In walked General Peter D. Loehr —now *Major* General Loehr, he had acquired a second star since I had last seen him in Charlottesville, and before that, during my military tours, in Afghanistan.

I pretended not to recognize him. "You're not my attorney," I said as I rose to my feet, reflexively. Which I regretted instantly because Tamsin Venables Bland did not leap up and snap to attention when men came into the room; she continued to nibble on her *amuse-bouche* or pick at her kale salad until, eventually, she looked up at the man with polite indifference.

"You'd rather talk to me."

I shot a pleasant glance his way. "Have we met before?"

He smiled mischievously. "You tell me."

I had to get out of Tami Vaduva mode and back into Tamsin

Venables Bland mode. Had I met him when I was a civilian? Then I remembered: we had. Once. "Yes. Now I remember," I said as I took my seat and regulated my breathing. "You're . . ." I leaned in and pretended to read his nametag. "General Loehr. Yes, of course. You were my husband's commanding officer in Afghanistan."

"Go on." The general sat down. He set the aluminum briefcase, handcuffed to his wrist, on the table.

"We met a few years back, when my husband and I hosted that Wounded Warrior fundraiser in Charlottesville. You arrived by helicopter. Made quite an entrance. On the night he . . ."

"Colonel Cletus Bland was a good soldier and a good American. He died a hero's death."

"I miss him every day. But not as much as our son, Cletus Bland IV, does."

We each took a moment of silence to honor my fallen husband, during which time the general sized me up. "Unbelievable."

I almost replied, *Sir?* But I caught myself. "Whatever do you mean?"

"What you pulled off. Truly unbelievable."

"I don't understand."

"I tip my hat to you, Master Sergeant Vaduva. If anybody could've gotten away with it, it could only be you."

"You were my husband's commanding officer, general, and he held you in high esteem. But—"

"'—*esteem*.' Now that wasn't one of your vocabulary words when you were Master Sergeant Tami Vaduva."

"I am Mrs. Tamsin Venables Blan—"

"—That I never put two and two together at that fundraiser

is a testament to your unrivaled skills at deception. Salt-of-the-earth Master Sergeant Tami Vaduva of West Virginia, the most highly decorated female in U.S. Army history, a sharp-shooter with fifteen hundred kills, not all of them official, and chest-full of medals, the most successful undercover operative in the military theater, goes A.W.O.L. from her post in Afghanistan. I've got men looking for her across a dozen time zones. Then, a year and a half later, unbeknownst to me, she's standing right in front of me, offering me a glass of lemonade with a little mint sprig in it, on her two-thousand-acre Virginia horse farm. She's blonde now. Green-eyed. Elegant. Poised beyond belief. All the rough edges sanded down. She's the young, devastatingly attractive, blue-blooded second wife of retired U.S. Army Colonel Cletus Bland—not the brunette who sites before me, with those legendary coal-black eyes."

"I'm the same woman I was when I was married to Cletus Bland. I just changed my look. Women do this all the time, general. Not uncommon when a woman is widowed and compelled to start over, either."

"For appearance' sake, you might at least have stuck with the disguise, master sergeant—including that fake British-aristocratic accent you were deploying when I met you at your fundraiser, which must have done quite a number on my old Anglophile pal Cleet." The general turned the combination wheel on the aluminum briefcase and popped it open. "This," he said as he slid the photograph across the table, "is your photo when you were in Kandahar, while under my command."

I glanced uninterestedly at the photo. "I can't say I see the resemblance."

"Your teeth were crooked back then. And if you don't mind my saying, rather on the yellow side. Not the perfectly straight, pearly whites before me today." He slid the photo back in front of him and studied it carefully, looked back up at me, then down at the picture again. "The underbite is gone. That must have cost a fortune. And then there's your nose—a regal new one, so it appears." He rolled his chair away from the table, leaned back, pulled a handkerchief out of his pocket and blotted his forehead. "So tell me . . . *'Mrs. Bland,'* what do you find so alluring about West Virginia as opposed to, say, London, or Rome, or Monte Carlo—which is where most European blueblood widows with fifty million dollars in stocks, bonds, and cash would make their new home?"

"I honeymooned here with my husband, floating on the New River, and was enchanted by the region's rugged beauty—which rivals Gonarezhou National Park, in Zimbabwe's lowlands, and, to some extent, the Verdon Gorge in Alpes-de-Haute-Provence, if you've ever been there."

"Listen to you: *'Alpes-de-Haute-Provence.'* How long did you have to practice pronouncing that one until you could say it?" He wiped his forehead again.

"You're very rude. Has anyone ever told you that?"

"Every day." He folded the handkerchief like a flag and tucked it in his pocket. "The Widow Bland. Working retail, at an AutoMotives store."

"I'm the owner. I have a store over in Dawson, too."

"You weren't an easy woman to find, I can tell you that. Last seen walking out of a Charlottesville with all your earthly possessions stuffed in a backpack. No forwarding address. No listing in any phone book. No email address. No presence in social media. Vanished. *Poof!* A blueblood widow inherits a twenty million dollar estate—which you sold to some queer antiques dealer for one dollar—then saunters out of town with the remaining fifty million dollars of her deceased husband's estate and decides to grab her princely son by the wrist and drag him to . . . Ninth Circle of Hell, West Virginia. Which, coincidentally, just happens to be the hometown of Master Sergeant Tami Vaduva, who went A.W.O.L." The general took his reading glasses from his pocket, folding and unfolding them as he continued. "Want to know how I found you?"

"The question presumes I was hiding from you."

He rocked back and forth in the chair. "The first point of contact after a soldier goes A.W.O.L. is of course next of kin. After you first went missing, I sent a man over to Thurmond, to see your mother and extended family." He plucked a manila folder out of the briefcase, laid it flat on the table and opened it. He scowled as he read. "I'm not going to repeat some of the more colorful epithets your mother . . . Luludja Vaduva, aka Velvet Vaduva, hurled at my representatives. But suffice to say your mother was *exceedingly* uncooperative. But if I am one thing, as you well know, it's persistent. So, I sent my men back, repeatedly, at least a dozen times, over a thirty-six-month period. The following three attempts were aborted after your mother unleashed a crazed and possibly rabid dog—a Rottweiler-Chow Chow mixed breed called 'Bitch' —on investigators. But we kept coming back. By which time our engagements became something of a game for her. She had a different story every time. 'She was always too big for her britches, too good for this place. You won't find her around here,' she said during one subsequent interview. You were always somewhere else: you mopped up crime scenes in Cleveland; you were a rodeo girl in Arizona; you were a palm-reader in San Francisco; an Avon Lady in . . ." He put his readers back on and scooped the word up off the page. ". . .

Petrești. Some remote Romanian village. The tall tales kept coming. But we didn't give up. You should be flattered, master sergeant. The Unites States Army never expends this kind of effort to track down an ordinary soldier who's gone A.W.O.L. But, then again, you're no ordinary soldier, are you? You're a prized asset. And your government invested a lot of training in you. So we kept going back. We threatened her with jail time. Velvet laughed in my MPs' faces, telling them she'd been jailed several times in the past and we were welcome to lock her up again, especially if it meant she could, and I quote, 'Get the fuck away from them dried-out old fossils in the bedroom,' end quote."

Mama's relationship with those "dried-out old fossils in the bedroom"—my grandmama Marlene and great-grandmama Charlene— had always been strained, but had in recent years deteriorated as my mama, who was not a natural caregiver, was now required to repeat things five times in a row, bring meals to their room, administer enemas, and perform other unpleasant tasks.

"So you ready to hear how we got her to talk?"

I sighed theatrically. "I'm profoundly uninterested."

"My men were down about a month ago. When they got on property, a van was there. Two men were on your mother's lawn, warding off that dog. My men confronted them. They announced they were there to re-possess one of those tabletop electronic blackjack machines, like you'll find in bars. Your mother was behind on payments. She told my MPs she'd disclose your whereabouts in exchange for the paying off the balance with the repo men so she could keep her video game. My men, the idiots, refused, explaining that under no circumstances did the United States Army pay rewards for information received concerning the whereabouts of absentees and deserters. Once I learned this, after my blood pressure settled, I decided it was time for me to make the trip. So, a week ago I choppered down from D.C.—with a payload that consisted of two pub chairs and one of those glass-topped wine-barrel tables with video games built into it: blackjack, poker, craps, roulette. Sixty games in all. When she greeted me at the door, I was shocked. I recognized her instantly. Know how?"

I did, but I wasn't going to tell the general that.

"I met her at the Wounded Warriors fundraiser you and Cleet hosted, when you were blushing newlyweds up in Charlottesville." He reached into his pocket and unwrapped a cigar—the same kind he taught Colonel Bland to smoke in Afghanistan. He bit at the tip. "Hard woman to forget. When I met her at your fundraiser, she was leaning against the side of a Brink's armored car, blowing smoke rings. She boasted about some sort of 'female surgery' she'd just had—and made some off-color remark about drunk cheerleaders." A sour look came over the general's face. "Now what on earth would a woman from rural West Virginia be doing at a fundraiser on a twenty million dollar horse farm in Albemarle County, Virginia? She wouldn't have known Cletus Bland or his fancy new supposedly British wife, would she?"

I sat there, stone-faced, pretending I was bored as I peeled the label back on the water bottle. The mistake in situations like these was to start talking, to make blocking or diversionary statements. I remained silent.

"Long story short, we haggled. For three hours. She said the gaming table was of no use to her if she didn't have cigarettes, Jack Daniels, a case of Bud Light Lime, and an ample supply of Flamin' Hot Nacho Cheese Doritos. So, I sweetened the pot.

Next thing I know, she tells me you're just up the road—at the AutoMotives store."

I reckoned the general could see my face was reddening. I was going to kill my mama next time I saw her. She'd been either stealing my money or trying to make money off me in unethical ways since I was a girl. I had been more than generous to my mama and hers since I had come into my inheritance, too. I deposited money in her account monthly. Of which she blew every penny, mostly on lotto tickets, cartons of Eve Menthol Ultra Lights 120s—which she had shipped from Alabama weekly by FedEx since you can't get them in West Virginia no more. She also spent lavishly on beer, Bob Evans takeout, country music cassette tapes at the truck stop, and imported paprika. She bought more than a dozen different paintings done by some local pothead artist she knew: pictures of a pug dog wearing various wigs (blonde, redhead, mohawk, afro). She spent on anything and everything—except paying her bills.

"And so, here we are."

Someone knocked on the door. The general consulted, in whispering tones, with one of the MPs, who handed the general an envelope. When he returned to the table, I said, "You've got nothing, general. Just the word of some crazy woman who claims I'm this soldier you're looking for."

"I've got this."

"What?"

The general opened the envelope and showed me its contents. "A locket of your hair."

"So?"

"Oh, I've also got this." The general reached into his briefcase and pulled a packet out. He waved it before me. "Your mother's hair. Cost me an extra twenty-five dollars, but worth every penny. Your mother said we'd find Gypsy—or Romani—DNA in her hair. And that we'd find it in yours, too. Not a lot of Romanians in these parts, is there? Something tells me her DNA will match the hair samples we sourced from your prison cell." He let his message sink in a moment, then shifted his tone from sarcastic to menacing. "I have the authority to put you in Leavenworth, Master Sergeant Vaduva."

It wasn't Leavenworth I feared but the realization I was out of options—especially when I considered the fate of my son. The time had come to surrender. "What do you want from me, general?"

"So the implications of Leavenworth sunk in, master sergeant?"

"I've been in far worse spots than prison—as you well know. With all respect, sir, what it is you want?"

"Your service."

"I served my country already."

"Better than anybody else. All those medals: intelligence work, enhanced interrogation techniques, weapons proficiency, languages, PSYOPs, surveillance, and chemical weapons expertise."

"I have a new life here. I'm raising a son."

"What do you suppose his father would make of you shirking your duty when called upon?"

"I fulfilled my duties, sir. And then some. I also have custody of a stepdaughter. Colonel Bland's daughter from his first marriage. My duty now is to my family, my employees, and my community. My deceased husband would honor me for that."

"*My* duty is to protect this country—and you're the only person I know who is capable of supporting me on this operation." He explained that he was now stationed at the Pentagon, as head of United States Army Special Operations Command.

"What operation?"

The general sifted through the briefcase and handed me a sealed gray packet stamped TOP SECRET in red ink. "Open it."

"No."

"What do you mean 'no'?"

"My son and I fly out of Dulles tomorrow night for Switzerland."

"Not if I send you to Leavenworth."

"It's parents' weekend at my stepdaughter Augusta's school. I'm not missing it."

"Do you not understand that you are in my custody, soldier?"

"I understand this very well, general."

"You'd really go to jail rather than miss parents' weekend?"

"If I had to. I have new responsibilities now."

"We're flying back to the Pentagon. Together. Now."

"I'm not coming to the Pentagon, general. I don't want to go to jail, but I am prepared to."

"Open the folder."

"Under one condition."

"What?"

"You furlough me for seventy-two hours, so I can go to Switzerland. After that, you own me."

The general drummed his fingers on the tabletop while he considered my proposal. "Granted."

"Really?"

"I waited this long. Three more days won't kill me."

"You're not worried I'd go A.W.O.L. in Europe?"

"Not in the least. I don't see you hiding out across the continent in five-star luxury hotels when you'd prefer to be in a one-room cabin in West Virginia. Nor do I believe for a moment you'd be of service to me in prison—which, let's not fool each other, master sergeant, you'd break out of twenty-four hours after your arrival. You're coming back into service because you love this country." He tapped his index finger on the gray packet. "And when you find out what these bastards are doing, you will say—as a solider, a patriot, and as a *mother*, 'I WILL NOT LET THIS STAND.'"

I studied the packet. I was not looking forward to the disruption the general was about to cause my family.

He pounded his fist on the table. "Open the goddamned envelope!"

I opened the packet, thirty seconds into my perusal I pulled back the tears welling in my eyes and said, "I'll see you in your office on Monday, sir."

"It's going to be dark in the tunnel, son."

"I ain't scared of the dark, mama," Cleet IV said.

"'I'm *not* scared of the dark,'" I corrected before silently chastising myself for allowing my son to spend so much time at his grandmama's house, where bad habits—grammatical being the least of them—were forged.

I chastised myself as well for letting the grammatical instruction I had so keenly taken to in Charlottesville—at my social mentor Shelby Nash's insistence—elapse. I needed to start listening to those grammar podcasts again, and do so double-quick.

When we emerged from the tunnel, the light was blinding as the sun ricocheted off the snow-capped Alps. Cleet IV observed that Montreux, Switzerland, looked a lot like Thurmond, West Virginia, which in fact it did: steep mountains, gray mist, and snaky roads with stone fencing to prevent drivers from veering over the cliffs and plunging to their death.

Looking down on Lake Geneva, I too was reminded of home—though the Lake was a lot bluer than the New River with its green-grey hue. I looked out the window and thought about my step-girl, Augusta. After her father, Cleet III, died, and her biological mother's repeated "episodes," culminating in her eventual abandonment of the girl, the courts assigned stewardship to me. I did my best to win her affections, but she would have none of it. At Digby Day, her school in Charlottesville, she fell in with a bad crowd, culminating, eventually, in her expulsion. I thought that fighting terrorists was exhausting business. A walk in the park compared to raising a teenage girl. All parties, in the end, agreed boarding school would suit her best.

I glanced over at my son, whose bright black eyes sparkled as he flipped through a Sally Mann picture book featuring pictures of naked girls his age—a birthday gift from his grandmama, who stole the book at a yard sale in Beckley, West Virginia.

"*Voilà!*" the taxi driver said. The iron gates to *'Institut de Dialectique,'* Augusta's fancy boarding school, stood right in front of the cab like a pair of upmarket prison bars.

After the guards cleared us and the gate, we entered the grounds. The school, a converted monastery dating back to the 1400s, was situated on thirty-five hundred hectares. After passing the stables, ski slopes, tennis courts, thermal baths, gymnasium, faculty apartments, academic buildings, science laboratories, amphitheater, infirmary, library, chapel, football pitch, rugby pitch, archery and shooting ranges, dining hall, and running track, we arrived at the student dormitories.

When Cleet IV and me exited the taxi, a lovely girl in riding attire—the future Crown Princess of Yugoslavia, according to the girl next to her, who boasted her daddy was CEO of the airline we flew to Switzerland—pointed to a nearby building and told me Augusta's room was on the third floor.

Cleet IV, leaping three steps at a time, beat me in our race to the top of the stairs. Halfway down the corridor, a hand-carved nameplate on the suite door read MADEMOISELLE BLAND.

"Bonjour, Augusta!" I shouted as I rapped on the door, which gently swung open. Her suite was empty: no bedding, no clothing, no computer or books on the desk, and no stuffed animals or skis stacked in the corner. The walls were stripped bare of the posters and other artwork I expected to see.

I directed cross-legged Cleet IV to the bathroom, then went to the window, where I scanned the grounds, sifting through the faces in search of Augusta.

"Madam Bland?"

I turned to see a silver-haired man, rail-thin, who stood erect in a suit so tight it looked as though a button would burst.

"We weren't sure you'd come," the man said in a thick accent. Mr. Christophe Saint-Dufay, the school's director, introduced himself.

"Where's Augusta?" I demanded, making sure to use my cosmopolitan accent.

He pushed his index finger into the bridge of his wire-rimmed glasses and looked disapprovingly through the doorway, where a knot of eavesdropping students congregated. "Perhaps we should go to my office, where I can offer you some tea and a light lunch. One imagines you're famished after all that traveling."

"Where's Augusta?"

"Let us adjourn to my office."

"Why is her room empty?"

"Yes, then. Please do follow me." The director, waving the crowd away, issued fancier versions of "Skedaddle!" to the students in English, Russian, Italian, and Arabic.

On the walk to his office, he avoided my questions and directed my attention to the pile of rubble that was once the swimming pool, apologizing for the mess and assuring me its replacement, designed by the same architect who built the pool for the 1992 Olympic Games in Barcelona, would be the grandest pool in Switzerland.

"I'm not so sure about that," I said.

Inside his office, for the fifth time, I demanded to know where my daughter was.

"She's perfectly safe, Madam Bland."

"Is she in hospital?"

"No."

"Was she expelled?

"No."

"Then where is she?"

"Nearby, to be sure. Always nearby." He served Cleet IV and me a cup of tea. "The occasional absence of our students, despite the extraordinary security measures undertaken to ensure the children are at all times protected on our grounds, is not uncommon at a school like this, I'm afraid. Our students—many of them rebellious teens, all of them with ready access to cash and credit—view the gated property, plainclothes guards, security cameras, and motion detectors as rivals to be outwitted. They slip away to go boating on Lake Geneva, or to Gstaad, after the first big snowfall, to ski. Their methods are as ingenious as they are maddening to school administrators. Smuggled out in laundry vans, food trucks, and FedEx vehicles—often after proffering lavish bribes. They build makeshift ladders and ziplines. They go into town on school busses with a duplicate set of clothes and pay local teens to impersonate them on the bus ride home." He poured himself a cup of tea and sipped daintily. "But they always come back."

"Except for Augusta."

"Who, I assure you, is safe." A team of chefs arrived, with

hot plates, bowls overflowing with steaming potatoes, baby pickles, onions, and cold cuts. "Please, Madam Bland, be my guest. Enjoy some *raclette*," he said as a white-gloved man served the vegetables then scraped warm, gooey cheese onto our plates.

I ignored the food. "Where *IS* she?"

"One of any number of hotels in Montreux." He consulted a legal pad. "She took a suite at the Hotel Des Trois Couronnes on the fifth of the month. Then, eight days later, moved on to Le Mont-Pelerin. She next took rooms at the Palace. And on the twenty-fourth hired the penthouse suite at the Eurotel. Our security team has her under constant surveillance."

"She keeps switching hotels. Is she being evicted? Are there boys involved? Drugs?"

"According to Prince Chai Son Thamrongnawasawat—one of her classmates—she keeps switching hotels in search of a cheeseburger that meets what are apparently her very exacting culinary standards. If it's any consolation, you'll be hearted to know she's eating well." Mr. Saint-Dufay handed me a stack of photographs, all sourced from the prince's phone: two dozen selfie images of grinning Augusta biting into cheeseburgers at various hotel restaurants.

"Where's she now?"

"At the Eurotel."

"Why wasn't I notified when all this started?"

"Oh, I assure you, Madam Bland, we've tried. *Repeatedly!* At the Charlottesville, Virginia, address and phone number we had on file upon Augusta's enrollment." He showed me the dates and times he had placed calls, copies of letters sent, and so on. "A Mr. Shelby Nash, the new owner of the home, was keen to help in any way he could, but said he had no idea how to reach you. It goes without staying, of course, that on multiple occasions we entreated Augusta to put us in touch, but she was, alas . . ."

"Unhelpful?"

"Quite."

"She blocks my calls."

"I take it, then, that you and your step-daughter are . . . *estranged*."

I stood and scraped the glob of cheese off my son's chin with my thumbnail. "For one hundred fifty-six thousand dollars a year, Mr. Saint-Dufay, I expect your people to know how to secure a compound. Summon a car and driver for me. I'm going to fetch my daughter."

5.

Augusta was not at the Eurotel. Nor was she back at the other hotels on Mr. Saint-Dufay's list.

"Look in the designer shops. Avenue du Casino," the general manager at the Le Mont-Pelerin said.

Cleet IV and I pounded the pavement, showing Augusta's photo to clerks at Gucci, Prada, Dolce & Gabbana, Cartier, Chanel, and Louis Vuitton. All of them smiled with recognition when they saw her photograph, though none could—or would—provide details on her whereabouts. The girl at Louis Vuitton said she saw Augusta earlier that morning, walking into the McDonald's on the Place du Marche. Augusta was wearing an Yves Saint-Laurent poncho. Beige. Made out of goat fur, she said, admiringly.

When I presented the photo to the manager at the McDonald's, he recognized Augusta immediately. A "client fréquent," he said. She had been in earlier, he reported. Had had a Double McBacon burger with frites and the *frappé saveur* vanilla. She arrived alone, he said, but met a man in his late twenties at the counter soon afterward. "'Un personnalité,' even by Montreux standards," the manager clucked, shaking his head disapprovingly as he described the man's open-chested white silk shirt and burnt-orange double-breasted suit, worn above blue crocodile-skin loafers.

I told the manager it was urgent I locate my daughter.

"She walks along the *Quai des Fleurs* after lunch. Feeds the ducks. We give her stale buns, no charge."

I did not like the looks of the *Quai des Fleurs*. At its entrance, police barricades were erected. Police cars, a fire truck, two ambulances. Gridlock traffic. A big mob of spectators gathered beside an overturned Citroën, where a paramedic was plucking shards of glass out of the forehead of an old woman who sat upright on the ground, her head bloody.

I elbowed my way to the center of the crash scene: No sign of Augusta, thank God. We forced our way through the crowd, weaving through the idling cars.

There was no sign of Augusta at the waterfront, either. Though I did notice that a cluster of ducks was demolishing a discarded McDonald's bag.

"Where you suppose she's gone?"

"I don't know, son," I said, squeezing Cleet IV's wrist harder than I should have as I dragged him along the sidewalk.

Ahead was a maze of buildings, cobblestoned passageways, delivery trucks, construction sites: she could have been anywhere. Or nowhere.

"Augusta!" my son shouted. Cleet IV spotted her on the Quai, riding shotgun in a red convertible.

Dashing to the car with Cleet IV in tow, I yanked open the passenger door. "Get out, Augusta!"

Shocked and awed—at first—her expression morphed into outrage. "What are you doing here?"

The driver, a man in an orange suit, threw up his hands in disgust. "Who is this crazy woman?"

"This 'crazy woman' is Augusta's mother!"

Augusta turned to the driver. "She's *not* my mother. She's my stepmother." Then she turned to me, scanned me up and down, and gasped. "My God, what happened to you? That hair! You were a blonde last time I saw you and now you look like Kim Kardashian!"

"You're coming with me!"

The driver hurled a one-word insult, something nasty in his native tongue—Spanish, Italian, Portuguese—something Mediterranean.

"Silenzioso!" I barked.

"I'm not going anywhere with you!" Augusta yelled. "I can do what I want. I'm a senior!"

I grabbed her by the wrist and dragged her from the car.

The driver reached over and attempted to break my grip and that's when I saw his hands. Tattoos. Three dots in a triangle formation on each middle finger. Right quick, I snapped the radius bone on his forearm, just below his elbow.

"Boceta!" he shrieked, as he bobbed forward in the driver's seat and shook his bloody arm.

"You have no idea," I told him. It wasn't the first time I had been called a "cunt." Among a certain set of recalcitrant perverters of Islam to whom I had issued one-way tickets either to Guantanamo or Hell, the insult had been directed at me in Farsi, Arabic, Urdu, Saraiki, Pashto, Sindhi, and Balochi.

I loaded Augusta over my shoulders in a fireman's carry.

"Put me down!"

"You're coming with me!"

"You can't tell me what to do. YOU'RE NOT MY MOTHER!"

I hauled her along the Quai. "I'm your legal guardian, girl. And until you're of legal age, I tell you what to do."

Augusta writhed and kicked. "Enough of the 'girl' bullshit, Tamsin. You're not that much older than me."

"Old enough to be your mother!" At least where I grew up, although I didn't elaborate on that one.

"*Step*mother."

The spiky goat fur on her poncho scraped against my cheeks and neck as the pedestrians disbursed. Near the entrance to the pharmacy, I yanked the purse from her wrist.

"That's a Birkin!"

I handed the bag to Cleet IV and instructed him to open it up. "I better not find cigarettes, weed, or birth control pills in there!"

"That's my property!"

The passport was at the bottom, below the iPhone, gum, breath mints, hand sanitizer, scrunchie, lip gloss, wrist wallet, dreamcatcher, hairbrush, tube of "Better Than Sex" mascara, iPod, iPad, earbuds, Toblerone bar, and sunglasses. "We're going home!"

Augusta was still kicking when I stuffed her into a cab. "To the airport!" I directed the driver.

"I need my clothes!"

"You'll get new ones."

"*Bitch!*"

I slapped her. "You don't talk to me that way!"

She burst into tears. Cleet IV removed the bandana from his pocket and handed it to his sister, who refused to look at me as she wiped her tears.

"Don't ever get into a car with a man you don't know. *Ever!*"

"He was just offering me a ride to my hotel. He's an artist. A rich one, too. He showed me pictures of his paintings on his iPhone. He drives a Ferrari."

"Probably stolen."

I squeezed her hand tightly; she had no idea the danger she was in.

She jerked her hand free. "Let go of me!"

"Did you see his nose?"

"No." She was still looking out the window—anywhere but at me. "Was it broken or something?" she mumbled.

"The big white ring around his right nostril. You didn't notice it? Cocaine. A lot of it."

"Gross!"

"I'm guessing you didn't notice his knuckles either?"

"I did. Cool tattoos."

"Yeah. Cool. Each middle finger. Three dots in a triangle formation. Know what those mean?"

A sheepish "No" from Augusta.

"He's *Rapazes Infero*. Potruguese mafia. Prostitution, gambling, drugs, arms-trading. They smuggle half the heroin out of Afghanistan, trading it for weapons that wind up in the hands of jihadists all over the Middle East: Syria, Iraq, Iran. I'm taking you home."

"No, you're not. *This* is my home. Besides, I don't *have* a home. You *sold* my home, remember?"

"To your new home, in West Virginia."

"Over my dead body!"

"It's where we live."

"It's where *you* live—with Cleet IV. I'm from Charlottesville. That's my home. If I'm leaving here, I'm going *there!*"

"No, you're not!"

"Why?" Augusta hissed. "Oh, that's right, I remember: because everyone there hates you for breaking up my parents' marriage and stealing all my dad's money?"

I slapped her, shocking her into stillness. "You don't know the first thing about my relationship with your father. I loved him. And I haven't spent hardly a nickel of his money. It's all in sitting in the bank—for you and your brother when you're adults."

"I'm not moving to some trailer in West Virginia with people who have no teeth."

"Your brother has teeth. And we don't live in a trailer."

"Grandmama Velvet, Great-grandmama Marlene and Great-great-grandmama Charlene have fake teeth," Cleet IV said.

I fished through my backpack and retrieved a bag of vinegar & salt pork skins, a peanut crunch bar, and a bottle of TruMoo chocolate milk, hurled the food at Cleet IV, then instructed him to please eat and keep quiet.

"You can survive your last year of high school in West Virginia. There's a private school near the Greenbrier."

"I bet it even has indoor plumbing. What's that?" Augusta asked, eyeing the gray packet in my backpack.

"It doesn't concern you."

She snatched it and read aloud: "DEPARTMENT OF THE ARMY. UNITED STATES OF AMERICA. TOP SECRET."

I snatched the packet out of her hand.

"What are *you* doing carrying top secret documents around?"

"That's classified."

"Are you a spy now, or something?"

"Hardly."

"Then what's in the packet?"

"It's a job offer."

"I wasn't aware you had any skills—other than yoga and spending my dad's money."

I almost smacked her but restrained myself. "You might find I'm full of surprises."

"Well, in that case you should take it! It might give you something other to do than ruin my life."

I took a deep breath and uncurled my fists. "As I learned today, my job, first and foremost, is to be a mother to you and Cleet IV." I snatched a handful of Cleet IV's pork rinds.

"This job offer, is it someplace fun? Paris, London, Buenos Aires, Sydney, Hong Kong, Singapore? Not some loser place like Moscow, I hope. The Russian kids at my school are *the worst!*"

"More likely someplace like Afghanistan, Pakistan, Iraq, Iran, Yemen, or Somalia."

Augusta arranged her thumb and index finger into the shape of a capital "L" and pressed the digits against her forehead. *"Looooooo-sers!"*

It was bedlam at the airport. Hostilities awaited me at the check-in counter, when I had to exchange tickets and buy a seat for Augusta. Total "Charlie Foxtrot" as we used to call it in the Army, a "cluster you-know-what" when translated into civilian parlance. Security was a nightmare, what with Augusta complaining the whole time she had to fly commercial, when all her classmates' families owned their own planes. Cleet IV was having sugar issues. An hour before the flight took off, in desperate need of a break from the kids, I scurried over to an empty seat in an unpopulated section of the gate area, where, confident no eyes or ears were on me, I got further acquainted with the contents of the general's packet.

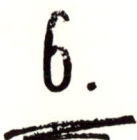

6.

The next morning, our taxi pulled up to the Air and Space Museum.

"I *hate* this place!" Augusta said. "It's the dumbest museum in Washington. I've been here a hundred times on field trips, like, since I was five!"

"Cleet IV hasn't been here. There's an exhibit on Cold War reconnaissance planes. Show him. They've got a U-2 and a SR-71 Blackbird."

Augusta stomped and huffed.

"Will you—just once—do something nice for your brother?" I gave the kids twenty dollars for snacks and told them I'd be back in an hour.

"Where are *you* going?" Augusta demanded.

"That's my business."

"If we're not here when you get back, we'll be at the National Gallery."

"No! You'll be right here when I get back. You are not leave the building. You will *not* walk on the Mall. You will *not* get into any cars driven by strangers!"

Augusta rolled her eyes and put those hands of hers – all manicured and the nails painted in pearl pastel colors – on her hips.

"My God, you are, like, the world's biggest over-reactor. Will you just chill? For once?"

Ninety minutes later, when the general's driver deposited me at Air & Space, I spotted Augusta, outside the museum.

"I told you to stay inside!"

"You're late!"

"Where's your brother?"

"In the gift shop," she said, not looking up from her phone. "I couldn't *take* it anymore. If I see one more stupid Spirit of St. Louis miniature airplane or its accompanying nerd-branded swag, I'm going to throw up!"

I grabbed her by the ear and dragged her back into the museum, where the hunt for Cleet IV commenced. We waded through the sea of tourists. After we found him, an hour later, hiding in the cockpit of the Enola Gay, the three of us walked across the Mall to downtown Washington, from one car-rental agency to another, in search of a fully loaded late model Chevy Suburban or Yukon—in either Navy or White. They had black, silver, green, and red, of course—though none of them would have passed muster where we were headed. The "iridescent pearl white" model was a temptation, but I knew in my heart it would be greeted with skepticism, at least on a subconscious level, in our new habitat. If there was one thing I learned doing my covert work in Afghanistan and Yemen and Iraq, if you got the tiniest detail wrong—how the hijab was wrapped, how the tea was poured—it could blow your cover and get you killed. And the culture I was about to infiltrate was equally complex.

Augusta hemmed and hawed when I announced we would continue our search at the car-rental agencies at the airport. But Cleet IV was delighted to ride the Metro over to Reagan National Airport. It was his first time on a subway.

In Alexandria, Virginia, we found a suitable Suburban. I aimed the vehicle south on I-95. The children badgered me unrelentingly as we exited the D.C. suburbs. They piled on their complaints: that I refused to disclose our destination, complaints about the Wi-Fi, complaints that I did not bring snacks, and complaints that they were being forced to listen to Ernest Tubb on "Willie's Roadhouse," the satellite radio station. Just above Quantico, Augusta shouted, "I *demand* to know where you're taking us!"

As part of the PSYOPs paces I was putting her through, my goal was to destabilize and anger her. Then drag red herrings across the trail to confuse and intimidate her. Then reward her, ultimately brining her to the place I intended to bring her all along.

"I've been giving some thought to what you said in Montreux and on the flight home," I began. "As much as I don't wish to admit it, Augusta, I know in my heart you wouldn't thrive in Thurmond—despite the fact Cleet IV loves his life there: carving walking sticks, crawdad-hunting in the creek, learning automotive repair, squirrel-hunting, and making bubbles in that metal above-ground pool we found on Beury Mountain Road. I think you might be right."

She looked at me skeptically. I could tell she was about to say something but decided instead to keep her trap shut, for once.

"We all want a fresh start," I continued. "What do you say we have one?"

"Like *what?* Or more importantly, *where?*"

"Let's not go to Thurmond."

"Good."

"But let's not go to Charlottesville either."

"What do you mean?"

"We're finding a new place for us to call home. But we need to find that place *together*—the three of us. A new place with good schools. New friends to be made. Good food. Good climate. Good culture. A place where I can focus all my attention on you two."

"Eww," remarked Augusta.

"Where?" said Cleet IV, who was always up for an adventure.

"Someplace south. Where would *you* two like to go?"

"You mean where do *I* want to go? Cleet IV has no vote."

"How about Jacksonville?"

"You've *got* to be joking," hissed Augusta.

"Daytona?"

"Not a NASCAR fan."

"Orlando?"

"I'm a little old for Disney World."

"Disney World!" Cleet IV shouted.

"Shut up!" Augusta barked.

"Birmingham?"

"I don't own slaves and never want to," Augusta continued.

"North Carolina?"

"I'm not in the Klan."

"How about Atlanta? I've always wanted to go there, ever since I was a little girl. Lots to do. Capital of the South. Yes, we'll go to Atlanta. It's settled."

Augusta's face lit up when I mentioned Atlanta. But once my enthusiasm was made clear, as predicted, she rejected it. "I *hate* Atlanta. Nobody from the South even lives there anymore."

"Charleston? No, skip Charleston. Too expensive. Too snooty, too much money, and too much free time. Too many great-looking young men in silly bowties and striking girls in pastel dresses doing nothing but drinking fancy cocktails on porches and going to parties. Who wants to live a shallow life there?"

"YES, Charleston!" Augusta said.

"Forget I mentioned it."

"A girl from my school just moved back there! Her mom was FURIOUS when she got sent home. She tried to transfer her to boarding schools around the world. Even the American school in Mumbai. Can you believe that? Like, who'd want to live in *that* hellhole? But nobody would take her—not after she got in the Interpol database."

"All the more reason not to go to Charleston, if unethical people like that live there."

"The houses are *amazing!*" Augusta retrieved her phone and scrolled through her friend's Instagram account. "They have *amazing* restaurants and *amazing* cobblestone streets and *amazing* polo fields and *amazing* beaches and—"

"Sharks?" asked Cleet IV.

"Charleston just doesn't sound like the right place for our family."

"I already know where Cleet IV and I can go to school: Peckham Hall. It's Episcopalian, like Digby Day was. That's where Channing goes now. I'm convinced one of the reasons she got into trouble was because so many of the kids in Montreux were atheists," she said, pandering. "They took her down a bad path."

"I thought you were an atheist, too?"

"Not anymore. I now see the value of an Episcopalian education like the one I got at Digby. Now that Channing's at Peckham Hall, she quit doing drugs. Though she's still sexting with boys. Like an *idiot* she sent pictures of herself topless to

Prince Chai Son Thamrongnawasawat, which he shared with *everybody*. They were totally disgusting. She has acne on her boobs! Like, why would you send pictures of your zitty boobs to people? It's so gross."

"This girl—whoever she is—doesn't sound like a positive influence."

"I want sharks!"

"Sorry, Cleet. While, yes, I'm sure there are sharks off the coast of Charleston, it's just not the right place for us."

"Sharks! Sharks! Sharks!" yelled Augusta, leading the chant. Cleet IV echoed his sister.

By the time we finished our burgers at the Steak 'n Shake in Richmond, the plan was fixed: According to the GPS, we'd arrive Charleston, South Carolina, at twenty-two-thirty-eight hours.

I spied a look at my phone while driving, which I know I shouldn't have done with kids in the car. The text from General Loehr instructed me to check in to the Garrison Hotel on Chalmers Street and request the Routledge Suite. Once installed in my room, I was to check under the minibar for further instruction.

I was back in the Army. Back on covert ops. And not regretting the decision for a nanosecond. The call to duty was strong in me. Stronger than ever after what General Loehr told me at the Pentagon briefing, which positively turned my stomach.

Just as the general predicted.

"We've got four more hours in the car," I told the kids when we were just below Florence, North Carolina. "I've got some podcasts I need to listen to." The world into which I was about to enter, or rather *re-enter*, undercover, as I did years before in Charlottesville, would require I present myself as a cultured, high-born woman. The clothes, hair, and makeup were always easy. And learning the natives' hobbies, habits, and manners—and mimicking them exactly—wasn't so hard, either. It was the language arts and vocabulary that always presented the biggest challenge, for I was not a particularly well-educated or well-spoken woman. "Augusta, put in your earbuds and watch a movie." I plugged my phone into the speaker system. "Cleet IV, I want you to listen to this." I put the phone on speaker mode and pressed play: "Conjunctions connect two words, phrases, or clauses. Common conjunctions are 'and,' 'but,' and 'or' . . ."

7.

Later that night, after the kids were asleep, I went outside, on the verandah, where I plopped myself down in a wicker chair, beneath a row of gaslight lamps that cast a soft, yellow glow.

I plugged the thumb drive the general gave me into my laptop computer. On my screen appeared the images of fourteen girls. Southern girls from Richmond, Birmingham, Raleigh, Wilmington, Atlanta, Tallahassee, New Orleans, Mobile, Nashville, Ashville, Jackson, Lexington, Baton Rouge, and Charlotte.

Southern girls—all of them Caucasian, eighteen, blonde and fresh-faced, with clear skin, perfect smiles and sparkling eyes: blue eyes, green eyes, hazel eyes. All of them posing in dresses haltered at the top, corseted through the middle, with big flowing hoop skirts below. All of them white-gloved, many standing in sultry power-poses: hands folded across chests or on the hips of their gowns of ivory white, scarlet red, purple, canary yellow, gold, emerald green, orange, elephant gray, fuchsia.

All of them debutantes, girls from prestigious southern families shown dancing with their daddies and beaux at the Orchid Ball, the Peachtree Ball, the Mary Anna Custis Lee

Society Debutante Ball, the Orange Blossom Ball, the Cotton Ball, the Triple Debutante Ball—and a half dozen others.

And all of them missing.

All of them taken from virtually every prosperous city in the South.

Except one, according to General Loehr: Charleston.

Charleston, despite the fact that its ball—the Masked Oracle Ball—was the oldest, most prestigious of the Southern balls.

Charleston, despite the fact that *Hound & Hammock* magazine, for the fifth year running, decreed the Masked Oracle Ball, with its "unrivaled glitz and glamour," the most important debutante ball in the nation. The ball where the most affluent, poised, and drop-dead gorgeous young women in America were annually introduced to Southern society.

Charleston, home to one of the busiest ports in the United States, and, according to the general's intel, Ground Zero for a diabolical human trafficking ring that kidnapped Southern white girls and smuggled them out of the U.S. to an unknown person or persons overseas.

"All roads lead to Charleston," the general told me earlier that morning, when he rose to escort me out of his office and return to the Smithsonian to collect my children. "I expect you to figure out how to penetrate what is certain to be a rich, insulated, hermetically-sealed social circle—the way you penetrated Colonel Bland's country club, charity fundraisers, coffee klatches, and all the rest. Spend whatever you need to and save your receipts."

On the verandah I sifted through a three-inch-thick file on the Masked Oracle Society. Newspaper clippings dating back to the nineteenth century, Xeroxed copies of recipes from the Society's wives' cookbook, and a pamphlet on etiquette for girls. Also included were recent academic essays and exposés from scholars at local universities, all of them critical, some of them downright hostile, that focused on the secret Society's exercise and defense of "white privilege."

A gentle breeze ruffled the leaves of the magnolia tree beside my balcony. I paused for a moment, recalling the breeze that propelled the canoe of my late husband, Colonel Cletus Bland III, and me down the New River in West Virginia, on our honeymoon. Not one for being overly nostalgic or sentimental—the past is the past—I reset my attentions and re-focused on my reading: the Society, I learned, was founded after the Civil War by prominent Charleston businessmen and their economic allies, the city's senior public officials. On its surface, the organization was devoted to civic virtue and charity—along with attracting investment. The men-only group's true purpose, however, was to maintain social order and protect each other's economic interests at the dawn of the Reconstruction Era.

These were not conflicting priorities in the founders' minds, the articles insisted. Society members fancied themselves role models for what they referred to as "the lower orders of Charleston." By encouraging industry and self-reliance, city fathers believed they could nudge the lower orders a rung or two up the economic ladder—and discourage uprisings or even downright revolution from below. The goal was to give the "lower orders" a taste of a better life, if not necessarily the good life, without actually having to let them into the city elites' social and economic circles.

I texted the general, knowing full well he'd be up. The price combat veterans pay for their service is never getting a proper night's sleep again. "Can you talk, sir?"

"Call now."

I phoned him. "I've read all the additional info you shared, sir. But a few questions remain."

"Shoot."

"First: why is the United States Army conducting clandestine activities on U.S. soil, sir? Isn't this the FBI's turf?"

"Technically, yes. And, on paper, it's clearly their remit. They've got someone down there on the ground now, absolutely first-rate. But progress is slow. The FBI director actually came to me looking for help, as they don't have a woman on staff who's quite up for this kind of assignment. Further, whoever is buying these girls is a person of interest to the U.S. Military's counter-terrorism authorities. While eavesdropping on known and suspected terrorists' audio communications across Africa and the Middle East, we've been picking up things, snippets, as part surveillance activities. Lots of chatter about 'more American girls coming soon' and 'blonde virgins in hoop dresses' and so on. But no definitive leads."

"Who is my FBI contact? Where and when do I rendezvous with him?"

"That's classified. And what makes you so sure it's a him?"

"Classified, sir?"

"The FBI director and I both agreed it was best to put you both on a 'need-to-know' basis—for your own safety. It's unlikely your paths will cross, but when two people are undercover on the same operation, the risks of a slip-up increase exponentially. A moment of unspoken sympathy between the two of you in a public situation, a shared reaction, the subtlest eye contact, and the risk increases. You stay in your lane, master sergeant, and the FBI's operative will stay in hers or his. Think of yourselves as separate, but equal, jaws of the same vise."

"Both of us out to squeeze a terrorist down in South Carolina who's at the center of all this. He shouldn't be hard to find given all the watch lists."

"Don't waste your time looking for you average Tariq, Dilaawa, or Hariz. It's someone local. We can't figure out who he is or how he does it, but our intel sources suggest the ringleader is someone of high social standing,"

"How do we know that?"

"These girls weren't snatched off the streets by middle-aged fat guys in wife-beaters driving windowless vans, but disappeared from ostensibly safe places—country clubs, Lacrosse fields, private music lessons—presumably by people they knew and trusted. Someone on the inside in cahoots with bad actors overseas."

"Do you have time for a few more questions, sir?"

"All the time you need, master sergeant."

"Why the masks, sir? Were they Klansmen?"

"The group's members were patricians and snobs," the general said. "Though surely racists would have been counted among their ranks over the decades," he conceded. He filled in the details: the myth of the Masked Oracle was cooked up for two reasons, the general explained. First, member anonymity was deemed crucial to the patricians. They met in secret, and in disguise, because they needed to maintain the charade that the town was a functioning democracy rather than the oligarchy it was. Had they all been spotted at public restaurants charting the town's progress—installing mayors, finding jobs for each other's often talentless children, fixing court cases, assigning property-development rights—the appearance would have been horrible. So, they met clandestinely in the basement of St. Margaret's Episcopal Church on Meeting Street—whose rector was himself a Society member—to avoid the gaze of the envious, who at any moment might issue calls for the guillotine.

"Second," the general continued, "the oligarchs knew the lower orders were suckers for pomp and exoticism—from watching a pharaoh glide down the Nile thirty-five hundred years ago to watching members of Britain's royal family wed on CNN today. So, the Masked Oracle Society invented an exotic fictitious figure from the Far East—bearded, berobed, mystical. A character steeped in magic, astrology, and alchemy, like one of the three Magi. A few years after the Society's founding, the myth was cemented in the popular imagination of Charleston's underclass. The Masked Oracle—a prominent Charleston banker, plantation owner, or judge rotated annually— 'arrived' in Charleston every summer, on the night of the solstice, as though he had just rolled into town on the back of a camel after months crossing the desert. On horseback he appeared, cantering down East Bay Street in his gem-studded turban, cape, and tunic, a muslin shroud concealing his true identity."

"And the crowds bought it?"

"Hook, line, and sinker. From on high, he tossed trinkets to the fawning crowds: silver coins, chocolate coins, scented bath soaps, pamphlets on hygiene, vials of perfumed oil, and children's textbooks. He brought progress and prosperity to all who encountered him."

At the winter solstice he returned, the general continued, but he didn't mingle with the masses on that visit. Instead, the Oracle presided over the city's exclusive debutante ball, where he anointed one lucky (i.e., most economically or ancestrally advantaged) eighteen-year-old Charleston virgin "The Queen of Charity and Chastity."

"What else can I tell you, master sergeant?"

"I've got enough to dive in."

"Head-first."

"Yes, sir."

After I ended the call, I picked up the hundred-year-old mask the general gave me when we were in his car on the drive from the Pentagon to the Air & Space museum and unwrapped the velvet sleeve that encased it. Fashioned out of porcelain, the mask was the color of burned milk. Spidery hairline fractures ran across its surface. The gold ribbons that secured it to a member's head were frayed.

I was just about to fit it to my head when Cleet IV, who rises with the sun, wandered out onto the verandah in his camo pajamas, scraping granola-sized specks of matter out of the corner of his eye. "Can we see the sharks, today, Mama?"

I put the mask carefully back into the sleeve. "Not until dusk. Wake your sister up and get showered, both of you. We've got a full day ahead of us."

8.

After I returned from my daily P.T.—a ten-mile run, two thousand sit-ups, and a hundred pull ups— my first priority was to get the kids out the door and enrolled at school.

But before I could do that, I had to make sure that I would blend in with the locals. I parked the kids in front of the TV, ordered them room service, and under the guidance of the hotel's concierge headed over to King Street, where I got my hair—all of it, even my "downstairs" hair—dyed ash-blonde.

On Broad Street, I bought a box of tinted contacts at the optometrist's. They didn't have the same shade of "envy green" that I wore when I was undercover in Charlottesville, but they had a close enough match: "gemstone green." Then I had my fingernails and toes painted coral. After that, I headed back over to King Street, to the Bitchy Belle boutique. I exited fifteen minutes later with two dozen outfits: tops, pants, dresses, skirts, sweaters, derby hats, and a variety of graphic handbags featuring little slogans stamped on their sides: "MY HUSBAND IS GIVING ME A HEADACHE!" and "THERE IS NO 'H' IN WINE!" just to name a few of the more than a dozen I purchased. Then I was off to Vineyard Vines, which I raided for the kids.

After we checked out of the hotel, I loaded the kids into

the Suburban and piloted them to their new school. There was a lot of friction with the headmaster. I put him on the phone with Mr. Christophe Saint-Dufay in Switzerland and Bernice, the retired schoolteacher in Thurmond who home-schooled Cleet IV. Augusta put up a stink—and embarrassed me greatly—when she said she wanted to board at the school. I told her that under no circumstances was that happening. She was living with me, where I could keep her under a watchful eye after the stunt she pulled in Montreux. The headmaster kept protesting that our situation was "highly unusual," and "not the way things are customarily done at Peckham Hall," and so on. But when I wrote the ninety-six thousand dollar check on the spot for the year's tuition, things sorted out quickly.

After a mid-afternoon wire transfer of $9,358,550—I owned a fully-furnished home on Legare Street.

At sixteen-forty-five, impressed with my productivity for the day, I sat in the queue outside the kids' school, which must have had fifty vehicles in it, one blue or white Yukon or Chevy Suburban after another—just as predicted.

The pick-up and drop-off protocols at Peckham Hall were quite explicit, the headmaster explained when we spoke in the morning. "Designed to guarantee for the children a tender transition between the school and home experience. Parents are required to remain in their vehicles. Car radios are to be extinguished. Parents are prohibited from being on their phones." Peckham Hall faculty and staff, I was told, would be stationed outside the entrance to the school (or just inside the door if weather was inclement) and would escort the children to their respective parents' cars, open the rear passenger door, load children into seats, and fasten the kids' seatbelts. Once secured in the vehicle, a school official would close the door and slap the car door twice. The vehicle was not authorized to proceed, he insisted, until after the two raps on the door occurred—even if the car door was shut.

The cars advanced—then stopped—at thirty-second intervals. While waiting, I busied myself on my phone, searching the internet for scout troops, soccer clubs, country clubs, lacrosse teams, tennis clinics, test-preparation courses, squash lessons, dining clubs, yoga studios, book clubs, piano instructors, yacht clubs, hiking clubs, running clubs, math tutors, and horseback-riding camps. The wider the net I cast, the faster Augusta, Cleet IV, and I would infiltrate Charleston High Society.

Ten minutes later, it was my turn. A stern young woman with a D.I.'s disposition marched across the lawn, dragging each of my children by the hand. In compliance with protocol, I extinguished the engine. Augusta tried to climb into the front seat but was ordered by the teacher's aide to sit in the backseat.

"I'm sitting up front! I'm not four!"

"It's your first day, Augusta. Are we really going to start on the wrong foot? Just do what she tells you to do." I was at that moment grateful for my military training, which trained me to obey dumb rules that had no value other than to teach you that in life there were many dumb rules to be obeyed—so you'd better get used to it.

Augusta snarled and huffed and climbed into the backseat.

The teacher buckled Cleet IV's seatbelt first, then attempted, unsuccessfully, to buckle Augusta's. "I can *DO* it!" Augusta yelled, as I turned over the engine.

"Kindly wait until the car door is shut, Mrs. Bland, and I have administered two raps to the door."

"Yes, ma'am," I said, extinguishing the engine.

After the raps were administered, I turned over the engine

again and put the vehicle into gear. Augusta leaned out of her window and shouted: "Talk to your mom, Channing!"

"I will!" her friend shouted as she was escorted to her family's idling Suburban, parked directly behind me in the queue. I looked in the rearview mirror and saw the girl's mom, a blonde like me—and every other mom in the queue—who waved enthusiastically.

"Channing wants to come over to the hotel tonight."

I told Augusta visitors were welcome, but not at the hotel.

"Great. You drag us to a new town and we're not allowed to have our friends come over?"

"If you'd kindly allow me to finish my sentence, you may not invite visitors to our hotel because we are no longer staying at the hotel. You are welcome, however, to invite Channing to . . . *our new home!*"

The kids shrieked when I told them about the house—a seventy-five-hundred-square-foot rose-colored Italian Renaissance mansion, with marble statues in the yard and a built-in swimming pool. Augusta texted the address to her friend, who replied seconds later. Augusta was vibrating with joy when she received her friend's reply. "Channing lives, like, the next street over from us!"

"Tell her to come for dinner."

9.

We mad-scrambled to get all the food home and displayed in a way that would impress Augusta's friend. After my time in Charlottesville, I knew enough about society women to know that they enlist spies—husbands, children, housekeepers, or tennis pros—to procure intel on newcomers. Channing's report to her mama needed to position the Bland family favorably.

We were lost for the first twenty minutes in the new kitchen—which was bigger than my log cabin in Thurmond. "Why ain't the paper plates inside the fridge like at home, mama?" Cleet IV complained.

"This *is* home, Cleet. And say 'aren't'—not 'ain't.'"

We found glass plates and cutlery. In the butler's pantry we discovered table settings and a stack of cloth napkins. We arranged everything prettily on the granite island in the middle of the room: pitchers of lemonade and sweet tea and bottles of Blenheim ginger ale, plus a big spread that included pimento cheese soufflé, slaw dogs, ham and cheese-stuffed pork chops, shrimp and grits, ginger and collard green fried rice, tomato pie, corn salad, dilly beans, simmered field peas, and, for desert, watermelon chiffon pie, peach cobbler, and sweet tea buttermilk pie.

The doorbell rang and we all went to greet Augusta's friend, Channing. The girl's mother pushed her aside and said, "So I finally wrestled an invitation to the Jeffrey Drane Kimbrell house!"

"You weren't *invited,* mom," Channing said all nasty.

Channing's mother made a theatrical gesture. "Oh, well. I'm here now. Introduce me, Channing."

"This is my mom, Pepper Boyell," the girl said in a monotone voice.

The mother sized me up as she stuck out a hand for a shake. "By luncheon today the whole town was talking about you, of course, which is probably *exactly* as you planned it. How this *gorgeous* woman with two *gorgeous* children bought the Jeffrey Drane Kimbrell mansion—the most gorgeous house in the city, with the best collection of antiques in Charleston—for an *unspeakable* sum of money. *In cash!* Every Charlestonian also knows what you paid for it, though of course we're too polite to mention it." The woman winked.

"Even though you just did, mom," said daughter Channing.

The mother barreled over the threshold. "If you haven't figured it out by now, this is a very small town and I'm its *biggest* busybody. But in a harmless way . . . *mostly.*" She winked again. "Years ago, I learned that while it pays to take an interest in others, taking *too* much interest can be costly."

She laughed as she tried not to appear nosey, ducking her head in the sitting room, and opening the closet door below the staircase. She seemed in a big hurry. "This food—which looks *delicious*—won't be eaten tonight, I'm afraid," she said after we entered the kitchen. "You're all coming with me to the Charleston Yacht Club! It's a full moon. We're cruising with a handful of friends, and I'm not taking no for an answer." Pepper Boyell started rounding up storage bowls and Tupperware containers, knowing instinctively which drawers to find them in.

When I grabbed my new purse with the words "Proudly, defiantly, permanently bitchy" printed on the side, Pepper Boyell lit up. "You've just made me eleven dollars richer," she cooed. On the walk to the yacht club, she told me all about her "little hobby business" making purses. Seamstresses across the South—usually single moms, women of color mostly—stitched them for her in their homes part-time, for supplementary income. "I don't make any money off it, of course," Pepper boasted as we scurried down the cobblestone sidewalks, "but it's my way of giving back."

⌒

We walked the gangway on to the *Hissy Fit*, Pepper Boyell's sixty-five-foot yacht, which she didn't want me to call a yacht. "It's just a little cruising vessel. And we got it *used,* so don't you get the impression we're rich—not on my husband's pathetic salary!"

Pepper Boyell's "couple of friends," which I estimated at three dozen, were crammed shoulder-to-shoulder on the yacht. Mrs. Boyell introduced the kids and me to her friends. Most of Mrs. Boyell's friends were Peckham Hall parents like me, she said, which made for a natural ice-breaker and gave Augusta and Cleet a chance to join the conversation. All the moms insisted Augusta and I looked like *sisters*, which I suppose we did—especially after I'd done and gone blonde and light-eyed like my stepdaughter. And our hairdos were similar, too (though Augusta's highlights were real).

I met husbands named Grady, Jackson, Austin, Aubrey, Harry, Charles, Houston, Walker, Crawford, Preston, and Wyatt before being introduced to wives named Olivia, Elizabeth, Alice, Nicole, Laura, Georgia, Margaret, Sallie, Hallie, Winn, and Amalie. Unused to meeting outsiders, us Blands were a source of fascination to them, I was told.

As an undercover operative in enemy territory, I was trained to get others talking. Before long, the Charlestonians were telling me about their favorite subject—everybody's favorite subject from Kabul to South Carolina: *themselves.*

The more I talked to these people, the more I was made to wonder if they too had been trained at covert ops. They were highly skilled at introducing into the conversation, in a casual way, the details they wanted me to know about them. After introductory chitchat, nearly everyone I met reported they were descendants of "The Lords Proprietors," "friends" of King Charles II sent in the 1600s to colonize the Carolinas. Every sentence or comment trigged some sort of historical response with these people: "They skimped on the sugar in my sweet tea," one of the Peckham Hall parents, Grady said, teeing up his wife to chime in, "Grady can never get enough sugar in his tea. His great-granddaddy was in the sugar business." Or timber, or tobacco cultivation, or indigo, or textiles.

Pepper Boyell hurried us along, from one person to the next on our social audition. Her champagne bottle in hand, she kept trying to refill my champagne glass, though I never swallowed a drop. "This is our skipper, Stallings," she told me as when we approached the bridge. "I call him 'Dumb-Dumb' but shouldn't," she said, laughing huskily, "especially since a) he's an elegant and accomplished gentleman with a Ph.D., and b) he also happens to be my husband." Pepper Boyell's eyes narrowed as she snatched the sour stout from her husband's hand. "No drinking and driving, Skipper."

I shook hands with the professor, whose scraggly, salt-and-pepper goatee reminded me why I prefer military men: they shave.

Soon we were on the starboard side, where three women, their backs against the rail, each of them in baseball caps, were posing for a group selfie. My heart skipped a beat when I saw them. My mind went blank as I struggled to recall their names. When the photo-shoot concluded, the one in the tangerine-colored hat with the word PINEHURST embroidered on the front locked eyes with me and shrieked, "You're alive!"

"Oh my God!" squealed the woman standing next to her in the lemon-colored Kiawah hat. She elbowed the third woman, clad in a lime-colored Bay Creek hat. "Willow, look who's here!" she declared.

At least I had one name: Willow, the one in the lime-colored Bay Creek hat.

Willow looked up and cried, "Tamsin Venables Bland!"

The three women all descended upon me for hugs and air-kisses as Pepper Boyell, her face knotted in confusion, looked on.

After registering their shock that I was now a resident of Charleston, Lemon-Colored Kiawah Hat scanned me up and down and in a mock-hiss said, "You *bitch!* You haven't gained a *pound* since I last saw you."

"Ugh!" Tangerine-Colored Pinehurst Hat moaned. "Don't even get me started on *this!*" She slapped her backside.

"Remember what Catherine Deneuve said, Caroline?" Lemon-Colored Kiawah Hat asked rhetorically. "At a certain age, you have to choose between your face and your ass."

"Thanks a lot, Sloan," Caroline replied. "This from the girl who has the exact same face she had twenty years ago, when she was Miss Virginia."

A wicked grin came over Willow's face. "It's not like she didn't get a little help along the way from Dr. Goulb."

"Not as much as you, Willow!" Sloan retorted.

To the extent the three ladies were able, in spite of various cosmetic procedures, Willow, Sloan, and Caroline smiled as they raised champagne flutes in a toast to Dr. Goulb.

After a big swallow of champagne, Willow took on a philosophical demeanor. "I chose ass. Nobody's going to tell me I can't have those yummy cheese straws they serve at Worthington with my cocktails. Life's too short to limit yourself to five asparagus spears a day, like Ginny Bland used to." She cupped the palm of her hand over her mouth.

"Nice work, Willow," said Caroline.

The ladies apologized to me for mentioning Colonel Bland's first wife. I accepted the apology with grace. Careful not to take the bait, I said nothing about the first Mrs. Bland and pretended to sip my champagne.

"Okay, I can't take it anymore," Pepper Boyell protested with a stomp of the foot. "How do you know these nasty, *nasty* women, Tamsin?"

"Sloan, Willow, Caroline, and I used to do yoga together up in Charlottesville."

Pepper Boyell cooed as she fiddled with the knot on her scarf, on which was printed elephants, giraffes, zebras, and monkeys. "I had no time to Google you before our little boating excursion, Tamsin. Now I don't have to spy on you via the internet; I can just go straight to these horses' mouths."

Willow made a braying noise and the ladies laughed.

Pepper Boyell turned to the yogis. "Tell me all about my new neighbor, girls."

The girls gushed about me. They told Pepper that before her stood an exiled member of the British aristocracy whose family's origins could be traced to a castle in Wiltshire England, how before my arrival in Charlottesville I had lived around the world, how I was an accomplished horsewoman, how I spent my youth as an "embassy brat" in Zimbabwe, Indonesia, and Turkmenistan.

"Tajikistan," I said, gently correcting Willow, maintaining the backstory invented for me by one Shelby Nash and his partner, Dr. Davis Warren, when I lived in Charlottesville.

"Are you still driving that fabulous Rover?" Sloan asked.

"It's up in Potomac, Maryland, now, with a collector," I informed them—skipping the part about how I had "borrowed" the car from said collector when I moved to Charlottesville and returned it in the middle of the night to his barn in Maryland two years later, when I left town.

Caroline welcomed a champagne refill from Pepper, to whom she said, "Tamsin was married to a war hero, you know. Her deceased husband, Cleet, killed some famous terrorist in Afghanistan."

"Mehdi Hashmi," I said.

"The Secretary of Defense gave him a medal for it."

Pepper Boyell lowered her head. "I didn't know you were a widow, Tamsin. I figured you were like so many of the other women here: divorced. I'm sorry for your loss."

"Cleet died of anaphylactic shock," Willow reported. "During a charity fundraiser Tamsin threw. He was rescuing their son, who was under attack by a swarm of frenzied yellowjackets."

"That's horrifying!" Pepper Boyell lamented.

Everybody was quiet for a moment, in tribute to Cleet. I, myself, said a silent little prayer for the man I'd loved. When the tribute ended, the ladies immediately started grilling me: where was I living in Charleston? Was I seeing anybody? And so on. I was cagey. My training taught me to acknowledge questions about the past quickly, then pivot to present or future times, which could not be challenged or verified. "I was in Switzerland. For longer than I would have preferred. The place is cold, the people are cold," I sighed. "Which is why I'm thrilled to call Charleston home now. Tell me more about your lives, who is in what grade at Digby Day?"

Each of the women chattered on at length, bragging about children that preoccupied them and husbands that annoyed them.

A waitress carrying a *hors d'oeuvres* tray came through. The yoga ladies each grabbed a nibble. Caroline leaned in towards Pepper Boyell. She tilted her head in the direction of the railing and said to Pepper in a low voice "Who's that *gorgeous* African-American gentleman in the white pants and the skin-tight t-shirt?"

Caroline re-threaded her ponytail through the opening above the slide buckle of her tangerine-colored Pinehurst hat. "OMG, those *eyes!* They're the color of apricots!"

"I want to dunk him in a vat of Old Spice and have my way with him," Willow purred.

Pepper laughed. "That's Gullah Jack. Decent to look at, if that's your thing, but hardly a riveting conversationalist. Trust me on that, ladies. He's helping Stallings with a book. An interview subject. A bit of a fish out of water with this crowd, I fear. He lives in a shed on Gatuh Island, one of the uninhabited Sea Islands, between Johns and Edisto."

"I *love* that the Gullah people have maintained their traditions after all these centuries," said Caroline. "Making those cute wicker baskets and whatever."

"I think they make brooms, too," added Willow.

"We should keep him company," said Sloan.

"Good luck comprehending anything he says," warned Pepper. "Trust me when I tell you he's far more interesting from a distance."

After sly reapplications of lipstick and hair-rearranging, the yoga ladies descended upon Gullah Jack.

I stole a final glance at him as Sloan put her hand on my shoulder and nudged me along. "C'mon, Tamsin," she said. "He might not be husband material, but he's definitely one-night-stand material." To be sure, he was a fine-looking man. Skin black and shiny as onyx. Clean-shaven, too. But I was on a mission in Charleston—not off duty or bored in an AutoMotives stockroom looking to pass the time and put out the fire in my belly. "Thanks, Sloan, but my kids are here."

I stayed behind with Pepper Boyell. It was time for me to burrow in to my reconnaissance work. "You've heard all about my husband and my life up in Charlottesville, Pepper," I said as we strolled the deck. "Tell me all about yours?"

Pepper Boyell refilled her champagne flute for the fourth time and said, "My life is gloriously boring. Nothing happens around here, which is exactly the way I prefer it. I wouldn't dream of boring you with details of Stallings' work; that's Stallings' job." She scanned the room for someone new to talk to before she returned her attentions to me. "Which he will, I assure you. Tomorrow night at seven, when you and the kids come over for dinner. We'll eat all those leftovers in your fridge, which will be far tastier than the Saltines we'd have been forced to eat for dinner after shelling out what we did to throw this party." Pepper waved to a pink-faced man in his sixties. "Now that I know you're in the market for a husband, I have someone you should meet."

"I'm not," I protested as she yanked me by the wrist towards the stern.

The Boyells' house was like all the others in the historic district of Charleston: symmetrical, built sideways, and stacked room-over-room. Augusta, Cleet IV, and I, leftovers in tow, banged on the brass lion's head door-knocker.

The help—an African-American woman named Flora—escorted us into the house. The inside of the Boyells' house was identical to mine: there were two rooms on each side of a short, narrow hall. Antiques everywhere, bright colors on the walls, fancy moldings, a fireplace with a big wrought iron grate.

"I've now made a whopping twenty-two dollars off you, Tamsin," Pepper quipped when she saw my purse with the words It's Wine O'clock Somewhere printed on the side.

"A gift for the hostess," I said as I unzipped the bag and presented her with a candy dish. "I hope you don't mind my re-gifting you, but there's so much stuff in my new house I can't even find a place to put my purse down."

Pepper's mouth sprung open like a jack-in-the-box. "That's no candy dish, honey." Pepper retrieved a pair of reading glasses from the living room and inspected the object's markings. "French Bronze Doré Frame, Chinese, easily nineteenth century. You sure you want to part with this?"

I shrugged. "There are a dozen more like it in the house. I

hate clutter. I'll probably give half of the stuff away." Having grown up in a home filled with clutter—Grandmama Marlene had a gnome collection numbering in the hundreds—I was happiest under a tent, with a cot and a trunk for my gear and nothing else.

"Don't you dare! Not without consulting me first. Every item in that house is *treasure*." Pepper Boyell gave me a big hug. "Best neighbor I've had in ages."

She dragged me on a house tour. When she wasn't talking about English Regency painted side cabinets, mahogany game tables and rococo carved giltwood mirrors, Pepper insisted on telling me the life story of her scarf: "It's vintage Hermès."

"Oh."

Had I noticed the one she wore the night before, on the boat, with the African animals? That one was vintage Hermès, too. "All those moneys and zebras, it's my favorite. So whimsical!"

"If you say so."

She leaned and forced me to inspect the workmanship of the one she was wearing on our house tour—mint-green with little golden horseshoes all over it. It was from the fifties, she said.

"Mm-hmm," I said, trotting out one of the "acknowledging phrases" taught me by my teachers, Shelby Nash and Dr. Davis Warren, when I lived in Charlottesville, Virginia.

She wouldn't stop carrying on about the scarves: she had dozens of vintage Hermès scarves, she boasted as we climbed the stairs to the second floor, each one hand-selected in little secondhand shops across the South, often in Goodwill stores, where clueless proprietors, unaware of the brand's "storied legacy," sold them for pennies on the dollar.

"Unbelievable," I said.

After she showed me the master bedroom suite and Channing's room—whose door was promptly closed and latched shut by the girls—we headed up to the third floor, where Stallings Boyell was seated at his desk. Next to him was that fine-looking black man I saw the night before on the boat. Both men grunted their way through re-introductions.

"Enough time spent today working on a book nobody will ever read, gentlemen," Pepper snapped. "It's cocktail hour."

After I sent Cleet IV out on the porch to watch videos on my phone, Pepper shook cocktails as Flora the helper arranged the food on platters.

"A red wedding for you, Stallings," she said when the men arrived. She looked at me conspiratorially, "Stallings won't touch anything unless it's overflowing with bourbon. And it's got to be Horsebit or nothing."

I was reminded of my late husband's affinity for Horsebit bourbon and a wave of melancholy rushed over me. I swallowed hard and kept my game face on as Pepper mixed, shook and served the next drink. "A witchdoctor for you, Gullah Jack. Chock-full of all those herbs your people fancy—to ward off the evil spirits!" Pepper winked. I think she winked two dozen times since I met her.

"The Gullah people are wary of witches," Stallings said, "whom they believe cast spells by slipping toxic herbs or roots under a person's pillow at night. On the Gullah islands there are specialists known as 'root doctors.' They're called in to protect the inhabitants from curses and—"

"—Oh, Lord, here we go. He hasn't even taken his first sip of drink and he's already being boring. I warned you, Tamsin."

Gullah Jack scowled. *"Dainjus!"* he said in his molasses-thick

Sea Island dialect as he pushed the drink away. Not a big talker, that Gullah Jack.

"Then we'll protect Tamsin from hexes and spells," Pepper said, handing Gullah Jack's drink to me. "She's going to need all the help she can get in this town!" Pepper brayed.

I pretended to sip the cocktail as I went to work on Stallings Boyle, asking him about his job at the university. When he said he was a history professor who specialized in the Atlantic slave trade, Pepper corrected him. *"Associate* professor, darling."

Stallings ignored his wife's remark and continued, saying he'd written fourteen books. Stallings could talk longer than one of them holds-you-hostage-all-day-in-church preachers. He had written books on how the Portuguese tricked tribal elders in the Kingdom of Kongo into believing they were friends, books about European-built forts—or "slave castles"—along the West African coastline, books on the Middle Passage, the triangular slave-trading route that began in Europe, stole Africans from their continent, then shipped them to the Americas; books on African tribal leaders' complicity in the trade, books on slaveship design and the deplorable conditions under which Africans were transported to the New World; books on the Old Slave Mart in Charleston, and books on the African diaspora in America, including the one he was currently researching about the Gullah people—whose African ancestors lived for centuries in the Lowcountry, on both the coastal plain and the Sea Islands.

"So, you're helping write the book?" I asked Gullah Jack.

"No write. Just talk. Got no *eddycashun*," he said, casting his eyes downward.

"Jack's source material," said Stallings Boyell. "His family can trace its origins in South Carolina to 1673. A walking encyclopedia, this fella. The lore-keeper of his entire family—of which he is the last remaining member."

"Dey wid da Lawd now," moaned Gullah Jack.

After the girls and Cleet IV arrived, dinner was eaten in the kitchen, standing up. Everyone hovered over the island, where Flora laid out the food. Cleet IV curled his lips after his first and only bite of pimento cheese soufflé.

We moved to the living room for dessert: watermelon chiffon pie, peach cobbler, and sweet tea buttermilk pie. Gullah Jack told the kids about the sweet grass basket-making tradition of the Gullah, passed down over generations.

"The baskets made on the islands were nearly identical to coil baskets made by the Wolof people in Senegal," Stallings said, hijacking the story. Just as Stallings was about to leap over the gorge from simply boring to becoming the Most Boring Fella of All Time ("Like the neighboring languages Serer and Fula, the Wolof language belongs to the Senegambian branch of the Niger-Congo language family. However, unlike most other languages of the Niger-Congo family, Wolof is not . . .") we were delighted to hear the chatter of a crowd outside, accompanied by the sound of clomping feet climbing stairs.

Flora opened the door and in came most of the people I'd met the night before on the boat—whose names and likenesses I had committed to memory, as I was trained to do during my Army days when I infiltrated garment factories, tea circles, and chemical weapons factories to collect intel on terrorist activities. I said hello again to Grady and his wife, Olivia. To Jackson and his wife, Elizabeth. Austin and his wife, Alice, as well as Aubrey, Nicole, Charles, Houston, Laura, Walker, Georgia, Crawford, Margaret, Preston, Sallie, Wyatt, Hallie, Winn, Harry, and Amalie.

All the men carried matching worn leather tubes that looked to be a hundred-plus years old. Documents—their tattered edges peering out from the leather folds—were stored inside, rolled up and tied with strings. The women carried matching beaded bags, equally old, all them faded burgundy, embroidered, with the same frayed tassels.

The group politely quizzed me and the kids about our experience on the boat the night before, our new home, and the kids' second day of school at Peckham Hall.

When the small talk ended, Pepper, whose mouth never stopped running, let the conversation lapse into awkward silence. "Maybe it's a good time for us to say goodnight to the Blands and Gullah Jack," she said as she stood and brushed imaginary crumbs off the front of her skirt. "Our drab, unofficial little community meeting is about to commence, and I know Jack's got to get back to his island and your kids have school tomorrow, Tamsin."

"As a newcomer to town, I'd be thrilled to learn more about civic affairs," I told her, hoping to wedge my way in.

Pepper was blunt. "We've got two hours' worth of *excruciatingly* boring agenda items to cover: next year's garden tour, a fundraiser to repair the façade at St. Margaret's. You'd never believe it, but a virtual war has broken out over the gaslight lamps—whether or not we need to upgrade to more energy-efficient bulbs, which will impact the color of the glow."

"Not in this lifetime," Amalie said, compelling the group to laugh.

"We shall spare you . . . *this time*," Pepper quipped as she nudged us towards the door. "Get settled and we will conscript you a month from now, when we have our next excruciating meeting. But I do have one small favor to ask . . ."

"Yes?"

Pepper nodded her head toward the sofa. "Those ladies' bags are stuffed with bourbon. This group can get a bit rowdy after a few belts. I'm worried about Channing being kept up all night. Would you mind *terribly* if she slept over at your place tonight?"

"Of course not."

While the hysterical girls raced to Channing's room to collect her gear, I went to the kitchen to fetch my bag. Flora, who was taking all my leftover food home with her, had everything packed in a Whole Foods Market brown paper bag. She and Gullah Jack and me and the kids said our goodnights.

As we headed out the door, the women in Pepper's living room all reached for their bags—which I did not for a moment believe contained bottles of bourbon.

11.

The walk home was an exercise in motherly multitasking. With one ear I tuned out the girls' chatter and Cleet IV's nonstop questioning as I electronically eavesdropped on the conversation in the Boyells' living room with the other ear—thanks to the transmitter I had fitted in the base of the candy bowl I gave Pepper.

I fiddled with the miniature dial until the muffled voices came in crisp and clear.

". . . he's never going to sell," said one of the women, whose twangy accent I remembered from the previous night. I reckoned it was Sallie, the woman who'd relocated to Charleston from Florida.

"Yes, he will," said the voice I recognized as Preston's. "Gullah Jack's people are uncomplicated people. They've been making wicker baskets for four centuries and eating oyster stew. His ancestors owned no stocks or bonds, invested in no 401(k)s, had no piles of rubies or diamonds stashed away in safe deposit boxes. All they ever had was that island. And it belongs to Gullah Jack now. He'll take the money and run. I guarantee it. And five years from now, there'll be condos, million-dollar beach houses, a half dozen James Beard award-winning farm-to-table restaurants and boutique hotels on that island," said Grady.

"We're ahead of ourselves," protested Pepper. "Stallings, start the meeting."

I heard a chorus of zippers as the women open their bags.

"Do we really have to wear these stupid masks?" Alice asked.

"We honor tradition for a reason," her husband, Austin, replied.

"Whoever owned this before me had a fat face," Houston complained.

A gavel struck the table and Stallings Boyell said, "Hear Ye, Hear Ye. It is my high honor to welcome each of you to this gathering of the members of the Masked Oracle Society of Charleston."

The group recited an oath —like Cleet IV's Cub Scout troop at the start of their meetings. Words like "industry," "charity," and "moral good" were repeated by the Society members.

After roll call was taken, agenda items were announced. Garden tours and light bulbs were at the top of the list. The following year's summer solstice parade and the upcoming Masked Oracle debutantes' ball would be covered next.

Forty minutes into the meeting, as I was supervising Cleet IV's teeth-brushing, the topic finally turned to the debutantes' ball.

"I'll kick things off," Pepper said. "You've all seen her twice now, last night on the boat and here in my home tonight. Impressions?"

"Before we get to that," said Harry, "I want to go on record—for the fifth time—that I think we should quit while we're ahead. Are we now forced to live in a dog-eat-dog world compared to a century ago? Yes. Has our influence and the esteem in which we are held in this community declined compared to a century ago? Yes. Have tech billionaires, Hollywood actors, and other vulgar outsiders swarmed into our community to dilute and disrespect our traditions? Yes. But even the dumbest dog knows that you don't shit where you eat."

Several Masked Oracle Society members indicated agreement with Harry.

After the chatter died down, Pepper cleared her throat and addressed the room. "There are two irrefutable, incontrovertible facts. Fact number one: everyone in this room is driving on fumes. Winn can't afford gas for his plane. Georgia can't even enjoy her own beach home for a measly week in August because she needs the rental income. Jackson lost his shirt investing in that doomed strip mall off of I-95. You think people don't notice these things? If Houston's family didn't own the bank, half the people in this room would've gone under a long time ago. Fact number two: we all agreed it's unacceptably risky to source debs from the same place twice. Nobody in Birmingham, Tallahassee, Lexington, or any of the other places we've been to has connected the dots. We take a second girl from any of those places and it's not just another random teenage girl who disappeared—one of thousands of cheerleaders, checkout girls, girls mad at their parents, or love-struck girls fleeing town with their boyfriends who disappear annually in this country—it's a second debutante that's missing, and that becomes a pattern."

"So why not source from other markets?" Laura asked. "Why does it have to be in our own backyard? This is unseemly. Why can't it be Boston? L.A.? New York? They have debutante balls, too."

"Because our client will know the second he sees her that she's not a real Southerner. And he's paying super-premium prices because he fancies Southern girls. He is an expert on their accents, their manners, their charms. Quit fooling yourself, Laura," Pepper scolded. "You really think you can send him Deborah Feingold from Park Avenue or Guadalupe Gonzales from L.A. and he's not going to notice?"

"I still don't understand why we can't just approach Gullah Jack now with the offer?" Laura pressed.

"Because we stick to the plan, that's why," barked Pepper. "We've got one hundred and forty million dollars parked offshore. We all agreed one hundred and fifty million dollars was the basement offer we could come in with—especially when the island is worth three times that. The longer we wait, the more likely some developer from New York or Miami will swoop in and steal it from beneath us."

"Why would he take one hundred and fifty million dollars when he could get four hundred and fifty million?" Austin asked.

"Because simple people like Gullah Jack are terrified of outsiders. Because Stallings has earned his trust. And because he's never seen so much money in his life, that's why." I heard a Zippo lighter click. "That," said Pepper as she exhaled, "and a little gentle nudging to be provided by Aubrey and his friends in the state capital, who have since our last meeting come up with a plan to make it impossible for Gullah Jack to say no."

Pepper turned the floor over to Aubrey.

"We don't see Charles Smith at these meetings much anymore—not since he moved to Columbia after the governor appointed him director of the Department of Environmental Control. But he hasn't forgotten that we made his daughter Queen of Charity and Chastity a decade ago—and we all remember what she looked like. He's indebted to us and he knows it. Nor is he immune to the lure of once-in-a-lifetime investment opportunities. Long story short, a state environmental inspector—Charles Henry's son, conveniently, who as many of you know was a Phi Theta at Clemson with Jackson and Elizabeth's son—will on a routine inspection of the Sea Islands discover unacceptably high levels of a compound called ketopoxin, a highly toxic environmental pollutant. It will be found in the soil on Gatuh Island. Gullah Jack will be notified, and informed that additional testing will be required, which will take about thirty days to complete. If the negative results are validated by outside inspectors from the EPA, he'll be told, the island will have to be completely evacuated."

"What if he challenges the findings?" Olivia asked.

"He won't. What do you think he's going to do in thirty days, Olivia? Go earn a master's in toxicology or environmental sciences then get on the Internet and review two hundred studies? The man can't even read."

"I don't think you have to be so nasty about it," Olivia said.

Pepper urged Aubrey to continue.

"It's during that thirty-day window that our little investment consortium—with Stallings as the face—knocks on the door of Gullah Jack's shed—a one-hundred-fifty-million-dollar offer in hand. Jack can't believe his good fortune. All of his relatives are dead: he's the sole heir to and inhabitant of the island. He's never seen more than one hundred dollars in cash. He takes the money and runs. Goes crazy, of course, and blows the fortune in six months: three-hundred-thousand-dollar watches and two-million-dollar cars and ten- million-dollar pop-up-mansions with basketball courts and bowling alleys in the basement. We break ground six months later, and everybody lives happily ever after."

"It could work," said Crawford.

"It will work," corrected Pepper. "Look, everybody, this is our last chance. The girl will fetch ten million dollars and we cross the finish line. We need alignment and we need it now."

"Better a stranger than one of our own daughters," said Hallie.

"Why do you think I brought her to you two nights in a row? Do you really think I roll out the welcome wagon to every interloper who swoops in on our community? Now," Pepper continued, "in the interest of getting through the agenda so we aren't all here until four in the morning, can I please get the group's impressions of the girl?"

The ladies' voices overlapped: "Darling." "Poised." "Statuesque." "Clearly well-bred." "Gorgeous skin." "Adorable."

"Gentlemen?" asked Pepper.

Platitudes about comportment and pedigree were repeated by the men until an exasperated Pepper interjected. "Oh, Christ, please, will you cut to the chase, gentlemen: Is she *fuckable?*"

The room was silent. Then, after a throat-clearing, Grady spoke on behalf of the gentlemen. "Oh, good *God,* yes!"

"Then let it be resolved: we shall recruit Tamsin Bland into the society and crown Augusta Bland this year's Queen of Charity and Chastity. All in favor say 'aye.'" After assent, the gavel banged and the meeting was adjourned.

I burst out of my bedroom, ran down the hall, and climbed into bed next to a sleeping Augusta, a loaded Beretta beneath my pillow.

12.

The following Saturday night, just after midnight as I snuck into Augusta's bed to keep watch over her again, a pebble struck her bedroom window. I put my hand over her mouth, awakened her, and discreetly cocked the Beretta so she couldn't see it. A second pebble, then a third, struck the window.

I peeled back the curtain. In the yard stood two dozen adults, all of them masked and cloaked in dark capes, each holding a candle. Their serenade barely rose above a whisper.

> *Who is kindhearted and fair?*
> *Of sturdy health and shining hair*
> *Her papa's pride and joy?*
>
> *Who is graceful, calm and wise?*
> *With her mama's fine and sparkling eyes*
> *The fancy of every boy?*
>
> *She of charity and chastity*
> *Will she wear the gilded mask with thee?*
> *Come forward, girl, pray not you be coy!*

We put on our robes. I tucked the Beretta into the waistband of my pajamas and unbolted the front door.

I did not know who was approaching me, as no one spoke, but it was a man. I slid my hand under my robe, ready to grab the Beretta. He bowed, untied the worn leather roll, and presented an ancient-looking parchment paper. Its appearance was deliberately smudged and worn, with ink blots and burn marks at the borders. In the center was an illustration of the masked oracle, seated on a velvet throne. It read: "Miss Augusta Bland is commanded to appear at the one hundred forty-ninth Annual Ball given in Honor of His Excellency The Masked Oracle and His Court of Charity and Chastity Saturday, Twenty-first December . . ."

I pretended to be confused and delighted as the Masked Oracle Society's members walked slowly backwards, each of them bowing, until they disappeared behind the gates and bushes of Legare Street.

Augusta, flattered by the attention and unaware of their intentions, was up all night as text messages flew back and forth between her and the girls at Peckham Hall. Most of her classmates were going to the ball, she learned. We laid in bed, the screen on her phone bursting with light every few seconds as a parade of emojis appeared: smiley-faces, tearful faces, stiletto heel icons, champagne flutes, puckered lips, vomiting faces, prayer hands, thumbs ups, thumbs down, hourglasses, martini glasses, bikinis, limousines, saxophones, cheeseburgers with red Xs stamped on them, tiaras, broken hearts, cherries, and see-hear-and-speak no evil monkey faces.

I'd never seen Augusta so delighted. For the first time since her late father introduced her to me, she seemed genuinely glad of my company. Only I couldn't enjoy it the way I would, as I was too busy making damn sure no harm would come to that girl.

The ball was a full six weeks out. During their meeting at the Boyells' house, the Society members made it clear that their intention was not to snatch Augusta until *after* her coronation as Queen of Charity and Chastity was publicized in the newspapers, thus certifying Augusta before the overseas buyer as "an authentic Southern debutante."

The soldier in me knew my job was to wait. We had nothing to do but dress-shop and kill time until the ball. But the mother in me was taking no chances with Augusta's safety between the time I learned about the group's intentions and the night of 21 December.

Accordingly, I put Augusta under twenty-four-hour surveillance, taking the notion of "helicopter mom" to new heights. In addition to sleeping with her, which infuriated her, every corner of the house—inside and out—was outfitted with motion detectors, security lights, cameras, microphones, and alarms. I insisted on driving her to and from school daily, despite the fact that she was a licensed driver and had indeed inherited her late father's BMW, which had been shipped down from Charlottesville days after our arrival. During school hours, I slithered across the wooded areas surrounding Peckham Hall, in full camo, monitoring incoming and outgoing vehicles and tracking Augusta's every movement with field glasses. I secretly installed NSA-grade GPS tracking and spyware on her iPhone. I collected DNA samples from the hairs she left on toilet seats and in the shower drain, if, God forbid, I should need them later.

With the general's approval, I conscripted Dalton and Dustin Crabtree, formerly of the 76th 3rd Stryker Brigade Combat Team, 2nd Infantry Division, to serve as the family's backup security detail. I quartered them in the carriage house, explaining to neighbors that they were artisan plasterers helping me on some rehab work. One of the brothers was always on Augusta's tail: on the parking lot at Augusta's nightly soccer practice or tucked away in the corner of a pizza parlor across from Washington Square where she and her friends from Peckham Hall congregated on Friday nights. The Crabtree boys' arrival reduced my stress immeasurably—especially late at night, after Augusta and Cleet IV were sleeping soundly.

Surveillance continued for weeks, during which Augusta and I fought like dogs from enemy packs. "What is your *deal?*" she protested when I denied her sleepover requests, prohibited dates, and escorted her to the movies (where, unbeknownst to Augusta and her popcorn-chomping girlfriends, the Crabtree brothers were seated behind and ahead of her, monitoring entrances and exits).

Gown-shopping, in particular, was a bloodbath. We shopped online. We visited dressmakers and bridal boutiques. We scoured vintage shops. Every dress had some disqualifying element: Augusta hated the beads, or the dress didn't have beads, or the pleats were too skinny, or too wide, or the fabric was ugly, or the length was wrong, or the embroidery, or the color, or the slit, or the drape, or the bust, or the way it fit at her hips.

Full of herself as she contemplated the prospect of becoming Charleston's next Queen of Charity and Chastity—she began lording the ball over her friends back in Charlottesville and Switzerland.

When they told her she hadn't a chance in Hell, as such balls were notoriously rigged in favor of the oldest and most prestigious families in the host-city, and she was a newcomer to Charleston, she struck back not at them, but by striking out at me. "You never had a coming-out party, did you, Tamsin?" Augusta sniffed.

"When I was your age I danced with presidents at embassies—not boys with spots" —the term Shelby taught me to use as a substitute for pimples— "who wear watermelon-colored trousers and baby blue gingham checked shirts."

"In Micronesia, or wherever," she snorted.

When I refused to fly her to New York to go dress-shopping, she accused me of being jealous of her and trying on purpose to make her less beautiful and refusing to spend any of my deceased husband's money on her, which she was legally entitled to. "You'll get your money, but not until you're an adult!"

"None of these dresses fit me right. I need a nutritionist *now*—not when I'm an adult!"

"P.T. with me in the morning before school and you can eat anything you want."

"Thanks, but disgusting sweat-circles under armpits look better on you."

"Then stop eating all that junk you eat."

"Huh, you're one to talk, stuffing your face with those *nasty* Cajun catfish sandwiches at Bojangles.'"

"My waist is smaller than yours, so I must be doing something right!"

"Channing's parents are renting the Stonewall Jackson suite at the Pine Knot Hotel. So are all the other girls. But you're too cheap to rent one!"

"I know what happens in those rooms. You'll come home and sleep in your own bed, young lady."

"Cut the 'young lady' bullshit, Tamsin!"

The bickering and complaining went on for weeks.

We were well into December and she still didn't have a dress, because, by this time, she had found a whole new set of crises to obsess over: makeup, hair, jewelry, shoes, and getting her teeth whitened.

After a dozen knock-down, drag-out fights, she finally settled on a pink dress from the Bitchy Belle—the first store we had dress-shopped in God-knows-how-many weeks prior.

At fifteen-hundred-hours the day of the ball, a crew came to the house to assist her: two seamstresses to fit her into the dress, a makeup artist, and a woman from the shoe shop, who brought a dozen different pairs for Augusta to try on, as the child was still undecided.

Panic struck as dusk approached. In me, silently, because I feared for my baby's safety at the ball, for Augusta, because she was still not ready.

Augusta was taking out her frustration on the helpers. "You're smearing my eyeliner!" she barked at the makeup gal. "Ow! You're pinching my boob!" The women, experienced as they were with stressed-out debutantes on their big night, were gracious in the face of Augusta's unrelenting criticisms.

Outside, a horn blared. "Your carriage awaits, Augusta," one of the ladies said.

Idling at the curb was a 1959 Rolls-Royce Silver Cloud, which I hired for the evening from an antique car-rental agency that specialized in weddings and winery tours—a two-tone mode, shell grey over dark blue. One of the Crabtree brothers, in white tie and tails, was stationed behind the wheel. I selected the car not for its style, but for its functionality: the car's gigantic trunk—which was twice the size of a US Army-issue two-man combat shelter tent—was packed with three M4 Carbines, a M107 Semi-Automatic Long Range Sniper Rifle, a half dozen M67 grenades, a half dozen M18 smoke grenades, a flamethrower—and a second armed, and formally-attired, Crabtree brother.

I sat in the backseat next to Augusta, who was snapping and posting photographs of herself, the car, and the driver nonstop.

"Ready to become the next Queen of Charity and Chastity?" I asked, my heart pounding as my adrenaline surged on the lead up to impending battle.

"Like I even have a chance," she grumbled as her thumbs flew across the iPhone keyboard like birds disperse when they hear a shotgun report.

I reached over and clasped her hand, squeezing so firmly I feared I'd break a bone. "You're going to be fine tonight, angel."

"For the tenth time: stop *touching* me!"

13.

A long line of vehicles clogged the half-moon-shaped entrance of the hotel, where the daughters of Charleston's most fancy citizens were helped out of limos by young men dressed in turbans and ankle-length velvet coats. Augusta extended a white-gloved hand to the turbaned greeter and stepped out of the Rolls into a burst of flashing cameras.

Inside the ballroom it was a mob scene, with flirting girls, half-drunk tuxedoed boys, and middle-aged parents milling about. An orchestra at the front of the room was playing music unfamiliar to me. Lots of brass instruments blaring. Mounted along the walls for the occasion were portraits of prior Queens of Charity and Chastity, dating all the way back to the 1800s. Children ran across the stage, waving dragon streamers. Dancers in flesh-colored bodysuits, oversized eagle wings strapped to their backs, fluttered through the crowd.

Pepper Boyell stood in a scrum near one of the half dozen bars scattered across the ballroom, alongside her husband, Stallings, and three other couples. Her neck was craned, scanning the room. When her eyes met mine, she pressed her martini glass into Stallings's hand and came hurling at me like a grenade fired out of a MGL-140 repeat-action launcher. The hug she gave me nearly broke my back. When she released me, she spun around and raved about Augusta's dress. "Bitchy Belle?"

Augusta said yes.

"Martha Broomley. Hottest designer in the South. She stitches all of her dresses by hand in Savannah." Pepper pointed to debutantes. "Channing, Sheridan, Tilly—half the girls in the room are wearing one."

Pepper guided Augusta and me through the crowd, back to her drinkers' circle, where I said my hellos to Stallings Boyell, Grady and Olivia, Jackson and Elizabeth, and Austin and Alice. Augusta begged to peel off and see her friends, but I kept her nearby, quite against her will, under the pretext that I wanted to show her off to my new friends.

Just when I was convinced I could endure no further excruciating small talk, bells chimed and Pepper said we all had to go to our tables. I consulted my invitation packet and located our table number. Pepper pretended to be shocked when a few minutes later Augusta and I pulled out chairs next to hers at Table 2. "The Oracle put you at my table!" she cooed.

Pepper insisted on sitting between Augusta and me. Every time Augusta rose to hug a girlfriend from school, or was introduced to some handsome young suitor, I slid my hand below the dinner napkin spread across my lap and felt for the Beretta holster-strapped to my thigh. When Augusta visited another table, I escorted her. When she finally hissed and said, "I can go to the bathroom by *myself*, Tamsin!" I monitored her whereabouts on the GPS at the same time Dalton and Dustin Crabtree, unbeknownst to Augusta, were walking either ten paces in front or behind her. Her bathroom trip lasted twenty minutes because she stopped every five seconds for selfies.

Back at the table, I pretended to be fascinated as Pepper

explained how she had chosen the evening's scarf, though I had not inquired about the topic. "As a rule, Hermès doesn't do much in the way of black—their colors are usually festive—so it wasn't easy finding something in black and white to complement my dress." She arranged the scarf draped across her shoulder. "I love that it's so big. Sort of halfway between a scarf and a pashmina," she said as she tugged it off her shoulder and dangled it in front of me, like a matador. "Behold the black cat! It's a jaguar, actually. Sort of a pre-Columbian Aztec civilization theme. Like it?"

"Gorgeous."

"Not as whimsical as my monkey-and-zebra number. But playful in its own right."

"If you say so."

When Augusta returned to the table, African-American waiters—some of them so old they tilted to one side—were delivering entrees and refreshing wine and water glasses. The diners at the table, who took no notice of the help, chattered away, the women and girls about their gowns and the men about guns, sports, and politics.

Stallings Boyell was boring all the other men at the table, his specialty. ". . . The boat was called *Temperança*. She set off at midnight on today's date—December 21—in 1571, from Lisbon, headed for Ghana, but never got past the southwest tip of Portugal. The waters are of course treacherous around there, given the S-shaped basin, which is uniquely treacherous given the region's coastline and seafloor topography. Just below the castle at Cascais, fifty feet down the flat-fronted cliffs, at Boca do Inferno—Hell's Mouth— the ship was sucked in and slammed into the cliffs, which within minutes turned the ship into a pile of floating matchsticks . . ."

A waiter stood patiently as Stallings droned on, careful not to interrupt.

"... at least that's the account of the lone survivor, a cook who..."

Finally, one of the other men at the table, Jackson, intervened on the waiter's behalf: "Still your tongue for just a nanosecond, Stallings, if that's possible, and let the man do his job."

Without looking up, Stallings Boyell pointed at his wine glass and indicated a refill was in order. He continued his story. "In the captain's journal, before the ship went down, there was nary a mention of—"

"—*Paa'd'n, Mr. Stallings, daa'k wine or da wide wine?*"

Stallings looked up, irritated at the interruption until he recognized the waiter. "Well, by golly, if it isn't Gullah Jack. What brings you to the Masked Oracle Ball?"

"*Workin' for da bittle,*" quipped Jack.

The men laughed heartily as Stallings indicated red.

After Gullah Jack exited, Stallings gave the men at the table a knowing look, as if to say, *"And you don't think he'll accept our one-hundred-fifty-million-dollar offer for his island?"*

After dessert was cleared, father-daughter and mother-son dancing commenced, which made things awkward for Augusta, who sat the dances out and scrolled through her Instagram feed.

"I wish your father was here. I'd give anything to see you two dance together," I said. "He'd have been floored by what a beautiful young woman you've become."

"I wish he was here, too," she mumbled.

After the awards presentations, one of the wives from Pepper's boat party—Georgia—took the stage and introduced a video about the Masked Oracle Society's charitable work in

Charleston. In the video, parents and debutantes were shown performing community service labors on Charleston's low-income East Side: sweeping up broken glass in front of liquor stores, planting flowers in front of derelict homes, and reading *Fancy Nancy* stories to elementary school girls. "The girls spent the summer giving back to the Charleston community," Georgia announced when the video concluded. "But tonight, it's all about them!" The crowd burst into applause, a cue to the men at our table to make their sly, silent exit. An exit unnoticed by most, but not by me.

"It's time to crown the Queen of Charity and Chastity," Pepper Boyell whispered conspiratorially.

All the girls were summoned to the rear of the ballroom. I was the only parent who chaperoned her girl, which attracted notice, but I didn't care: I was not letting Augusta out of my sight.

After the girls were assembled, a gong was struck. Red and gold lights flashed onstage. Musicians played ancient Persian rhythms on drums that look like gigantic goblets and strummed pregnant-looking banjos with bows. The Masked Oracle's court began its procession onstage.

Everybody lined up on either side of the Oracle's throne—all gold-painted carved wood and velvet. Then the music stopped. The room went completely black, at which time I clasped Augusta's wrist. She tried, and failed, to jerk free.

When the lights came up, the Masked Oracle, adorned in in his turban, was seated on his throne. His chest-length fake beard spilled out from below the chin of the mask. His velvet cape was draped across the shoulders. Next to him was the empty seat that awaited his Queen.

Orchestral music began as down the middle of the ballroom,

where an elevated runway was installed, the girls began their procession.

One by one the girls' names were called:

Winn Acton.
Mercer Ashby.
Mallory Bailey.
Augusta Bland.
Channing Boyell.
Sheridan Brewer.
Morgan Carter.
Tilly Clemons.

I was not happy about sending Augusta down the runway unescorted, but she would have been mortified if her stepmother walked with her, like a kindergartener on her first day of school. Besides, there were spotlights on her and the Crabtree boys, steps away from the runway on either side, along with two hundred and fifty witnesses, were watching.

Each girl walked unsteadily down the runway. Not used to being in high heels, most were gawky and un-fleet of foot, like newborn giraffes. Cameras flashed and the girls smiled, until they reached the stage. Before the Masked Oracle, each bowed. After an acknowledging nod from the Oracle, the girls, among them my Augusta, exited stage left and excitedly scurried back to the rear of the ballroom.

Fifty girls later, the last girl had made her bow. At which time another man in a turban appeared onstage to consult with the Oracle. The proceedings were all very official and top secret. A roll of parchment was unspooled. With a big peacock feather, the Oracle pretended to inspect the document carefully, then rendered a mark on the paper before leaning back, satisfied, on his throne, like a man who just finished a feast. A herald walked halfway down the runway. "Ladies and gentlemen, His Excellency the Masked Oracle of Charleston has named this year's Queen of Charity and Chastity."

The room went dead quiet. The parents at the tables leaned forward. The girls in the back with me were vibrating. The herald, who dragged it out as long as he could, finally decreed: "His Excellency the Masked Oracle commands to the stage, as the 149th Queen of Charity and Chastity, the lovely and gracious . . . Miss Augusta Bland!"

Augusta shrieked, jumping up and down as she was hugged by Channing, high-fived by her new friends at Peckham Hall, and looked at with suspicion and resentment by other girls, who had always known each other and had never even heard of Augusta Bland. The debutante behind me grumbled that as someone not born in Charleston, she shouldn't have been eligible for the title.

Augusta mustered all the poise at her disposal and glided down the runaway a second time. When she arrived at the stage, another attendant appeared, this time with an emerald green pillow, atop which was placed her crown. On bended knee, Augusta leaned before the Oracle, who placed it upon her head. She stood, leaned in towards the Oracle, and took a selfie. (Teenage girls and their phones: it was like they were welded to the palms of their hands). The Oracle, who was not keen on being photographed at close range, curtly directed her to the empty throne at his left. She sat there, fidgeting, unsure what was expected of her. Moments later, the attendant reappeared with a bouquet of flowers fit for a Queen. A Queen of Charity and Chastity.

Her golden crown was visibly uncomfortable. It must have weighed twenty pounds: metal, banged out by hammer in the nineteenth century. The crown's gemstones—diamonds, rubies, and emeralds—were all the size of half-dollars. From the top of the crown, sprouting up like weeds, were oversized crosses and *fleur-de-lys*—those fancy French symbols that look like lily flowers, whose name I would never have known were it not for the fact that my mentor in Southern culture, Shelby Nash, took me to a restaurant in Charlottesville once by that name, and, after teaching me how to pronounce the word, taught me its meaning. The thick, antique veil that draped from the crown—which looked like the gauze bandages medics would have wrapped around soldier's legs in World War One, and probably date to that era—fluttered every time Augusta breathed.

The orchestra struck up the theme music for the ball, a cue to the Masked Oracle that it was time for him to escort Augusta to the center of the dance floor. A look of terror swept over her face and I regretted that I never bought her dancing lessons before the ball. Once the dance commenced, she was a disaster, stepping on the Oracle's black velvet slippers and tripping constantly as he twirled her around.

The song concluded with a jarring halt, at which time the Oracle dipped her with gusto as an explosion of light bathed the two dancers: green, red, yellow, blue, and orange spotlights circled about them at high speed. Then, at the same time the orchestra mimicked the sound of an explosion, a big puff of black smoke engulfed the center of the ballroom floor and the room went black.

I rushed towards the dance floor. As did the Crabtree brothers. By the time me and the Crabtree boys got there, The Oracle was . . . *gone!*

But my Queen was still there, standing in the middle of the

room, dazed, confused, but loving every minute of the attention showered upon her.

The room exploded in applause. She cupped her hands over her mouth in excitement, almost ripping off the fragile veil, as the debutantes and boys swarmed her. The mob surrounding her was five-deep. I kept her squarely in my sights, refusing to let any of the commotion surrounding her distract me. It was no different than the many times I was stationed on a rooftop in Kabul or Karachi and had to take out an insurgent in a crowded bazaar.

The crowd finally receded, and I approached Augusta, who was utterly indifferent to my advances.

"I know we've had our ups and downs over the past few years . . ."

Half attentive, she made an acknowledging grunt or two as she snapped more selfies.

"I just want you to know, I've never been prouder of you than I am tonight."

She took another selfie. "Whatever."

"Did you hear what I said, Augusta?"

"Yeah, I did," she replied. "Thanks for the compliment, but you should probably give it to Augusta instead of me."

"Huh?"

The Queen of Charity and Chastity lifted her veil. "It's me, Mrs. Bland," Channing Boyell said before twirling around and snapping another selfie.

I grabbed Channing by the shoulders. "Where's Augusta?!"

"Ow! Stop it!" She swatted me away. "Backstage. It's all part of the show."

14.

I scrambled to locate my phone and dial Augusta. I heard the familiar ringtone of her phone—a high-pitched, aching phrase from some teenage girl singer —and patted my pockets and scanned the floor for Augusta's phone. Channing slapped the iPhone into my palm. "It's for Augusta. Will you give this back to her, Mrs. Bland?"

I charged towards the front of the room, blasted past the Oracle's throne, and searched backstage. Augusta was nowhere. One Crabtree brother was dispatched to the hotel entrance. The other was instructed to sweep the kitchen and the lobby. Back in the ballroom, I sifted through the mob in search of Augusta.

Minutes later, one of the Crabtrees reported he had penetrated the hotel's security offices and was monitoring all entrances and exits, plus each of the hotel's eight floors. Still no sign of her. I sent the other Crabtree up the fire escape while I commenced a floor-by-floor search. On the top floor I passed the entrances to the suites: the Robert E. Lee Suite . . . the J.E.B. Stuart Suite . . . the Nathan Bedford Forrest Suite. I recalled Augusta mentioning during one of our arguments that the Boyells booked the Stonewall Jackson Suite. I sprinted down the hall in search of the entrance.

Beretta drawn, I leaned in and pressed my ear against the door. Pepper was on the phone. I overheard her ask, "Where did you tell her I was? Good. Keep her at bay. No, just leave her to her friends. She'll be preoccupied for the next hour."

When I burst into the suite, Pepper was standing by the window, flipping shut the burner phone. "Where is she?" I shouted before plunging the cocked pistol into her neck.

"Who?"

"AUGUSTA!"

"Have you gone *mad*, Tamsin?"

"WHERE IS SHE?!"

"Why are you pointing that *gun* at me?"

"You switched the girls."

"Tamsin, are you drunk?"

"Where is she?"

"I don't know. Downstairs somewhere, I imagine."

"Channing was wearing her crown!"

Pepper made a face. "And that means . . . *what?* That crown ends up on twenty girls' heads by the time the ball is over."

"You switched the girls: on the runway, on stage, during the dance with the Oracle. I don't know where or when or how, but you switched them! The crowns were different. Augusta's had crosses and *fleurs-de-lys* on top; Channing's had only metal crosses—no *fleurs-de-lys*. What was it, trapdoor on the floor? Is that how you made the switch?"

"You're not making any sense, Tamsin."

I cocked my head and looked around the room. "Is she in here?"

"No, of course not. Why would Augusta be up here?"

"Why are *you* up here?"

"Because it's my *room*, Tamsin. I had a *splitting* migraine and realized all the flashing lights and smoke was just making it worse. Am I entitled to a break from the ball?"

"Where's Stallings?"

"I think you need to leave now, Tamsin."

I jammed the Beretta into her mouth. "Where's Stallings?"

"Mmphffm."

"Excuse me?" I asked, sliding the Beretta slowly from between her lips, which she promptly licked before beginning to sniffle and tremble.

"Backstage, changing out of the Masked Oracle's costume. What on earth is the matter with you? You've gone insane!"

"For the last time: WHERE. IS. AUGUSTA?"

"For the fifth time: I. DON'T. KNOW! Probably making out in a stairwell with some boy. Alice and Aubrey's boy, Spencer, most likely. He's been flirting with her all night, if you didn't notice. And she's been flirting right back. Now will you kindly get that gun out of my face and take your psycho shitshow somewhere else so I can take a gigantic gulp of my martini, draw a scalding hot bath, and cure this miserable headache?"

I landed a sharp punch to Pepper Boyell's temporal lobe, two inches from the corner of her eye, laying her out flat on her back.

I barricaded the entrance to her suite before overturning the Boyell women's four suitcases, sifting through bras, jewelry boxes, and backup dresses in search of the materials I needed.

Ten minutes later, when she came to, Pepper Boyle, still groggy, mumbled, "What's happening?"

I switched on the radio. "Stand up."

"I can't see!"

"That's not an accident." While she was out, I triple-wrapped her gigantic Hermès "jaguar" scarf around her head and knotted it tightly near the ear.

"Get this off my head! Do you hear me? You're ruining my scarf!"

"I think the look suits you; it's 'whimsical.'"

She tried to free her hands, but her wrists were pinioned to the leather belt wrapped around her waist. I spun her around in circles, keeping her steady, as Channing's canvas belts were wound tightly around her thighs and ankles.

"Walk!"

"Don't make me scream, Tamsin."

"Nobody will hear you, not with Hank Junior blasting. Besides, something tells me you don't want to attract the attention of hotel management."

"You have completely lost your *mind!*"

"Shut up and walk." I guided her to the bathroom. The ironing board was already laid out inside the tub, titled downward at an angle, its narrow end resting atop the porcelain at one end and its wide end wedged into the bottom of the tub at the opposite end.

I maneuvered her into the tub, upside down, pressing her back and shoulder blades against the ironing board, ensuring her head was positioned below her heart. With a bed sheet I swaddled her tightly to the board, mummy-style. Despite her wiggling, she couldn't move an inch in either direction.

"Where's Augusta?"

"I don't know!"

I went to the sink and filled the ice bucket with lukewarm

water. "Let me tell you how this works, Pepper. We'll do fifteen seconds on, take a fifteen second break, then do fifteen seconds on again until you talk."

"What are you going to do to me?"

"You're about to get waterboarded."

"Water-*what?*"

"You're going to tell me where my daughter is."

She said nothing, but she was breathing hard. Her face was trembling beneath her Hermès scarf making the jaguars look like they were dancing. I sat on the edge of the tub and gently tilted the ice bucket over her mouth and nostrils for five seconds. The water seeped gradually through the enveloping fabric of her scarf.

I waited to hear choking.

She issued no verbal protest, nor did she react physically. Which baffled me. Until I figured out she was holding her breath. "You won't outlast me, Pepper." I pinched her nostrils and waited five seconds. Then ten. Then fifteen. Finally, she exhaled forcefully through the mouth, which caused the scarf's fabric—a little swatch of coiled jaguar tail—to balloon up before, a half second later, she inhaled reflexively, sucking the damp patch of scarf deep into her mouth. "Time for your second dose." I poured the water over her mouth, a light stream, in curlicues, tracing the jaguar's tail. Her nostrils flared. Panic began. She jerked violently on the ironing board and gasped repeatedly.

"Where is she?"

"Spencer. Alice, Aubrey's son."

"What about Spencer?"

"Making. Out. Stairwell."

We took fifteen seconds off. I checked her vitals. Her

heartrate was off the charts. Sweat was streaming down her arms. B.O. enveloped the bathroom. "You're having an adrenaline rush, Pepper."

Even though I hadn't used more than three ounces of water, and the ice bucket was full, the person on the receiving end of a waterboarding session is prone to believe a gallon of water has been poured down his—or her—throat. I went to the sink and turned on the faucets for maximum psychological impact. "Ever heard of Farzaad Shah and Ibad ur Rehman–Ullah?" I asked as she hyperventilated. "From a teashop in Kabul, these fellas plotted an attack on the Empire State building. I was part of a team that waterboarded them at a CIA black site before the scheduled blast. They were a lot tougher than you. We had to waterboard the fellas a hundred times—each. If you think your B.O. stinks now, wait till you get a whiff of the urine and diarrhea that'll be squirting out of your business an hour from now. Anyway, I learned about patience during that interrogation. In due time, we got the intel we needed, which is why the building's still standing. Calm down and hold still now." She jerked and writhed as I repeated the ritual. Once the water seeped through the scarf, her body thrusted and slammed yet again against the ironing board as she groped for air. I elevated her head. "This is only my third application. Ninety-seven to go. Now breathe. Relax."

After Pepper leveled out, I spoke in a gentle voice. "She was snatched during the dance with the Oracle, right?"

Pepper nodded yes.

"Trap door?"

Pepper nodded no.

"Rushed backstage when the smoke bomb exploded?"

A yes.

"And Channing was backstage, waiting to make the switch?"

Yes again.

"So, Channing's in on it?"

She violently shook her head no.

"Augusta was drugged?"

Pepper didn't respond.

I walked over to the faucet. She heard the water splashing in the ice bucket. "I'll ask again. Augusta was drugged?"

Pepper nodded yes.

"What did you give her?"

"Dilaudid," she gasped. "Mist. Sprayed. On. Veil."

"Where is she now?"

"I don't know. I swear!"

I titled her head downward, putting her head below her heart again. "Stop!" she begged.

I dribbled more water. After her shaking and coughing fit, I said, "I forgot to tell you what happened to Farzaad Shah and Ibad ur Rehman–Ullah after we were done. Do you know what the side effects of sustained waterboarding are? Oxygen-deprivation does a number on the lungs and brain. Where is she?"

"Port of Charleston!"

"With who?"

"Stallings."

"What's the pier number?"

"I don't know."

"You'll be unconsciousness after the next one." I titled the bucket over her mouth and nose. The water cascaded. She flailed and gasped and jerked violently. I poured too much too fast and worried I might drown her.

"Huuuuuuuuuuugh!"

"The pier number. Now! Or I'll turn you into a vegetable!"

After I got my answer, I burst out of the hotel room and sprinted the fifteen blocks to Pier 39, where the *Fidelidade*, an unmoored container ship, was crawling out to sea.

15.

I tripped the ball gown off my shoulder, stripped to bra and panties, wedged mine and Augusta's mobile phones into my holster beside the Beretta, and dove into the ice-cold waters of the Atlantic.

The wake was fierce, yanking me under and spinning me around. But after a half-minute of flailing, I got my bearings, applied the techniques I learned as a girl, when I taught myself to navigate Class V rapids on the New River.

I captured a big gasp of air, dove underwater, and went plank stiff, feet first and parallel to the surface. The tides thrust me forward until I was propelled out to sea.

The *Fidelidade*'s blades were groaning loudly as I got closer, at which time I flipped over onto my belly and furiously began swimming, perpendicular to the tide. I was only five minutes in, but exhaustion was beginning to overtake me. After a couple hundred yards of freestyle swimming, I managed to catch up to the ship, just past the stern on its starboard side. I looked for a ladder, a rope, a raft—anything I could hoist myself up on. The deck was forty feet up. There was no way to get there.

The ship was gaining speed as my energy waned. I was pulled backwards by the tide, towards the stern, where I was enveloped by a group of sea otters. They were leaping up at the ship, hurling themselves into its side.

Clustered along the side of the ship were hundreds of baseball-sized barnacles. The otters leapt repeatedly, nipping—unsuccessfully—at the barnacles. They were rock-hard, those barnacles—like pegs on a climbing wall. Provided I could get my hands and feet on one, I could scale the ship.

But like the otters', my attempts to grab at them were failures, too. The riptide kept smashing me into the side of the ship each time. I made twenty attempts until finally I managed to grab one and hoist myself upward. As I gripped the orb, the pincers of the rock crab that lived inside sliced an inch-deep gash into the flesh of my palm. But I held on, despite the excruciating pain. I threw my leg up and landed a foot on a second barnacle. I was, for the first time, above water. I looked up, trying to discern the path of my climbing wall. It was slow-going, that climb. Between foot-slippage, near falls, and the ship getting jostled by the waves, I spent more than three hours climbing. I kept chanting my mantra, one from a decade prior, when I scaled Afghanistan's Koh-i-Firoz plateau, where Taliban warlord Abdul Kaziz Fazl was holed up: "If you *think* you can . . . you won't. If you *know* you can . . . you might."

I finally got close to a lifeboat suspended by thick ropes attached to a pulley above. I climbed the rope that dangled ten feet below it. I pulled myself over the hull and collapsed into the bed of the boat. I was there, recuperating, for the better part of an hour before I summoned the energy to continue my trek northward to the deck.

I climbed the ropes and gripped the pulley's iron hardware, which was housed in one of the underdecks. I was officially aboard ship. Once on the top deck, I was overwhelmed by an entirely new problem set: Stacked from bow to stern—fifteen wide and high—were shipping containers: blue ones, red ones, orange ones, green ones, and gray ones. The big ones ran twenty feet long, eight feet high and eight feet wide—about the size of Augusta's dorm room in Montreux. There were between fifteen to twenty thousand containers, I reckoned. And Augusta—the needle in the haystack—was locked up in one of them.

I ducked into an electrical room below deck and called the general to brief him. Pepper and Stallings Boyell engineered the transfer, I reported, but all the members of the Masked Oracle Society's executive committee aided and abetted. "Right now, she's in the Stonewall Jackson suite, Pine Knot Hotel. Secured to an ironing board. She's the only one who knows we're onto them—so far. The Crabtree boys will need to get her out quickly and quietly. As far as everybody else in the Masked Oracle Society is concerned, I recommend we let them believe everything is proceeding as planned."

"I agree, master sergeant," General Loehr said. "We'll put Pepper on ice and keep the others under surveillance."

"Except for Stallings Boyell, sir—who I believe is aboard ship."

After I provided the ship's name, I heard the general's aide banging away on a computer keyboard. "Registered to a holding company in Portugal," he reported. "*Fidelidade*'s destination is Lisbon."

"When I gave you this mission, master sergeant, I didn't expect that it would be a member of your family that'd be seized," said the general. "I regret that I've put you in this position."

"Thank you, sir."

"What do you need from me, master sergeant?"

"Can I get a list of every container on this ship: what's in it, who sent it, country of origin, and destination?"

"You'll have it within the hour," the aide said.

"And when you find Augusta, master sergeant—assuming you do?"

"I'll find her, sir. And when I do, and I'm assured she's safe, we go to Lisbon and complete the mission."

The general was silent. "The risks are unacceptably high. I'm sending in the Second Fleet for a carrier intercept."

"Permission to speak freely, sir?"

"Permission granted, master sergeant."

"Sir, if we do that, we get the bad actors on one side of the Atlantic, but the bad actors on the opposite go free. And we both know that once they're alerted, we'll never get another crack at them."

"And you think your eighteen-year-old daughter has the capacity to allow herself to be . . . *sold into sex-slavery?*"

"I will allow nothing of the sort to happen, sir. You leave that to me."

It was silent at the other end of the phone.

"I do have one other request, though, general."

"Name it, master sergeant."

"My son, Cleet IV, is probably wondering where I am. Could you arrange that one of the Crabtree boys gets him boarded at his school—Peckham Hall in Charleston—while his mama is away?"

"Done, master sergeant." The general cleared his throat and dismissed the aide. A door shut and the general resumed the conversation. "Do you have faith, Master Sergeant Vaduva?"

"In the mission's success or in my ability to complete the mission, sir?"

"In God."

"I wasn't raised religious, sir. Except for a short time as a young girl, when my mama was mixed up with the Pentecostal Tabernacle of the Holy Ghost's Testimony church, in McDowell County, West Virginia. Though she viewed churchgoing more as a business venture than a call to prayer."

He lowered his voice even lower. "This is not something I customarily share with the soldiers under my command, but I am an ordained minister in my church."

"I didn't know that, sir."

"May I give you a blessing, master sergeant?"

"Of course, general. I'd like that." Which was true. Though I was not a regular churchgoer, I was indeed a believer. It only took about two seconds in a foxhole to turn you into one.

"Go with God, master sergeant. May you go with God."

Within the hour, as promised, the container list appeared on my phone. In an electrical closet below deck I reviewed the single-spaced, twenty-five-page manifest, cataloguing shippers, contents, and container numbers and location aboard ship.

No clues emerged. Stallings Boyell and Augusta could have been concealed in any of them: containers supposedly filled with blue jeans, beer, furniture, building supplies, medical equipment, computers, electronics, phones, canned foods, and automotive parts.

The journey across the Atlantic would take five days, I reckoned. Even if I pried open each container in broad daylight—which of course I could not do without altering the ship's crew and Augusta's captors—there was no way I'd find Augusta before we docked in Lisbon.

I squatted in the electrical closet for fourteen hours, shaking out a charley horses as I read and reread the list. The answer was in there, buried somewhere deep in the manifest. I just had to find it. After my tenth review of the document, I realized my mind was fatigued. So, I began on the last page and went backwards. And then, there it was, on page twenty-two, as shiny as a quarter laying in the bed of a spring-feed creek: Container 4853F17KZ, in Row Q, Slot 15B and Container 9287J51GX, in Row D, Slot 9A. Both were registered to a company called Antebellum Accessories, LLC, and contained "graphic handbags manufactured in VA, AL, NC, SC, GA, FL, LA, TN, MS, and KY." I got on my phone and looked up the company. I clicked on the OUR STORY button on the company's website, and, sure enough, my suspicion was confirmed: "Founded by Pepper Boyell, a Charleston native whose ancestors first arrived on the shores of South Carolina in 1683, when King Charles II dispatched his 'Lord Proprietors' to the colonies . . ."

I rounded up materials from the kitchen, boiler room and crew quarters to use for camo: an electrician's dark jumpsuit, motor oil, rotting foods like carrots, tomatoes and greens, which imparted color when smeared on clothing and skin. I commenced my search after sundown, stealthily moving through passages and slinking down corridors below deck.

Container 4853F17KZ, in Row Q, was nearest. It was on deck level. Six containers were stacked atop it. When I got closer, I heard the muffled sound of voices from inside, all of them Southern. But I did not recognize them as either Augusta's or Stallings'. Nor were they voices I recognized as members of the Masked Oracle Society. Yet, somehow, they were familiar; I had heard those voices before—albeit from way back in my memory. There were a bunch of them in that container—as maybe as many as five, all of them talking over each other. I drew the Beretta and pressed my ear against the side of the container.

"... How about a slice of blueberry cobbler?" an old woman's voice asked.

"Reckon I will! Thanks, Aunt Bee," replied the second voice, a boy's.

"What about you, Andy?" the old woman asked.

An adult male replied, "Not after all that cornbread."

"If Sherriff Taylor don't want none, I got room," said another man in the container who snorted as he talked. His West Virginia accent was instantly recognizable to me. What was he doing with those Carolina boys?

"You've had three helpings already, Barney!" the woman they called Aunt Bee said.

The conversation about cobbler went on for five minutes. I kept waiting to hear Stallings Boyell speak up, but there was no trace of his voice.

As time elapsed, more than a half dozen people revealed themselves to be in the container. How they all fit in there I could not divine: There was, in addition to the man they called "Sheriff," that Aunt Bee woman, Barney the West Virginian, the boy, a fella named Gomer—he talked goofy, that one—a slow-talker named Floyd, and a drunk-sounding man they called Otis.

After the voices stopped, they all started playing music. Someone began whistling and snapping fingers. Then drums and a bass kicked in, followed by horns. When I heard that music, that's when I realized how I knew the people's voice's—*from the TV!* When I was a little girl, Great-grandmama Charlene used to watch rerun marathons of that show; Stallings Boyle was watching old-time TV shows on his computer.

When the show ended, I heard buttons pressed on a phone. "It's me again. Where the devil are you, Pepper? Look, when you get this, call me back."

So it was established: Stallings Boyell was in Container 4853F17KZ. The question: was Augusta with him?

16.

I reckoned I'd better check the second container before going into Stallings', guns blazing.

Under the bright glow of a full moon—the enemy on a night like this—I traversed the passageways and crammed myself into narrow walkways between containers.

The second container was located in the middle of the stack. I climbed up. There was no sound coming from inside. No light neither. It took two hours, but with a screwdriver I found below deck, I popped the lockbox. At the bottom of each door I disengaged the knuckles, releasing the vertical lock rods.

Beretta in one hand and my phone's flashlight in the other, I swung open the door, expecting to encounter at least one and perhaps as many as three armed guards.

It was like a morgue in there.

I heard the muted humming of an electrical generator, next to which was placed one of those power cord extenders, into which an oxygen pump and nightlight was plugged in.

Augusta was in the middle of the room, in a four-poster canopied bed, tucked beneath a patchwork quilt, perfectly still. I teared up when I saw her. I placed the palm of my hand over her check. It was reassuringly warm. "Augusta darlin', can you hear me?" She laid soundless and still. After I checked her vitals, I inspected the two IV drips connected to her arms. One to keep her nourished and hydrated, the other doped-up.

I aimed the light around the room. Everything—the embroidered antique fainting sofa off to the side, the carpet, the bed linens, the little makeup table with mirror in the corner, even the porcelain bedpan—were color-coordinated, a matching shade of faded peach. The walls and interior doors were covered in heavy velvet draping (behind which was placed duct-taped foam-padding, a foot thick, to soundproof the container).

I walked around the container, hearing only the sound of my bare feet slapping on the metal floor. Eighteen hundreds-era paintings of Southern women wearing big hats and carrying parasols, all of them in big gold-painted wooden frames, were hung along the walls. The whole room was done up like a plantation-girl's mansion in the 1800s.

Her Masked Oracle crown was perched on the fainting sofa, along with her wilting Queen's bouquet. The orchids still smelled sweet and perfume-y.

Just as I picked up the crown, a forearm wrapped around my neck. I felt the blade in my back, poking into my spinal column.

"Whatever Stallings Boyell is paying you, I'll pay you double."

He tightened the grip at my neck.

"Put the gun down."

"Okay. You're the boss." I slowly bent forward to place the gun on the fainting sofa.

"Faster!"

I laid the weapon at the sofa's edge, at an angle, knowing

it would fall. I prayed it wouldn't discharge when it crashed to the floor and kill Augusta or myself. When, as expected, it hit the floor, the gun, thankfully, did not discharge.

"Pick it up!"

I bent forward, slowly, and maneuvered myself into a modified version of Big Toe Pose from yoga. I folded myself in half, clamshell-style. He gripped tighter at my neck. By the time my open palms were planted flatly and firmly on the floor, his feet were elevated slightly off the ground. With a fierce thrust of my left hip, I flipped him over my head into the wall, onto which he crashed with a thud. He bounced off and landed on the fainting sofa, whose claw-footed legs collapsed instantly when his two-hundred-and-twenty-pound-frame, pure muscle, came crashing down upon it.

I dragged him to the floor. Half-conscious and sprawled before me was Gullah Jack.

He reached for the gun. I kicked it away and I pressed the ball of my foot against his windpipe as I clinched his wrist and stretched out his arm, preparing to dislocate his shoulder, if necessary.

"Now it's time for you to start answering questions. The Boyells are the brains of this scheme. You're the brawn, is that it?"

He shot a blank stare at me. Tilted his head up proudly. "You don't know what you're talking about."

"Liar. You put my girl on this ship. You've been working for them all along. You were on the *Hissy Fit;* you were at the Boyells' the night we ate leftovers; you were waiting tables at the Masked Oracle ball. It was you that snatched Augusta backstage, wasn't it?"

"It's *you* in cahoots with them."

I yanked on the arm, but he was indifferent to the pain. I grabbed his knife off the sofa and waved it over the zipper of his trousers. "If you want to keep what's below deck, you're going to tell me everything. Where is she going after we land in Lisbon? Who's buying her? Where's the payoff? What do they plan to do with her? Talk!"

"Like you don' know. You're the one who sold the girl to them."

"Answer my question!"

Gullah Jack was defiant. "Answer mine first."

"I'm asking the questions."

"Just one."

"What?"

"Where'd you learn to flip a man like that? Not at no yoga class," he snorted.

It was not my habit to provide answers to people I interrogated—whether they were Taliban fighters or South Carolina kidnappers. But, given Gullah Jack's size and fearlessness, I reckoned his learning more about my combat credentials might dissuade him from attempting to overpower me later. "In the United States Army. Joint Special Operations Command."

He laughed. "You're no JSOC! You're country club."

I eyed him with suspicion. "How do you know JSOC? Civilians don't know that acronym."

He remained silent.

"I'll yank this arm right out of its socket. One, two . . ."

"I know because I was United States Army Rangers, 3rd Battalion, 75th Ranger Regiment."

"Liar."

"Test me."

"What's a 'ground pounder'?"

"An infantry fighter."

"What's a 'dash ten'?"

"All U.S. Army technical publications are assigned a number that ends in 'dash-ten.'"

"You're not talking Gullah anymore."

"I was an officer, a major, in the United States Army. I hold a bachelor's degree in comparative literature and a juris doctorate from Princeton and Yale, respectively. I'm now a special agent with the Federal Bureau of Investigation. Forgive me if I picked up a few words of Standard English along the way."

If I was being played, this guy was a master.

"The knife you're poking into my crotch is a U.S. Army-issued tactical spring assisted folding knife. How much longer do we have to keep playing Army trivia?"

"Who was head of JSOC when you were over there?"

"General Peter D. Loehr."

I loosened my grip—but not entirely. What's your real name, Gullah Jack?"

"The same as my Gullah name: Jack Capers."

"You're not a Gullah."

"I'm Gullah, alright. One hundred percent. My family has been on Gatuh Island for three centuries, which afforded me entrée to Stallings Boyell. It's why I was tapped for this assignment."

I removed my foot from his neck.

"Can I get up now?"

"You're the FBI's undercover man?"

"Yes. You knew I was here?"

"I did."

"Would've been nice if somebody told me the Army sent someone, too."

"It was classified."

He sniffed. "It always is." He shook his head disdainfully. "And now here we are. On a slow boat to China."

"Portugal."

"And nobody bothered to tell us we were on the same team. Classic U.S. government at work. All that 'need-to-know' bullshit," Gullah Jack said as he rubbed his shoulder.

"Our bosses speculated one or both of us will be killed if we worked in tandem."

"Yeah, right." He rotated his neck. "Assuming we didn't kill each other first."

17.

After confirming she had plenty of oxygen and nutrients, we sealed up Augusta's container. "If anybody spots you or me coming in and out of that container, it's game over. So, we don't go back in there; she's perfectly safe," Special Agent Gullah Jack declared.

"Agree."

Jack, who realized I had caught him staring at the lace on my bra, averted his eyes. "Beg your pardon, soldier."

"No offense taken. It's not your fault you ended up working with a half-naked woman. I had to strip when I swam out to ship and board it." I tried to adopt some form of modesty, bending my arm at the elbow and covering myself, as though I was placing my hand over my heart and reciting the Pledge of Allegiance. "How'd you get on?"

"The old-fashioned way, I guess: I just followed Stalling Boyell. Boarded the ship about sixty seconds after he did."

"What do we do about Stallings? What if he goes wandering above deck?"

"With a bunch of Portuguese merchant-sailors hanging around chain-smoking and peeing over the sides? He knows better. He'll be quite happy where he is. I'm sure he's got a week's worth of chow in there. Fresh water. A bed. Power, so he can watch movies on his laptop. A porta-potty."

After we sealed Augusta's container, we slinked through the passageways.

"Where do we hide?"

"We'll find a room below decks. Half of them are unoccupied."

Jack was right about that, although the rooms he spoke of were tiny. But at least they had real toilets and showers.

Once we got ourselves settled in one of the cabins I asked, "Who's at the other end for the other handoff?"

"I don't know."

We played the speculation game: who was the buyer? A sheik? A Russian gangster? An African warlord? How would we get off the ship undetected? Jump overboard? Hide in a container? How would we spot the buyer's middleman in port? How would they transport Augusta's container terrestrially?

After our speculations ran their course, Jack said, "Can't speak for you, but I need food. Wait here and I'll scrounge up some chow."

"Too dangerous."

"It's not. Skeleton crew. Everyone's asleep."

While he was away, I took a scorching hot shower and washed all the sea-salt out of my hair. Still clad in only bra and underwear, I needed to find some clothes. The cabin's dresser drawers and closets were empty, but down the passageway, outside the captain's quarters, in a laundry bag left there for pickup, I found a navy blue wool sweater, a gold anchor and four bars stitched on its shoulder board epaulets. The captain was mighty fat, I was grateful to discover; the sweater stretched down to mid-thigh level.

Special Agent Gullah Jack returned with an industrial-sized tin can, food splashed over its sides. He handed me a spoon. "Made you some authentic—well, mostly authentic—Gullah Grub. No okra or ginger aboard ship, I'm sad to report."

I stirred the contents of the can: a stew of shrimp, pork, chicken, big chunks of onions, rice, and broth.

He pulled chunks of bread and apples out of his pockets. "Brought sides and dessert, too."

It was the first time a man ever cooked for me—*that* was for certain.

He sat down beside me on the sofa. While we ate, we talked more about what we expected in Lisbon. After we exhausted every speculative scenario, we rewound the clock and talked about Augusta's abduction, and how she was targeted by the Masked Oracle Society.

"When you rolled into town and those people—who *hate* strangers and let *no one* in their circle—took an instant liking to you, I figured you must have made a deal with them, sold them Augusta."

Jack shook his head in disgust when I told him about the Saturday night, just after midnight, when cloaked, candle-holding Society members serenaded Augusta, praising her as "kindhearted and fair" and flattering her "sturdy health and shining hair."

"That's just sick. Women take gestures like that seriously. To pervert it the way they did. It's just not right to mess with a female's head that way. Especially a teenage girl's."

"No one ever serenaded me when I was growing up," I declared. "Though there was plenty of perverts."

As was the custom on multi-day stakeouts, as conversational topics were exhausted, the talk grew increasingly personal. He wanted to know all about my childhood in West Virginia.

I asked about his boyhood on Gatuh Island. We talked about gator-hunting, before covering cars, guns, and fitness routines.

When that conversational course was complete, I asked if he ever married or had children. "Never. My career is my mistress," he said with a sly grin. "Is it really true that you're a widow? Or was that just your cover story?"

I told him about my marriage to Colonel Cletus Bland III and our children.

"If you don't mind my asking, how did your husband die?"

"I prefer not to get into specifics. The memory is painful. But I can tell you our son, Cleet IV, is the spittin' image of him—and a natural-born killer, to boot," I said with motherly pride. "He's already a legend back home, a BB gun sharp-shooter who can drop a squirrel off an electrical wire. When he turns eighteen, he'll serve in the United States Army, like his parents."

Jack asked about Augusta. I picked a bit of shrimp shell out of my teeth. "That's a complicated story. After she was abandoned by her mentally-unstable mother, I became her legal—"

"—you're not her biological mom?"

"No. We're nothing alike. Isn't that evident?"

"You're both blonde. You both have green eyes. You're the same size. Looked like a mother-daughter combo to me, if I ever saw one. More like mother-sister, actually."

"I hoped to keep her near me. Raise her as my own. When I left Charlottesville to return to West Virginia, with Cleet IV, she didn't come, of course. There was no way she was relocating, she said, even though I found her a good school. So, she stayed on in Charlottesville, with her aunt. But then she got expelled from the Digby-Emmanuel Day School in ninth grade. Which led to Swiss boarding school and the subsequent trouble she courted there, which lead to her second school exit. I had genuinely hoped she might make a fresh start in Charleston at Peckham Hall. She's still a little girl under all that sassy teenage attitude."

Jack wiped his mouth with his hand. "What happens to her when all of this is over?" He averted his eyes before he spoke the next line: "Assuming all turns out okay?"

"It will, I have no doubt about that. I reckon she'll do what all the women in her bloodline do. Go to some fancy private college in the South. Find a rich boy with good teeth and clear skin who works for his daddy. Join a country club. Have kids. Do yoga. Go to parties."

"You think she'll come around, become closer to you after she grows up?"

"No. She's counting the days until she can be done with me and Cleet IV. That saddens me, because I think of her as my daughter now. But her mind—and her personality—looks to be fixed. It will be especially hard on Cleet IV, though. He idolizes her."

Outside the porthole the morning sun was beginning to show its hot yellow face. Jack stood and peered through the porthole, directing my attention to four dolphins, who leapt in and out of the water in formation.

He began inhaling and exhaling deeply as he swirled in slow-motion.

"What are you doing?"

"Silat," he said. "I'm in knots."

"Tai chi?"

"Not on your life. Deadliest martial art in the world."

"Never heard of it."

"Makes taekwondo and kung fu look like ballerina class. From Malaysia. None of that zen-spiritual-get-in-touch-with-your-inner-energy nonsense; it's pure violence; it's all about breaking bones."

"I'd like to learn how to do it."

"I'll teach you."

I stood and copied his moves. He asked me how I found my way to the Army. "Illegally, before my eighteenth birthday," I told him. "My mama, who is an expert in such matters, made me a fake I.D. Got me into the West Virginia National Guard. Then I joined the Army."

I asked him about his journey into the military and, later, the FBI. After he won his scholarships to Princeton and Yale, he planned to go to New York and become rich and powerful and fancy. "The 3C's," he said, "cars, cufflinks, and co-ops." But after a few years among people he spent his childhood dreaming to become, he knew he belonged somewhere else.

He was a charmer, that Jack was. Handsome, humble, easy to talk to. "I bet the girls were after you something fierce." I teased. I was beginning to develop affinity for Special Agent Gullah Jack beyond the strictly professional. This happened a lot during combat situations. Put two people in a bunker together, both of them getting shot at, and you couldn't help but to get familiar, to want to seize a part of their life to sustain yours—and vice versa.

"The girls were after me, alright. But for all the wrong reasons. And definitely not at first. When I showed up on an Ivy League campus the first day, they thought I was some gang-banger from the Bronx sent there to rape them. The girls nervously crossed the street when I approached from the opposite direction. But after the first week, they knew they'd seen me around—and felt safer. Of course, they thought they'd remembered seeing me clearing tables or raking the lawn. At least they were no longer afraid; they just became indifferent, treated me like I was invisible. Realizing I was a serious fish out of water, I went out and bought some clothes that looked like theirs. Khaki pants, a pair of Ray-Ban Aviator sunglasses. When they saw me all decked out after my shopping spree, it was like it was the first time they saw me. Then they all wanted to sit next to me and make their Very First Black Friend. They invited me to parties, where they didn't know what to say to me until they were drunk, which they always were. That's when the girls gave me phone numbers and told me to text them any time after ten at night, any night of my choosing, if I ever wanted a hook-up. Not go on a date, not go to a dance—only hook up. After I'd had enough of that scene in college and later, on Wall Street, I enlisted. Maybe it was the Boy Scout in me. Once an Eagle Scout, always an Eagle Scout."

We sat down and exchanged war stories, at which time the mood grew somber. He told me about defending Combat Outpost Loughlin in Nuristan Province, when the base was rocked with enemy machine gun and rocket fire. He lost his best friend on that day, he said. He also told me about patrolling Afghanistan's deadly Kunar Valley, and how it all went wrong after two dozen enemy fighters fired rocket-propelled grenades at his platoon, killing five. I already knew the story about how he stopped a suicide bomber inside a public library in Iraq; I read about it in *Stars & Stripes*. He won a Medal of Honor for his bravery. Though I did not mention that, as such mentions were always a source of embarrassment for soldiers.

I told him about my surveillance work in Al-Karkh and capturing Mehdi Hashmi.

"You were part of the team that got 'Corned Beef Hash?'"

"Affirmative."

"That raid is *legendary!*"

Reciting the story got me to thinking about how me and Colonel Bland were smuggled out of Karz after the mission, in that food and medical relief convoy. It was on that journey that we fell in love.

I walked over to the porthole and looked out on the water in hopes of seeing the dolphin pack. They were gone. I kept my back to Jack, mindful that I was becoming sentimental for my deceased husband. I swallowed hard, spun around and said, "Did I tell you about the time they had me infiltrate a seamstresses' group in Ghazni Province?"

When my story was complete, he said, "You're very skilled at covert ops, master sergeant. When you showed up in town, you had me totally fooled. I totally bought your cover. That you were some sort of Charlottesville socialite—like those three drunk women I met on the boat in the golf-resort hats."

I raised my eyebrows in a playful manner. "Did you get an invitation for an after-ten hookup from any of them?"

"You bet I did."

I was keen to know which one—or ones—but didn't want to seem too interested. My guess: Tangerine-Colored Pinehurst Hat, who was obsessed with his eyes. "Technically speaking, I was a Charlottesville socialite," I resumed, putting the conversation back on a safe and familiar track. "I married the local aristocrat, Colonel Bland. I joined a country club. I hosted fundraisers. Fancy private schools."

"Less pressure posing as a socialite there than in Charleston,

I imagine. Must be hard, using your kid as bait. Don't know that I could do that."

"I never intended to use Augusta as bait. They came to her, not the other way around."

"Still, a lot of people would have turned tail and ran."

"That's not what I do."

He looked me up and down. "*Damn,* you're a strong, independent—and if you don't mind my saying—*fine* specimen of a woman. Just curious—if it's not too personal—how a woman like you didn't find herself remarried after her husband passed. There must have been scores of rich, eligible bachelors in Charlottesville after you."

"Those men are not my type," I told him. "I could never be with a civilian. Military men only for me. Well, that's not entirely true. I tangled with a civilian or two in high school, but that was a lifetime ago." Though I did not mention Ricky Ray Jeeter and Scooter Skinner by name, I told him about our teenage skinny-dipping adventures in Beryl's Hole, the fresh-water spring about a mile up in the hills from Mama's place in Thurmond. "But once I joined the military, I lost interest in men who just want bigger trucks and more beer and bigger TVs and will do anything they can to get out of having to get a job. I like men who are in service to higher ideals, men willing to fight and die for them."

I realized, as the time passed, our eye contact was becoming more sustained. I asked him about his romantic adventures as a teenager on Gatuh Island. His did not include skinny-dipping sessions with the opposite sex. His mama made sure of that, he said with a laugh. His family was devoutly religious. And his parents were strict! He said he spent most of his childhood in church—"the praise house"—he called it, where his papa was pastor and long hours were spent in communal prayer, song, and dance. He missed his parents, who both died while he was still in high school, something mighty. With no siblings or relatives left on Gatuh Island, it was lonely there. Which was why he was so keen to get out when he could—first to college, then to the military, and finally to the FBI. "But now that I am back there—even if, like you, I'm undercover and on assignment from the general—I take great comfort and solace in that island. Guess where I spend almost all my free time?"

"At the beach, gator-hunting?"

"In the praise-house. You must think I'm hopelessly old-fashioned and square."

"You're an Eagle Scout for a reason. Besides, I honor people with faith. I wish I had more of it myself."

His faith was the most important thing in his life, he said, the thing that kept him on a straight and narrow path. It kept him away from crime and liquor and tobacco, too, he said—not in a holier-than-thou tone, but with genuine gratitude.

"My mama and her mamas weren't church people," I replied when he asked about my faith traditions—or lack thereof. "Except for once, when my mama was dating a pastor at the Pentecostal Tabernacle of the Holy Ghost's Testimony church, in McDowell County, West Virginia. I learned a scripture passage there. And only one: Mark 16, verses 16-18: 'Whoever believes and is baptized will be saved, but whoever does not believe will be condemned. And these signs will accompany those who believe: in my name they will drive out demons; they will speak in new tongues; they will pick up snakes with their hands; and when they drink deadly poison, it will not hurt them at all; they will place their hands on sick people, and they will get well.' That's the passage I know. Which I was made to memorize and repeat about ten thousand times."

I asked if he was Episcopal, like all the people in Charlottesville and Charleston.

"*Piskubble,*" he laughed. His religion was a mix of the Christianity pushed on his people by white masters, who, yes, were Episcopal, jumbled in with a generous dose of traditional African beliefs—what he called "juju" and "hoodoo practice"—which his ancestors brought from Angola to the New World.

"One of the black helpers who worked at one of the big houses in Charlottesville was named Juju. Would she have been named after the religion? The way Mexicans name their sons Jesus?"

"I hope not. It's African witchcraft. Black magic."

"Stallings and Pepper Boyell gave you that witchdoctor drink at their house. She was making fun of you?"

"Yes. But it's no joke."

"I believe you."

I stood and stretched. Slow-motion silat had done nothing to alleviate my joints, which still ached from swimming and sleeplessness. My mind was so fatigued it was getting harder to process what he said in conversation or remember what my point was when I spoke. I needed to snap out of my daze. "I need some P.T. Care to join me?"

"I never pass up an opportunity to P.T.!"

In that tight little cabin, side by side on the floor, we did two hundred and fifty squats first, calling them out as we went: 187, 188, 189, 190 . . . After that, two hundred and fifty lunges, two hundred and fifty pushups, two hundred and fifty side planks, a thousand sit-ups, progressively slower, until we were both on the brink of collapse.

"Looks like you're struggling to keep up, soldier," Jack quipped when he saw the grimace on my face.

"My stomach's on fire, the muscle burn."

"Then you're way ahead of me, master sergeant. The whole left side of my body is on fire—from armpit to toe—from those nasty side planks. Ready to quit?"

"Never!"

"Split squat to cross crunches, two-fifty. Go!" he barked.

We huffed and puffed, both of us struggling to catch our breath, before adding another two hundred and fifty bicycle kicks, followed by two hundred and fifty dolphin planks, two hundred and fifty leg rotations, two hundred and fifty seated lunges, two hundred and fifty Russian twists, two hundred and fifty mountain climbers, and two hundred and fifty taekwondo kicks.

"Ready to surrender?" he taunted.

"I can do this all day. Don't test me."

"How's the heartrate, master sergeant?"

"Ready to explode."

We were almost done with the taekwondo kicks when he finally mumbled, "Enough." He lowered himself slowly to his knees. He tilted sideways, like a tree 99-percent chain-sawed through, and planted his palm on the floor to break his fall. He did everything but creak, like splitting wood, as he gradually rolled onto his back. "Everything hurts. My shoulder hurts. My arm hurts. My neck hurts. My *hair* hurts."

I stood over him and executed the remainder of pledged taekwondo kicks, calling out the numbers—147, 148, 149 —just to rub it in. When I finished, I said, "You surrendered with dignity. There is no shame in that."

He started wheezing. "Don't make me laugh. It's hard

enough to breathe as it is." He sucked in three long, deep breaths and eventually leveled out.

After the workout, I gave him first dibs on the shower. "It's the sportsmanlike thing to do, seeing as I won and all—and won handily, if you don't mind me reminding you of this painful fact."

"I'd tell you to go do something to yourself if I used expletives, but my mama had no tolerance for foul language. Washed out my mouth with soap—a palm load of Fab powdered laundry detergent when I was five. I'll take the memory of that foul chalky soap in my mouth to my grave. It was the first—and last—time a bad word has passed these lips of mine."

"I don't care for curse words neither—but for the opposite reason: my mama, and hers before her, were and remain to this day world class cussers."

I pretended not to be looking at his back—a perfect "V" shape—as he peeled off his shirt. On either side of his spine, the deltoids, traps, and scaps bulged out like as though a surgeon slid rubber orbs beneath the skin.

From the sofa, where I pretend-scrolled through my phone, I watched him pace back and forth in the bathroom. After his trousers and skivvies were off, I caught a glimpse at his backside: a firm rear end, about one third the width of his shoulders, mounted above muscular thighs almost as wide as those shoulders.

He moved to the sink, a towel wrapped around his torso as he fished through the medicine cabinet in search of a razor. I approached and stood behind him, in the doorway. "We something in common—especially when it comes to black magic."

He grinned at me through the mirror. "Is that so?"

I told him about my family's Gypsy traditions: love spells,

money spells, protection spells and charms, ancient Gypsy curses, and hex- and curse-removal spells.

He twisted the knobs on the shower. As the room got hot and steamy, he told me about juju spells: how good or bad luck was summoned with herbal bath crystals and ritual conjuring oils. In Gullah language, to *"bad mout"* someone was to put a curse on them. He told me spells could be applied for good, too: before important guests she wished to impress arrived at her home, his grandmother would sprinkle African juju powder in the living room, Jack said, reciting the 23rd Psalm as she swept cobwebs from the room's corners.

"I should know that prayer but don't."

"'The Lord is my shepherd; I shall not want. He causes me to lie down in green pastures; he leads me beside—'"

"'—still waters,' I continued. 'He restores my soul; he leads me in paths of righteousness for His name's sake.' I do know that. Command Sergeant Major Moellering, who was with me on the Corned Beef Hash capture mission, whispered the prayer about a hundred times on the chopper ride to Karz. He must have had an inclination it was his last mission. He talked of becoming a Roman Catholic priest when he got out. Fancy that."

"The Army, the church. They're both a kind of a priesthood, I suppose."

We each made our reflections silently.

"I'm going to get in the shower now, master sergeant. I'd very much like to invite you to come in and do my back for me, but there are two sound reasons not to."

I looked up. I had to chew on the inside of my cheek to keep from smiling. "What are those?"

"First, I fear you'd put a spell on me."

"I actually have the power to do that, believe it or not."

"Oh, I believe it, alright."

"And the second reason?" My private lady parts were beginning to twitch.

"I don't know quite how to say this . . ."

"Say it."

"I'm a virgin." He looked me square in the eye and held his gaze. "I made a promise to my mama to stay pure until I find the right woman to marry. I fear a shower with you would cause me to violate my oath."

"Your fears are warranted. But even if they were not, there's a third reason we won't be having a go this morning."

"And what's that, sergeant major?"

"When your kidnapped, drugged daughter is out cold in a shipping container, it's just not right to be chasing amusements by having a go with a man when she's being held captive about five hundred feet away from you. Even if that go is with a man as fine-looking as you."

He leaned in and kissed me. The towel at his waist slipped and he grabbed a knot of fabric and hoisted it back over his hips at the last possible second, sparing us both a likely violation of our respective oaths.

I smiled at him. "I'll just head back to the cabin now and do another five thousand sit-ups until it's my turn to shower."

He smiled back at me. "You go do that, you surly little . . . female dog!"

18.

Four days later, after hours' and hours' worth of nonstop foxhole conversation about every imaginable topic in the world—from fish-frying techniques to his love of a musical style he called "1960s soul jazz" to my affinity for the sound of CSX freight trains rumbling down the mountains of West Virginia—we arrived in Lisbon.

On the day of our arrival, Jack and I, crouched behind a container, watched as Stallings Boyell made his sly exit from the ship and supervised the unloading of Augusta's container.

A beautiful, scowling woman stood opposite him on the dock, her silky red pantsuit flapping in the breeze. But not her hair: it was pulled back severely in a thick, long braid that hung to the small of her back, slicked down with what must have been a quart of 10W-40 motor oil.

After the customs man—who was chummy with the woman in red—cleared the container, it was loaded onto the bed of one of those compact tractor-trailer trucks ever present throughout Europe and the Middle East.

"I don't see any of our people. The general knew the ship's destination."

"They're here, I assure you. An army of them."

The woman in red gave envelopes to the customs man and

to Stallings Boyell. As the group disbanded, Stallings Boyell attempted to hug the woman in red, but she rebuffed him. She refused even to shake hands. Stallings walked in one direction, alone, and the woman, alone, climbed into the truck.

"We need a car," I said.

"Why? Let's just hitch a ride with our guys. Once she pulls off the lot, you're going to hear about fifty mid-sized black sedans' or SUVs' engines turn over," he said.

"Which is exactly why I want my own car. Something less obvious."

He looked out over the pier. "It doesn't exactly look like there's Hertz counter around here."

I scanned the parking lot. "We're looking for an old car. Or truck, or bus, I don't care. Any vehicle at least twenty years old or older."

He pointed. "That old FIAT looks thirty."

"More like fifty. Run!"

The tires squealed as I jammed the car into gear. Jack, who I slammed into the passenger door when we fish-tailed off the lot, pulled up a road map on his phone. "Where did you learn how to hotwire cars, master sergeant?"

"Buckle up and I'll tell you."

"Catch up to her," he said as the seatbelt clicked.

"No." She's still in my range. "And to answer your question: I learned as teenager in West Virginia, where I could've been thrown in juvie for it. Then I put it to good use in the Army, where they gave me medals for getting overturned Humvees re-started after they were shelled."

"Impressive."

"I need to check in with the general."

"And me with the director."

We called our respective bosses.

"Who's the lady in red?" we both asked.

Her likeness was being run through various agencies' facial recognition software programs as we spoke, each of us was told. Jack and I each provided our briefings.

Ten minutes later, while following the woman in red truck, the general texted me. "Her name is Minodora Grigorescu. Romanian."

"I knew it!" I shouted.

"How could you tell?"

We went through the tollbooth and entered the A5 freeway. "I knew the second I saw her—big eyes, square face, high cheek bones and jet-black hair. We're unmistakable. Did you not believe me when I told you on that ship I was from Gypsy stock?"

"I figured you were jerking my chain."

"My birth name is Luludja Văduva."

"You'd never know it. Not with that blonde hair and those green eyes."

"It's camo. I look a lot more like that Minodora woman in real life than those women in Charlottesville and Charleston. But since they all look alike, I got their same dye-job, haircut, and yoga pants to blend in. Where's Stallings Boyell going?"

"FBI HQ says he's flying to Atlanta, then over to Charleston. FBI's already got someone booked on Boyell's flight to keep an eye on him."

A text came in from the general: "Nothing on Minodora Grigorescu beyond a name and face on a passport. No addresses, work history, nada. Stay tuned for more."

"Not a surprise."

"What do you mean?" Jack asked.

"You don't have experience with Gypsies the way I do. The Romani across Europe are especially skilled at the art of un-documentation; they have been for centuries. No credit cards or bank accounts, no home mortgage loans or car loans or permanent addresses. It's all cash and bartering—among other things. Nothing's going to come up."

He angled his head away from his window. "The sun here is brutal."

"Get used to it. She may drive for hours."

Jack looked down at the map. "No, she won't. This highway dead-ends in twenty minutes, at the beach, a little resort town called Cascais. Maybe they're transferring her to another boat?"

We got to speculating, when, suddenly, I realized I had lost the woman in red's truck. I opened up the FIAT, whose engine sounded like it was on the brink of explosion.

"Slow down! Did you see all those motorcycle cops on the roadside? They're everywhere. She won't be speeding, not with Augusta on the flatbed."

I eased off the gas. A few minutes later, we spotted the truck, which, as predicted, was crawling along at seventy-five kilometers per hour. Surveilling from a safe distance, we relaxed. Jack gazed out at a billboard advertisement on the A5, one for a Portuguese beer. "Not much to look at around here, is there?"

The traffic congested as we approached Cascais. The Renaults, Peugeots, and Volkswagens creeping along were packed with young couples and families, kids in the backseat sandwiched between rafts, beach balls, and towels.

We turned off the A5 and went through the historic city center, navigating roundabouts where bronze statues of kings and saints stared forlornly back at the visitors. We snaked past cafés, churches, boutiques, and tabacaria shops, all of them painted white, or yellow, or pink, each with flowering vines on their facades.

The tractor-trailer downshifted with a mighty grind and eased its way up the gentle sloping hills towards the seaside cliffs. The houses were grand, all of them behind walls and gates.

We kept two or three cars back.

The truck idled at the top of a hill, at a guard's station at the mouth of a long driveway that climbed even further up into the hills. Surrounding the property was a fifteen-foot-high stone retaining wall crowned with barbed wire.

Men in suits, badly concealed weapons bulging at hips, stood at the gates. A panel of security cameras, stacked vertically, lined the wall of the gatehouse. Upon seeing Minodora Grigorescu, the men stood erect and sprang into action. Iron gates swung open and the truck's gears ground once more as she entered the compound.

I pulled a supermarket insert off the visor and pretended to consult a map as I crawled past the compound at ten kilometers per hour and casually looked up the long, winding driveway. Whatever was at the top of that hill was not visible, shielded by a thick grove of pomegranate, orange, and plum trees. As we passed the driveway, affixed to the retaining wall was a polished bronze placard: "New Beginnings Healing Centre."

⁓

"We'll go into town, regroup, and eat."

We had at least a bit of time to refresh ourselves as we both knew Augusta wasn't going anywhere. "That Minodora gal will need to check her vitals, make sure the merchandise isn't damaged. She'll be comparing her likeness to news photos from the ball to make sure she wasn't baited and switched. She'll have a bunch of phone calls to make after that. We'll call the general and put a watch on the front gate just in case there's any movement."

We ditched the car in town and looked for somewhere to find chow and formulate our attack plan.

Outside the car, Jack gave me a head-to-toe once-over, as did half the pedestrians passing by. "Do you think it might be time to upgrade your . . . *outfit?*" I was still clad in the captain's sweater, bra and panties, forgetting I was half naked. "You need some clothing. Something boring. You're attracting the wrong kind of attention."

"I've got no money."

He reached into his wallet. "This debit card has got ten thousand dollars on it. Don't spend it all in one place."

I pointed at a seafood shack on the water. "Meet me in twenty minutes at that restaurant. Order me anything, but a lot of it."

When I returned and sat down in my cargo shorts, T-shirt, and sneakers. Jack was internet-surfing. We hastily shoveled Portuguese stew into our mouths as he read aloud. "An eating disorder is the expression of emotional distress," he read. "New Beginnings Healing Centre was created to alleviate that distress, and put teenage girls and young women back on the path to recovery and wellness . . . Anorexia and bulimia are eating disorders which typically occur during adolescence . . . Privileged teenage girls, in particular, face a unique set of stressors: anxiety, depression, volatile friendships, difficulty coping with puberty, navigating social media minefields, mood swings, friction with parents, and academic pressure to win coveted seats at elite colleges . . . Come to Portugal, high above the sea, to a private, secure, luxurious medieval castle, where addiction treatment solutions are hand tailored for clients whose individual and familial reputations require the utmost discretion. Receive expert treatment from a staff fluent in the languages and customs of an international clientele sourced from Europe, America, the Middle East, and Asia. With a limited number of spaces and a two-year waiting list, our exclusive treatment center isn't for everyone."

"Girls going in and out of there all the time. Perfect cover. None of the locals look twice at them when they arrive, either: They assume they're all on the brink of death by starvation when they're actually drugged."

Jack was chewing on a piece of fried bread when he said, "Jackpot!" He showed me the picture gallery. The grand reception hall contained overstuffed furniture, statuary, mirrors, and tapestries. The dining hall's twenty-seat table was centered, below a mural-painted ceiling. Plush sitting rooms, where counselors met with patients, contained vases stuffed with yellow and purple wildflowers. There was a medieval library with floor-to-thirty-foot-ceiling built-in bookcases, filled with what looked like three-hundred-year-old books, and a hand-carved spiral staircase climbing to the upper balcony. A gloomy chapel.

The patients' rooms, depending on size, ran from five thousand to twenty thousand dollars per week, bedroom walls covered in ornate, gold- or blue-colored tiles. The beds, bureaus, and side chairs were carved of thick mahogany, everything covered in red, green, or gold velvet. There were photos of tiled bathrooms with gigantic claw-footed tubs, lit candles surrounding them.

"Show me the outside."

"Oh, this is not good. Not good at all. Holy . . ." His voice faded as he handed his phone to me and directed my attention to a sequence of exterior photographs. "It's a medieval castle!"

The perimeter walls, reinforced by square and cylindrical towers, were covered by a battlement. A watchtower stood intimidatingly at the northern end. To the west, a line of walls rose above the mountainous cliffs, reinforced by large, rectangular towers. The castle was three hundred feet high. The windows didn't begin until one hundred and fifty feet up—and were narrow, vertical slits. Jack tossed the phone on the table. "There's no way on God's earth we're getting in there without choppers, tanks, and ground support."

"There's always a way."

We war-gamed our options: approach by water and climb the cliffs, then scale the retaining wall at the opposite end of the property; drop in by parachute; storm the gate in a pickup. One bad option after another was discussed. Each was dismissed because no element of surprise was available. No option was available that would not give Minodora Grigorescu ample time to hide—or worse, "dispose" of—the evidence, which in this instance happened to be Augusta.

"I think we call the general. Get him to requisition the house across the street. For now, we wait and watch," he said.

I took another sip of the fizzy water they make you drink in Europe. "No disrespect, but my daughter's in there. I'm going in tonight. Alone if I have to. I have a plan."

"And what's that?"

"I don't know yet. But I will have one when I come back in an hour. I'm going for a walk. Clears the mind. Makes room for fresh ideas."

An hour later I returned to the restaurant. "What's the word from our surveillance people? Any movement at the gate?"

"None."

"Good. I told you they'd keep her on ice for a while."

"What's in the bags?"

"The plan. A change of clothes for the evening. I'll show you in a little while. After you're stinky."

"After *what?*"

"I'll explain when you get back. No time now. Meet me here in forty minutes. Between now and my return, you need to make yourself as smelly as possible. Sweat, grime, B.O. Run five miles, roll in the mud, smear dog poo under your arms, make yourself nervous, do whatever you need to. But you need to smell *bad* when I come back to get you."

"And become repulsive to people?"

"And become *authentic* to people."

19.

The sun had only recently descended, the light was fading. "So, what's the secret to hotwiring a Lamborghini, master sergeant?" Jack asked as the car climbed the winding road that leads to the New Beginnings Healing Centre.

"No idea. The valet left the keys in it."

I downshifted and the Lambo growled up the hill.

"You reek," I said. "Nice job."

"And you look like a Russian hooker. That's some pair of boots."

"Let's hear your accent again."

I had explained to Jack on the drive up the various characters we would assume for Minodora. He was to say as few words as possible in response to questions. H grunted a few words in dialect. "Excellent."

Moments later, we idled at the gate. "I do all the talking from here on."

Jack issued an affirming grunt.

A Portuguese guard approached the car. *"Propriedade privado,"* he hissed before shooing us away.

"Tell Minodora Grigorescu that Vera Renczi is here to see her."

"No Minodora Grigorescu here. Go."

"She's expecting me."

"Go, or there will be trouble."

"Tell her Vera Renczi has come all the way from Romania to see her. Or I slice off your *caralho e culhões* and stuff them down your throat! Vera Renczi from Romania. Call her. Now!"

He sneered and entered the gatehouse. My and Jack's faces, filmed from various angles, were displayed on the four security monitors. A second guard got on a second phone. Five minutes later, the guards approach us. "Get out, both of you," said the first, who grimaced as he frisked Jack—who did smell right terrible just as I asked him to—while the second guard rummaged through the car, checking glove boxes and below seats. He cursed as he tried to figure out how to release the trunk—if there was one. After sweeping below the car with a mirror, the guards waved us in.

"Past the first gauntlet."

"Only fifty more to go."

We crept up the drive, past all the trees. "I never knew it was possible to plant so dense a forest on ten acres," he said. "Japanese pear trees, Middle Eastern dates, Vietnamese tea trees. That whole groove over there is imported from Africa: guava, fever trees, marula trees, whistling thorns: somebody spent a fortune importing all of these trees."

We approached the castle. Off to the side, Augusta's shipping container was still on the back of the flatbed truck. We parked. A pale yellow glow emanated from the narrow window slits.

Chains cranked and unspooled as the drawbridge lowered. We saw nobody. A rusted iron grill protecting the front door groaned as it raised. Still no one to be seen as the wooden doors swung open. I extinguished the engine. "Remember: I do all the talking from now on. You just grunt."

Jack made a grunting sound.

"Perfect."

We stood in the grand reception hall, which I recognized from the photos. It was cool in the castle, bordering on cold. Ten minutes passed and still no one greeted us. Along the walls were the eating disorder clinic's "staff diplomas," expensively and identically framed: psychologists, psychiatrists, therapists, nurses, physicians, nutritionists, fitness instructors, life coaches, and so on.

On the many display tables, framed portraits of teenage girls, all of them vibrant and healthy, were displayed. I inspected the photos, wondering if Augusta might be featured. I could tell upon closer inspection that the girls weren't patients; some were even familiar to me, as the pictures were ripped out of the same teen girls' fashion magazines strewn about Augusta's room at home.

"Correction: you don't look like a Russian hooker; you look like a witch," whispered Jack through clenched teeth.

"Good."

I pulled a compact out of my bag and applied a fifth coat of lipstick, adjusted my false eyelash, and shook out my freshly-dyed ink-black hair. Through the compact's reflection I could see the rotating security camera mounted on the wall, recording our every move. There were a half dozen of them scattered across the grand reception hall.

I heard the heels clacking across the floor before I saw her. *"Nu v-am mai văzut de mult,* Vera Renczi," Minodora said as she breezed into the room.

"Long time, indeed," I replied in English.

"Ah, you would prefer to speak English? Very well. Let us all have a glass of champagne and get acquainted. But first, who is this mouth-watering *negru?*"

"Jack."

"Jack?"

"He told me his full name once," I said with indifference. "I can't pronounce it."

Minodora purred. "Where did you find him?"

"In Angola."

Minodora scanned Jack up and down. "He is your lover?"

"He is more my . . . *helper*. More or less permanently."

Minodora grinned. "Ah, I see. Whatever you paid for him, he's worth double! Perhaps there will be a bidding war for him before our reunion is over." She walked up to Jack and smoothed out the shoulders of his shiny purple suit, then fastened his jacket, her fingers teasing the buttons playfully. "Smells like a man of Africa, too. Earthy. I love it. No amount of cologne can mask it—even the expensive stuff." She sniffed dramatically. "Bulgari pour Homme?"

"Good nose," I said approvingly.

"A good nose pays in my business." She brushed her palm across Jack's smoothly-shaven cheek. "As a rule, men do not amuse me—except for business, of course. But with this one . . . I could make an exception." Just as quickly she grew bored of Jack and turned her back on him. "Come, let us sit."

We took our places in front of a ten foot-by-ten-foot stone fireplace. A half dozen silver candelabras, all lit, lined the interior of the fireplace. We sunk into the sofas. A young man pushing a cart, which seemed to come out of nowhere, appeared. Silently, he unloaded a bottle of Țuică, an alcoholic drink from Romania whose label I recognized. Four ruby-red

Bohemian crystal shot glasses were lined up. The purple liquid was poured. Next, the cheese platter was arranged. After he distributed plates and napkins, I expected him to leave. But the young man—who poured a glass of Țuică for himself—was apparently staying.

Minodora pointed at the cheese selection. "Local fare for my new friends: Azeitão, Évora, Pico, and Serra da Estrela. Nice with the fig jam and marmelada. And especially for you, Jack, almonds and walnuts. Your people have a tradition as foragers, no?"

Jack grunted.

She lifted the lid on a silver box, plucked a cigarette, and leaned forward, awaiting a light.

"You won't eat?" I asked.

"I hate food." Her servant bowed and lit Minodora's cigarette with a gold lighter. She nodded at him. "This is João."

I glanced up at João to appraise him in the same cool, but indecent way in which Minodora appraised Jack. His face was veiled by the shadow of a large fern next to me, but I made sure my eyes ran good and slow over the curve of his buttocks.

"You might say he is my *helper,* too," Minodora said with a sniff. "He brings me things." She expelled a thick cloud of smoke. "And then, when the time is right, takes them away." She laughed huskily as she leaned back and sunk into the sofa. After taking a sip of the plum liqueur, Minodora said to Jack, "Do you know why when I saw your boss 'Vera Renczi' I said, 'Long time no see'?"

Jack nodded no.

"Of course not. One suspects that, of your many attributes, a command of Romanian history—or any history further back than what you ate for breakfast— isn't one of them. I said,

'Long time no see' because the Vera Renczi I know, the legend, the most notorious woman in the history of Romania, has been dead for almost a century." She paused, delighting in the silence as she stared me down. "So, can you imagine my surprise when the guard rang and announced that Vera Renczi—the infamous 'Black Widow,' the 'Chatelaine of Berkerekul'—was at my doorstep?"

Jack made a face that suggested he didn't understand a word Minodora was saying.

"Has your boss told you Vera's tragic story, handsome Jack?"

Jack indicated I had not.

"Come with me on a journey back to Bucharest in the 1920s and '30s. Vera Renczi was high-born woman from one of the best families. *Astonishing* beauty. A very passionate woman, she was. But with one weakness, which turned out to be her undoing: her appetite for validation from men was insatiable. Poor dear." Minodora flicked an ash on the stone floor. "Vera was *insanely* jealous of her men. The minute a man she believed to be under her spell even so much as *glanced* at another woman, he was exterminated. Always the same way: arsenic-laced red wine. By the way, neither of you have touched your Țuică. I urge you to try it."

Jack and I sipped from our shot glasses. Cautiously.

"Despite her high pedigree," Minodora continued, "she was undiscriminating when it came to men: aristocrats, bank clerks, other women's husbands, farm hands, high government officials, day laborers, dog-groomers—she fucked them all. And every one of them vanished. *Poof!*"

Minodora took her first sip of Țuică.

"She did this for almost twenty years, until the police finally landed on her doorstep. Soon thereafter, they discovered thirty-five coffins in her wine cellar. At her trial, she confessed that she liked to venture down to the cellar at night and sit in her armchair amidst the decomposing corpses. She liked being surrounded by her former suitors, she told the judge." Minodora squashed the cigarette in a crystal ashtray. "And now, who is here before me but her ghost."

"Romani women's stories are all the same," I said. "Not many happy endings. Only the names and dates change."

"And what is the name of the Romanian woman who sits before me who most definitely is *not* Vera Renczi?"

"Luludja Văduva is the name that would appear on my birth certificate—if I had one. We Romani have never been big on record keeping or registering with the authorities, have we, Minodora?"

Minodora raised her shot glass and tilted it in my direction. "This is how we retain our mystery. Though mine is not maintained with you—who knew my name before I knew yours. This puts me at a disadvantage. I loathe being at a disadvantage."

"I come bearing a proposal that will be to our mutual advantage."

She took another sip of Țuică as she studied me carefully. "Your accent. I can't place it. South African?"

"The only place my ancestors haven't been."

"Tell me about all the places they *have* been."

"We started out in Petrești, in southern Romania, if you know it."

"I do."

"My ancestors had a blood feud with a rival clan from the next village."

"Gherghești?"

"That's the one."

"About?"

"The Văduva women were fortune-tellers. So were the women of Gherghești. Competition for customers was fierce. I don't know if it was the Văduva women who were poaching their neighbors' customers or the other way around, but the rival village women put a curse on the Văduva women."

"Those are never good. Let me guess: money or sex? Or maybe both? Perhaps they made it impossible for Văduva women to keep a man, which in turn would guarantee a lifetime's poverty and whoring if they wished to eat?"

"Something like that. Our women kept moving to other villages, and later to other countries, searching for men we could keep. Poland in the 1500s, then, over the centuries, on to England. Then Ireland. Then Canada. Then America. All those places live in my voice, I reckon. We Romani, we move around quite a bit."

"That's the truth," Minodora sighed. "'One step ahead of the posse,' isn't that the phrase one hears in American cowboy movies? And stop calling call me 'Romani.' I detest this modern castrato of a word. I'm a Gypsy—and proud of it."

She took another cigarette from the silver box and leaned forward, João's signal it was time for a light.

It wasn't until João bowed this second time, putting his face in a direct beam of afternoon sunlight, that I noticed his shiny skin and the ultra-groomed stubble he wore. My eyes went right to his hand, where I spotted the three-dot triangle formations tattooed onto each middle finger. João was the boy in the Red Ferrari who lured Augusta in his car in Montreux.

I glanced up at his face again—a mistake.

20.

João returned the gaze with contempt. "I know you. From Prague? Or was it Milano?"

"I don't think we run in the same circles," I sniffed. "Something tells me we haven't found ourselves sipping Kir Royales at the Hotel Paříž in Prague or seated side by side at Dolce & Gabbana's Ready-to-Wear Collection in Milan," I said dismissively.

Bristling at the insult, João's curiosity morphed into contempt as he poured himself a second shot of Țuică. He must, in his line of work, have seen the faces of a thousand women, on a thousand street corners, inside retail shops, restaurants, bars—"things to bring Minodora," all of them. Of course, none of those women had snapped his elbow joint and dragged a fresh-faced teenaged blonde out of his car, but our meeting had been fast and furious. Satisfied I was no threat, or, more likely, too lazy to overheat the hard drive of his memory, he helped himself to a lump of cheese, which he chewed with gusto, mouth open.

"Tell me, did the hex put on your women by the rival clan stick?" Minodora asked, her tone playful as she pulled her long braid over to the front side, dangled it over a breast, and picked at her split ends.

"Five centuries later, it's still in effect."

"Tragedy. So, you are single, of course?"

"Yes."

"Your mother?"

"Yes. And her mother and her mother and her mother before her."

"So this explains your affinity for Vera Renczi, a Gypsy woman unlucky at love—just like you."

"Unlucky at love, but lucky in business, because I know two things Vera did not."

"And those are?"

"First, men were not made to validate me, only to surrender what's in their pockets to me."

"Spoken like a true Gypsy woman." She gazed over at my chest, for the fifth or sixth time. "Second?"

"Unlike Vera, I know how not to get caught."

She sighed. "I'm not sure I am so interested in learning about your business ventures. As I am simply a health-clinic operator with no grander aspirations."

The conversation halted. From another room, I heard the faint sound of a pan flute and multiple violins. I took another sip of Țuică and pretended to savor it. When I made eye contact with Minodora, she cocked her head and said, "Why are you here, Luludja Văduva, sitting before me so stylishly, with those elegantly crossed legs, concealed from my hungry gaze by those glossy thigh-high Versace boots with all those marvelous studs and buckles?"

I placed a hand on one of the buckles and petted it. "Because I want in."

"In what?"

"I can get you girls."

"I have girls. There's a two-year waiting list to get into this clinic. Every month a fashion magazine is published. And every month another fourteen-year-old girl sees a skinnier, prettier version of herself. The virtuous circle spins. I don't need more girls."

"Not those girls. Who only fetch five or ten thousand a week in one of your velvet-bedspreaded upstairs rooms. I mean the other girls: the girls you sell."

"Now I think someone has been putting something in *your* wine, my dear."

"I can get you girls from America, the fairest girls of all. Girls with spirit and spunk—not the trash João snatches from mildewed ladies' rooms in Prague discotheques, or the ruddy-faced sluts he lures out of pubs in the British Midlands."

"I told you, I have plenty of patients already."

"Plenty is never enough."

"I think you are in a very different business than me, Ghost of Vera Renczi." Minodora stood. "Thank you both for coming," she said. "I always enjoy chatting with someone from the old country. I so rarely get the opportunity to do so. João will show you out."

Jack and I connected eyes as we stood.

João was armed, that was confirmed. Minodora, possibly. We could overtake them. But then what? How long until the guards in the gatehouse—who were watching our wine-and-cheese soirée on security monitors—would appear with AK-47s? And how many others were in the house—behind curtains, in closets, perched in stairwells, playing Gypsy folk music in other rooms—guns trained on us already? Jack and I gloomily proceeded to the door, under the watchful eye of João, who grimaced a bit as he rubbed his elbow.

Suddenly, Jack turned on his heel and flashed for Minodora a wide, menacing smile, revealing the 18-carat gold star fitted on his incisor. "We get you Southern girls," he grunted. "Rich girls white as snow, with blonde hair and pale eyes. From Atlanta, New Orleans, Nashville. Fresh, tasty virgins."

Without giving her a chance to react, I expanded on Jack's pitch. "Girls with perfect smiles because their parents spent two thousand dollars on braces in sixth grade. Girls with flawless skin, because their parents spent a fortune on Accutane in eighth grade. Girls who've had every imperfection corrected: crooked noses, flat chests, meaty thighs, and saggy asses. Rich girls, cultured girls, educated girls with impeccable manners."

Minodora approached—cautiously. She tightened the back of her black feather-drop earing as she walked. "The clinic has a robust patient pipeline—girls with eating disorders from around the world." She stroked her braid as she collected her thoughts, then issued an exasperated sigh. "That said, we're projecting fewer patients from the U.S. in the months ahead. For the past year or so, I've had a mutually beneficial relationship with an intake coordinator in the region. A contractor to my firm. She sent me a steady stream of high-quality patients. One a month. Every month. Always from the American South, where, sadly, girls suffer from eating disorders at a disproportional rate. Unfortunately, she has hinted that she is keen to retire. Despite the fact—or perhaps because—I have compensated her so lavishly. I suppose she believes she has earned plenty," she said, shaking her head disapprovingly.

"Plenty is never enough."

She walked over to the display table and inspected one of the framed *Teen Vogue* portraits. "Further, she claims there just aren't enough girls. Even if there were, she contends, the logistics involved transporting them from America to Portugal are considerable. Travel costs, she says, are skyrocketing."

"I can send you fifty a month—not just one. Every month."

"Really? And how's that?"

"Do you know what rich American girls in the South do in their spare time?"

"I have never been to America. Not a travel visa I'm eager to apply for. May I presume they attend fancy masked balls?"

"No. That's a very small cohort of girls. A dozen, maybe two dozen per city. What they really do—the rich girls in the American South—is play soccer. What you call *futbol*."

The expression on Minodora's face remained distant, yet polite, even a bit bemused. I followed her to the display table. "American girls' soccer is not the soccer you know, the soccer of street urchins in crumbling housing projects on the outskirts of Rome. In the U.S., rich girls join private all-girls' soccer clubs. Clubs priced so high that the riffraff can't afford to join. Nothing but elite, well-educated girls with silky hair and fine teeth. Girls from Virginia to Memphis to Miami, they play. Tens of thousands of them. And here's the part that will most interest you, Minodora: they don't need to be coaxed or cajoled into European travel. Because entire planeloads of them fly to Europe twice a year—willingly, enthusiastically, *on purpose*—to participate in international soccer tournaments in Italy, Spain, France. They fly direct to your doorstep."

"I imagine some of them have eating disorders."

"This could be a very profitable relationship, Minodora—for both of us."

The cogs were turning. Her eyes grew larger, blacker, more menacing as she approached me. Our noses nearly touched. "I know nothing about you. And you expect me to enter into a business arrangement with you? To trust you?" she growled in a low voice. I could smell the plum liqueur on her breath.

"It's not like people in our line get five-star reviews from satisfied customers on the internet. That said, I can get you referrals, if you wish."

"Those can be faked."

"If your fear is that I'm some kind of law enforcement agency like Interpol or FBI, take a good look at me. I'm a Gypsy, like you. Do those agencies hire people like us? They hunt us, not hire us."

"Why would I fear Interpol or the FBI? I run an eating disorders clinic."

"If you need assurances we're not, I have a way of proving so. Definitively and conclusively."

"Really?"

"Would an undercover Interpol or FBI agent go upstairs and fuck one of those girls? In front of you? And invite you to film it and post it on the internet? No, he would not. Because he'd be criminally prosecuted for rape by his superiors." I pointed to Jack. "But Jack would be happy to oblige. He could fuck three of them if you want him to. At the same time. I've seen him do it before. Right, Jack?"

Jack flashed his 18-carat gold tooth.

Minodora summoned João from the front door. "Frisk them both again. Confiscate their phones."

"We don't carry phones. Ever. That's how you get caught."

She issued more direction to João: "Get a last name out of Jack. Give their names to our friend. Tell him to cross-check against every law enforcement agency in Western Europe, the States and Asia. Facial recognition, known addresses—all of it. Get a blood sample and hair sample from the woman. Javier

Gomes Machado is still downstairs, in the infirmary. Have him do DNA tests and confirm she's a real Gypsy. Work up a 23andMe on this Jack fellow, too. See if he's really from Angola. I have to call some people in Bucharest." She instructed us to sit on the sofa. "Don't get up—not even to go to the toilet. If you do, there will be permanent regret."

Her heels clacked across the stone floor as she began dialing a number on her mobile phone.

After she ascended the staircase, we sat, careful not to speak, mindful of the rotating security cameras in the corners.

João returned five minutes later with scissors, a syringe and a rubber tourniquet. He procured hair and blood samples from each of us.

An hour later, we heard the clacking heels that announced Minodora's return. "It's show time, Jack."

21.

We followed Minodora and João down a long passageway, to the opposite end of the first floor. Then down a stone staircase into the industrial-sized kitchen. Against the wall stood an old Aga stove—the same kind Colonel Bland's wife had in their kitchen, though about a hundred years older. Its top was caked with splattered sauces, its doors dented. João unscrewed and disconnected the exhaust pipe that sprouted from its stovetop. "You, *negru*," he said to Jack, "help me push."

The stove was un-wedged from the wall, revealing yet another stone staircase, this one far narrower and steeper. Minodora flicked the light switch. João's pockets rattled as we descended the stairs.

I expected to see a dungeon—with bars and cold stone floors and rats scurrying about. The doors to each of the girls' rooms were indeed barred and locked, but the rooms were brightly lit, carpeted, and handsomely furnished. Pictures from teen fan and fashion magazines were taped to the walls: images of European boy bands, teen TV stars, models, and professional athletes. Most of the girls were seated Indian-style on their beds, watching TV, or listening to CDs with headphones. They appeared healthy and well-fed—not starving, filthy, and rag-clad.

We walked down the corridor, looking into each of the rooms. As we proceeded, I was desperate to shout, "Augusta! Augusta! Mama's here!" but I knew that would be her death sentence. And mine.

"Most of our patients at the moment are Greek," Minodora lamented as we passed the third cell in a row housing a black-haired girl. "Any one of these girls will do."

"No," said Jack. "See *all* merchandise."

"You don't get to choose."

"What Jack's really saying is we need assurances you have experience moving high-end inventory—that you're not simply an off-loader of inferior Greek-made junk, sold at cut-rate prices."

Minodora took offense. "Look around. These girls all leave here better than they came in. Nutritious food three times a day. Workout videos. Free dental work. The first good haircut of their lives."

"We're offering you *princesses,* Minodora," I said, testing my bargaining power, "not street urchins with a fresh coat of lipstick."

We passed more girls, Portuguese, Spanish, Central and Eastern European. Blondes and redheads began to appear. "That one with the stringy hair, João actually *did* find her in a discotheque," she quipped. "Though not in Prague."

"Brno," João mumbled.

We kept walking. Still no sign of Augusta. She couldn't have been outside in the shipping container all this time?

We approached the end of the corridor, where, in the last cell, my baby had to be.

A moist-eyed young woman from Senegal rocked on her bed, singing a traditional lullaby.

"You have now seen our inventory. I shall now select a girl for you."

"I no get three?"

"Absolutely not. I don't need you stretching all my girls out."

"No like these girls."

"Bicha," sneered João.

Jack ignored the insult and trained his gaze on Minodora. "I want American."

"Don't we all? But I don't have one to give you."

"Give me American to taste."

"Out of the question. Even if I had one, I'd never let you touch her."

"If you really expect me to deliver fifty high-quality girls a month, I need to see at least one girl who isn't some diseased hooker or junkie you found in a slum somewhere," I said.

Minodora took offense for a second time. "My girls are clean! Our doctor checks each and every one out."

"Then give me best girl."

Minodora looked hard at me. "You do realize that if we don't agree on a deal, you don't leave here alive?"

"Of course I realize that. Which is why it's decision time, Minodora. You can kill us. Or you can show us the good stuff you keep under the counter for your preferred customers."

At last a bell seemed to ring in her severely styled head. When it comes to choosing between cold-blooded murder and a guaranteed eight figures of cool, clean cash every month, all but the hardest sadists and fanatics will opt for the latter.

"Stay here," Minodora said. She walked to the end of the corridor and punched buttons on her phone. When she returned, she nodded at João. "Follow me."

We walked past the Senegalese girl's cell, into what appeared to be a dead end. João directed Jack to help him move a carved mahogany library table, atop which were stacked dozens of books, CDs and DVDs. The Persian rug beneath it was rolled up and the hatch door was lifted. "The presidential suite is down here."

There were only three cells on the corridor. Minodora guided us to the one at the end. She slid back the iron cover on the peephole. "Take a look."

Jack blinked, indicating I should look first. Inside, Augusta was propped upright in the four-poster canopied bed, a half dozen pillows behind her. She was bobbing back and forth, half-catatonic.

She saw only my eyes, but her own flashed with recognition. She whimpered, "Mommy! Mommy!"

"That's what they all say," said Minodora with a wave of the hand. "All day, all night, "Mama, Mummy, Mère, Mandinka."

I fought back a tear as I stared at Augusta, blinking intensely, like I was sending her a message in Morse code, assuring her she was now safe.

"She's still under the influence of the narcotics, but coming around slowly," Minodora said. "A beauty. Spectacular green eyes. Pert tits. A tight virgin."

I turned and faced Minodora. Restraining myself from grabbing her and putting her in a choke hold, I instead whispered, "Where's she from?"

"She came with a file. Lives in a ten-million-dollar mansion. Goes to a very expensive school in South Carolina. A dozen pictures of her playing soccer—you were right about that. Pictures of her being crowned at a debutantes' ball. She's the genuine bauble."

"Get a good look at her, *negru*," Minodora said, "because you won't lay a finger on her."

Jack pressed his forehead against the door and looked in on Augusta, for what seemed a long time.

"Satisfied?"

"Ready now for girl."

⁓

"You'll fuck one of the Greeks," Minodora said as we climbed the stairs. "I'll let you choose."

We walked down the corridor and Jack indicated his choice.

João pulled a jailer's keyring out of his pocket and opened the door. Everyone entered and João locked the door behind him. Minodora walked over to the girl and pulled the strap off the top of her shoulder. "This one is called 'Filomena.'" Minodora dragged a chair across the room, sat in the corner, and procured the cigarette case from the pocket of her suit jacket. "Watching men fuck girls bores me. I will smoke." After João lit her cigarette, Minodora started issuing commands. "You," she pointed at Jack, "take off your clothes." "You," she pointed at João, "Get ready to film."

Jack looked at me, his eyes begging for help.

"Do as she says," I barked.

Jack started with his shoes and socks, looking up at me repeatedly, like a dog waiting for his owner to come home. Then he unbuttoned his shirt, his fingers fumbling at the buttons, and pulled it over his shoulders.

"Trousers," barked Minodora.

Jack removed his trousers, folded them, and stacked them on a side table, like a patient in a doctor's office. His military-issue skivvies, which I should have swapped out for a pair of skin-tight European-style bikini underwear when I bought him the purple suit, came off next. I was waiting for Minodora or João to notice our mistake—and put a bullet through each of our heads—but they were busy checking camera angles for filming.

Jack stood naked.

"Oh my," Minodora said when she returned her attention to Jack. Minodora leered at the Greek girl. "What do you think of *that*, Filomena?"

A look of terror swept over Filomena's face.

"She's all yours, Jack. Make it fast."

Jack looked at me again. His color has changed. He appeared nauseous. Sweat beads lined his ribcage.

"Your *negru*, he glistens," Minodora said approvingly.

I waved him on. He skittishly approached the bed.

"Get him ready, Filomena," commanded Minodora.

Filomena looked at all of us, her eyes pleading.

"She is in need of instruction," said Minodora, who in turn provided it. The terrified girl began cautiously to lean forward when Minodora shouted, "Stop!"

Jack and Filomena each retreated. Minodora stood up. "I think the millions of lonely men in front of their computer screens would find it more interesting if Jack was serviced by two girls.

"I will fetch another."

"That won't be necessary, João. I think my new Gypsy friend, Luludja Văduva, should join the action."

I protested. "I'm a businesswoman, with a reputation to protect. I don't appear in porno films."

Minodora reaches into her pocket and produced a Ruger LC9. "Take off your clothes," she said, waving the gun at me.

22.

The bangles on my forearms rattled as I removed the leopard-print blouse. When my breasts spilled out Jack averted his eyes, João and Filomena expressed indifference, and Minodora's eyes swelled like a full belly. "Very nice," she purred.

After I removed the skirt, I stacked my garments beside Jack's.

"I have always been a sucker for garters on a woman," Minodora growled as she waved the gun at my privates. "Step out of those panties."

"I can't with these boots on."

"I want them on during the filming. João, cut her panties off."

"I don't have my knife."

"Then tear them off."

"These panties cost a fortune," I protested. "Boots off, then panties, then I'll put the boots back on."

"Do it."

"You know as well as I do, Minodora, that a woman can't get out of boots like these by herself. That's the whole point of them. You need a man, ideally two, one for each leg, to yank them off."

A sour look swept over Minodora's face as she visualized me with two men. She snapped a finger, directing João to assist me. He approached.

"If you think I'm allowing that trash to touch me, you've seriously mistaken, Minodora."

She hesitated for a moment, then, "Come."

She directed me to sit on the stone floor before her and instructed me to loosen the buckles. I raised the left leg first. Minodora, cigarette dangling off her lip, leaned forward. The Ruger in her right hand was trained on me, leaving only her left hand to assist. She tugged and wedged, cursing in Romanian, until the boot popped off. She liked what she saw, her eyes rounding over my calf muscle.

"Other leg now," she said as she removed the cigarette and turned towards the cell's corner to toss it on the stone floor, at which time, like a mongoose striking a cobra, I simultaneously thrust my bottom upward, drew in my knee, and executed a taekwondo kick to her abdomen, knocking her off the chair. As I rolled away the first shot fired by João whizzed past me, ricocheted off the stone floor and pocked the cement wall. Before he could get off the second shot, Jack smashed João's windpipe.

João was dead before he hit the floor.

I grabbed Minodora's gun and trained it on her. "Stay still!"

Jack took the keys and gun off João.

Filomena scurried to the corner of the cell, where she rolled herself up in a ball, biting her nails. "Get Filomena out of here. Take her downstairs to Augusta's room. Lock the door behind you," I said to Jack.

Minodora was still doubled over when I grabbed her by her braid and dragged her across the room, the way lady-wrestlers do. I stood her up, punched her in the stomach to knock more wind out of her, then pushed her on the bed, where she lay flat on her back, moaning and winded. The nose of the Ruger pressed to her forehead, I ran my hands along the box spring, below the bedspread, until I found two pairs of shackles, just as I expected. I fastened her at the wrists first, ankles next.

"You know who that girl is downstairs? The blonde with the 'spectacular green eyes and pert tits'? That's my daughter."

"Any self-respecting woman of our kind would just have another daughter. Or steal one."

I slapped her. "You're an insult to Romani women across the globe!"

She groaned and called me "whore" in Romanian.

"Your 'patient-intake officer' from the States, Pepper Boyle, is already in custody—along with her husband and all the people in Charleston who enabled them. João is dead. This is over."

"This is hardly over. You have to get out of here. I have an army upstairs. Outside, too."

"I have an Army as well, Minodora. The United States Army. They know all about you and this place. They're patrolling the coast right now. In boats and choppers. Cascais is crawling with troops, who've done a dozen drive-bys already tonight. You're going to jail . . . if you're lucky. So, it's time for you to tell me: who were you selling my daughter to? Who's your high-roller client who collects debutantes from the American South?"

She spat in my face.

I leaned over and wiped my cheek on the sleeve of her red suit. "I'm trained in enhanced interrogation techniques. I know them all. Take your pick. I've got as much time as it'll take. But I'm going to get an answer to my question."

"You'll be dead within the hour. You and that *negru*. But not your daughter. Your tasty virgin daughter—yes, I wasn't lying about that! She's still a virgin, we checked—she will live. In fact, given all the trouble you've caused, I'm raising her price to fifteen million dollars. "Hazard pay." Isn't that what they call it in the military?"

I put her in a facial hold.

"Finished yet?" she mumbled as I applied further pressure to the squeeze. "Do all your tricks. You will not break me."

Over the course of the next hour, I applied a combination of hard and soft tactics: abdominal slaps, deception, cramped confinement, suggestibility, stress positions, and pride-and-ego games. But Minodora, as promised, did not yield.

I heard someone outside the cell door. I took cover at the side of the bed. The fumbling of keys. The sound of a weapon cocking. When the steel door swung open, the trigger on my pistol was about half squeezed when still-naked Jack yelled, "It's okay!"

I panicked. "Where's Augusta?"

"She's safe. It's okay. Still half out of it." He walked over to the table and snatched his pants and skivvies. "She was spooked when I burst into her cell, naked. I settled her down. She hugged me so tight she almost broke my back. Delusional. Kept saying, 'Mommy came for me.'" He buckled his belt. "She's making friends with Filomena, to the extent they can communicate." He looked over at me, topless, clad only in my panties and thigh-high boots. "You should put some clothes on," he said, handing me my brassiere.

Minodora sneered at Jack as he buttoned his shirt. "You couldn't even get it up, *negru*," she hissed, the darkened blood from her broken nose hardening above her red-painted lip.

"We need to talk," I said.

Outside the cell, I stood in the corridor with Jack. "She's

immune to enhanced interrogation techniques. I've tried them all."

"Even waterboarding?"

"No. Not yet."

"Do it!"

"Go back to Augusta. Stay with her. I can waterboard Minodora on my own. Everything I need is upstairs in that kitchen."

Forty minutes later, Jack stood at the entrance to the cell, studying Minodora, whose hair was sopping wet, a moist dishrag stuffed in her mouth.

"Let's go outside."

In the hallway Jack asked, "How'd it go?"

"Badly. I waterboarded Abdul Kaziz Fazl, Farzaad Shah, Ibad ur Rehman–Ullah, and Pepper Boyle. I know how to do this work. I get results. But I'm getting nowhere with her."

"Give her another round."

"I can break her, I don't doubt that for a second. But we don't have forty-eight hours. She says she doesn't care if she gets lung or brain damage. Says she never expected to live to forty."

"She's different than those ISIS boys," Jack said. "They were jihadists blinded by ideology. Convinced they had to do evil to do good. That's a hard nut to crack. But it's crack-able, because they have moral grounding, at least in their minds, even if it's supremely twisted. But for someone like Minodora, there is no high ideal, no praise for Allah and a big reward from Him in the afterlife as she flies her 747 into the tower. She's utterly amoral." Jack checked his watch. "You're right, master sergeant. Someone's going to come looking for us very soon—and it won't be General Loehr and his boys. We need a Plan B, master sergeant, and we need it now."

"Everybody has a breaking point. Even Minodora Grigorescu. I just haven't figured it out yet. Go look in on Augusta. I'll come up with something."

23.

Jack returned. "Augusta wants you."

"I'm aching to see her, but she'll have to wait."

"What's the plan?"

"I'm working on it."

"We *need* one. *Fast!*"

"First, we need to go upstairs and find out if Minodora really has an army in the house."

We slinked up the stairs to the kitchen. Nobody there; a good sign. Jack waved his gun at the staircase that ascended to the main floor. We tiptoed up the second flight of stairs. The Gypsy music no longer played. Silent as an empty church. We listened for footsteps, the sound of conversation, a television. A dog barking, a cat, a bird chirping. Any sign of life. Nothing.

I stepped one boot onto the fancy marble and onyx floor tiles, flinching at the clip-clop echo my heel made. From behind a French door, I saw the flash of gun metal and dove to the floor, rolling behind a big velvet sofa. Jack got out a round, and I heard the crunchy splat of a bullet hitting a forehead. Then the thump of a body as it hit the tiles. More shots rang out – not from Jack this time. These came from where we had entered, as more goons from Minodora's "army" burst in.

I covered Jack with a spray of fire as he jumped behind a

leather club chair the size of a throne. We met eyes and nodded, each of us knowing what we had to do. He and I had been down this road a thousand times.

I laid on my back, ready to spring, and counted to three before leaping at a Chinese vase, which I proceeded to hurl across the room, shattering it against the skull of a thick-necked thug with a skinny black mustache and a thick carpet of curly hair. I rolled back behind the sofa. It was quiet and still for a moment. I heard men communicating in Portuguese. When I heard one of the men eject the cartridge on his Glock, I leapt up and put lead in two of Minodora's men—one in the chest, the other in the groin—as Jack took out another three more with damned perfect head shots.

Jack helped me up and we walked over to one of thugs, the one with the mustache, who got a vase in the head. He lay there whimpering like a hound. I raised up my boot and brought it down slow to his forehead. My heel made contact with a shard of glass lodged in the flesh. I applied the slightest trace of pressure. He shrieked.

Jack asked him, in Portuguese, if there were others in the house.

"No!"

Jack signaled me. I applied more pressure with my heel.

"You better not be lying," Jack said to him.

The man said the others had left. They were at the port of Lisbon.

"More girls?" Jack asked.

"No. Drugs."

I removed my boot and Jack crouched down over his bloody face. "There's no one else?"

"Just the gatehouse. Nowhere else."

"How do I make sure of that?"

The man's mustache twitched as he gritted his teeth in agony. "Library. Monitors there. You'll only see the gatehouse men, I swear," he said. Then he passed out.

"Stay out of camera range," Jack reminded me as we snaked through passageways.

When we arrived at the library, crawling on our bellies, peering only slightly into the room, I pointed to the bay of security monitors stacked on the desk. He pointed to the rotating camera in the corner, above the monitors. "If we go in, they see us and come," he said.

I tracked the camera's arc. Halfway through its third rotation, I zeroed Minodora's Ruger LC9. "Time to roll the dice. Either this will be the shot heard round the world or we'll find out our one-nutted friend was telling the truth. You ready for a gunfight?"

"Bring it."

I discharged the weapon. Sparks flew as I put a clean shot through the camera's lens.

"They'll have to storm the place if they see a camera's been put out," Jack shouted as we ran across the library.

"Good. That'll flush them out and we do them like we did the others."

We looked at the monitors. All the upper-floor hallways, bedrooms and bathrooms were empty. As was the rest of the house.

"One of the screens in the gatehouse just went black," said Jack. "The guards will troubleshoot. One minute, max, before they come up here to check it out."

I pulled Minodora's phone out of my pocket and called the Special Forces men surveilling the gatehouse. "Intercept now.

Just the guards at the gate. Come no further. Nobody comes to the castle until green-lit from us."

"We're coming in."

Jack grabbed the phone out of my hand. "This is FBI Special Agent Capers. No, you're not. We took down eight total, and if any more were in here, they'd have shot at us by now. The guards at the gate are the only guys left. Nobody storms us until we green-light you, is that understood?"

It was.

I paced the library and considered my PSYOPs options. "She is immune to pain. What can we bring her? Hope? Money? What will motivate her to cooperate?"

"She's never going to talk."

"Everybody talks . . . eventually." I was pacing something fierce, walking in circles. On gigantic iron bookstands, spaced at ten-foot intervals, thick, oversized, leather bound books were displayed. Ancient books from the Middle Ages and Renaissance era, all of them in Latin. Bibles, illustrated encyclopedias of saints, art books, books with philosophers' pictures on the pages, each page longer and wider than an extended arm. Suddenly, my eyes fixated on a picture-book.

"The answer's not in those books, sergeant major."

"It just might be."

Jack approached, wanting to know what I was looking at. "Ah," he said, *"Locupletissimi rerum naturalium thesauri accurata description."*

"Huh?"

"Cabinet of Natural Curiosities, by Albertus Seba. Very famous book. They had a copy of this in the biology lab at Princeton." He flipped through the pages of the illustrated encyclopedia as dust particles floated up into the air. "My God,

this must be worth a fortune. Wonder who she stole *this* from." Jack turned the pages, each cataloging objects from the natural world: spiders, birds, bats, porcupines, butterflies, turtles, snakes, amphibians, rocks, fossils, seashells, coral, fish species . . . and plants. Dozens of pages of plants: mulberry, hazel, milk-weed, palms, sunflower, ragwort, spurge, and sun-rose. I slammed shut the cover of the book.

"Follow me," I said as we sprinted across the main floor to the steps leading down to the kitchen. "It's time for Plan B."

I rummaged through the pantries, sweeping cans of soup, boxes of breakfast cereal, bags of rice and other foods to the floor.

"What are you looking for?"

"Herbs. Spices."

"Why?"

"We're going to feed them to Minodora and get the truth out of her."

"Gypsy hexes?"

"African witchcraft. Take your pick. Between us, we're going to make her talk."

"You've already tortured her. You think she's going to respond to some herb?"

"Enhanced interrogation—not torture. I'm not looking to inflict more pain. I want to loosen her up. Something to relax her, make her tell the truth. I want herbs that cause visions and loosen lips."

"Paging the roots doctor," said Jack as he searched the cabinets for dried mushrooms. "If my grandmother could only see me now. What we really want is Coltsfoot Leaf. Member of the daisy family. But it's toxic. Destroys the liver."

"I don't care about Minodora's liver. Any dried-out daisies around?"

"I'll look upstairs on the main floor. Maybe some poking out of a flower vase somewhere."

Jack returned empty handed five minutes later.

"See if you can find a liquor cabinet. Look for gin. Juniper summons truth."

Jack scoured the cabinets. "No gin."

"Found the spice drawer!" I said as I slid it open. I rummaged through the onion powders, mustard seeds, oregano, none of which were any use to us. I fumbled through more jars. "When I was a little girl, my mama used to have me scour the banks of the New River for maidens' weed, which she said I should eat to protect myself from syphilis."

"That's not the kind of motherly advice I was given."

"Don't get me started on Mama." I came upon an entire row of Asian spices. "What about these?"

"Asian spices contain galangal, but that'll give her more strength—the last thing we want."

"There's a bunch of oils in here. What's patchouli?"

"It's a kind of mint oil. Has its uses, but they're all the wrong ones. At least for our purposes. According to my grandmother, Gullah women on the prowl for husbands used to spike men's rum with it. Used for love and sex spells. Powerful aphrodisiac. That and oils from hasta plants."

"Dill makes men frisky, too, according to my grandmama Marlene. First step towards emptying their pockets, she always said." I froze in my tracks and looked over at Jack. "If Minodora won't respond to pain, maybe a love spell will make her talk?"

"Something tells me she's not exactly the lovey-dovey cuddling type. My vote: this cast-iron meat tenderizer." Jack pounded the mallet into the palm of his meaty hand.

"Men have said things to me in moments of passion they never said to nobody in a million years."

"Which is why most things are better left unsaid." He rummaged through the spice drawer some more. "Dill, jasmine, saffron, nutmeg—they're all aphrodisiacs, according to Gullah lore. But if you're serious about going down this road, what we *really* want is yohimbine, nature's original date-rape drug, if you don't mind my saying so, and promise not to file a 7279 against me for saying it. It's an indole alkaloid, extracted from the bark of . . ."

Jack let the spices in his hand fall to the floor. He searched the kitchen for the biggest carving knife he could find.

"What are you doing?"

He rushed towards the stairs. "Outside. Those African trees in the orchard. I swear I saw a Pausinystalia yohimbe."

While he was away, I found a knotty, gnarled ginger root the size of a witch's fist. I was at the sink chopping it up when Jack returned with the bark. Into a blender our ingredients went, along with overturned jars of dill, jasmine, saffron, nutmeg, a bottle of mint oil, three cans of smoked oysters, and a splash of Perrier mineral water.

"Save a chip of that bark for me—for if we get out of here alive," Jack said.

Civilians who have never experienced the stress of combat would not understand, but moments of levity occurred frequently during moments like the one we were in the middle of, but it was precisely that levity that calmed nerves and lowered adrenaline levels, and thus protected soldiers from over-anxiousness and twitchy trigger-fingers.

After the blender's engine growled its cutting blades through the tree bark, I poured the goop into a vessel and handed it to Jack.

"I know, I know," he groaned. "It's show time."

24.

We unlocked Minodora's cell door.

"It's time for us to find out who your client is, Minodora," I said.

"*Rapazes Infero* will cut you up and sell your limbs in pieces, like someone who steals a car and sells it for spare parts."

"No Potruguese mafia here. We checked. João's dead. The men in your gatehouse are in an airline hangar somewhere by now, hooded and handcuffed. We're all alone."

"Not for long."

"We brought you some refreshment," said Jack, pointing to the plastic cup I was holding.

She clinched her jaw.

"Ah, we figured you might not be thirsty," Jack said. "So, we brought something to help make the medicine go down." He removed the plastic kitchen funnel from his pocket.

"Don't let her bite you."

Jack approached cautiously.

Minodora jerked and twisted.

I approached from the opposite side and wedged her face between my forearms. I squeezed tight as Jack began to pry her teeth apart and stuff the funnel in.

"Remember when we were upstairs having cocktails earlier?"

Jack said as he tried to wedge the funnel in. "You posited my knowledge of history doesn't go any further back than breakfast. Actually, it goes much further back. It may surprise you, but I'm co-authoring a history book about the Atlantic Slave Trade. Or, more accurately, I *was*. Before my co-author—your former business associate Stallings Boyell, eminent historian of the Middle Passage—was captured."

She hurled yet another gurgled insult.

"After Portuguese slave-traders collected their cargo in Senegal, Guinea, Nigeria, Ivory Coast, and elsewhere," Jack continued as he attempted, for the third time, to pry apart Minodora's teeth with the neck of the funnel, "the biggest challenge was to deliver them alive in Charleston. Legend has it that many slaves went on hunger strikes, believing if they died, their spirits would return home to Africa. As you can imagine, this did not please slaveship captains. So, they developed an instrument called 'the Speculum Oris.' It was shaped like a pair of scissors. The crew would insert the Speculum Oris into the recalcitrant slave's closed mouth and turn its thumbscrews, forcing the jaws open so they could force-feed the slaves. We couldn't find one in your kitchen—God knows you've probably got one—so this will have to do. Jackpot!" he said when he successfully wedged the mouth open. With the palm of his hand Jack crammed the funnel into Minodora's mouth. She shrieked as her cheeks ballooned. Jack smiled at me. "Ready when you are, master sergeant."

I dribbled the goopy liquid down her throat.

"Your belly's about to become the Garden of Eden," Jack said.

Minodora violently shook.

After the vessel was emptied, Jack attempted to remove the funnel. But Minodora kept trying to bite him.

"Just leave it in," I said.

Jack and I huddled near the doorway. "I don't have much experience with this sort of thing," Jack said. "Recommendations on the best way to do this?"

"Yes. Leave."

"Huh?"

"I don't think you want to be in here when this interrogation gets underway."

"*You're* interrogating her?"

"She made it pretty clear she fancies women."

"And you fancy *her?*"

"Who I fancy or don't fancy is beside the point. We have a mission to complete."

He looked over at writhing, furious Minodora. "You don't have to do this."

"Yes, I do."

"You sure it'll be safe for you to be alone with her?"

"It's going to be nasty, I won't lie to you. Jack, you don't want to be here for this. I don't want Augusta anywhere near this. Lock me in. Come back in an hour."

"They don't give out medals for this part of our job."

"That's not what I'm after. Now go. But before you do, will you drag João out to the hallway? He's not good for the mood I need to set."

After the door locked behind Jack, I sat motionless for a quarter hour, waiting for the herbs to take hold, directing only a penetrating stare at Minodora.

She stared back, with equal ferocity, and a generous dose of hate. This was a woman who knew how to stand her ground, that was for certain. Finally, I rose and waltzed over to her. "You and I need to get better acquainted, Minodora."

I stroked her hair.

Minodora gurgled and scowled.

"Shhh." I turned my back to her and unfastened and removed my bra, dangling it over her face before placing it on the side table. "Getting hot in here, don't you think?" And it was. Sweat was pouring out of me. I twisted around, employing the yoga stretch I'd learned back in Charlottesville, then looked into her eyes as I began to massage my breasts, slowly, in big circular motions. "Ah, that's better."

When her face began to flush, Minodora screwed her eyelids shut and angled her face to the wall.

"Come on, have a look. I know you want to."

Her eyes opened, then shut as quickly.

"Feeling frisky yet?" I walked around to the side of the bed, where her head lay. I leaned over and lowered a breast onto her cheek; swishing it back and forth like the ocean's tide. "Recognize that smell? I borrowed some of your Jasmin Rouge. The perfume, mixed with perspiration, is nice, isn't it?"

Minodora jerked.

"Soft, aren't they? I wish more than anything that you were unshackled and could squeeze them. Or kiss them."

She swung her head in the direction of the opposite wall, eyes clinched shut. I walked to the opposite side of the bed and did more of the same for a few minutes, laying my opposite breast on her opposite cheek.

"Who is Augusta's buyer?"

She shook her head no.

I walked to the bottom of the bed. I continued taunting her verbally. "I bet you're burning up in that suit." I crawled up her legs, to her torso, and unbuttoned the jacket and blouse. "That's better, isn't it?"

Next, I slid my hands beneath her back and unfastened the bra. She opened her eyes and watched as her breasts spilled out, then squeezed them shut again. "Now they're free. Aren't those lovely?" I moistened my thumbs and forefingers with saliva and went to work. Minodora's nostrils flared as her breathing and heartrate accelerated.

"I think I'll get more comfortable myself."

When she heard the rip of fabric, her eyes burst open again. I removed what was left of my panties, then my garter belts. She was blinking wildly, greedily taking me in. "Should I keep my shiny boots on?" I asked. Her face screwed up tight. I brushed her inner thigh with my fingertips as I exited the bottom of the bed and walked around to the top. The front was flush against the wall, so I pushed it out a few feet so I could wedge myself between the front of the bed and the wall. Slowly I climbed aboard the mattress, jungle cat-style. I knelt over her, gently squeezing her ears between my thigh-high boots. At her abdomen, I lowered my head, exhaling small, warm bursts of breath. Minodora began to writhe. When I fiddled with the button of her trousers, a groan blasted through the funnel. When the shuddering ceased, I whispered, "Who are you selling Augusta to? What's his name? Where does he live?"

She made "no" grunts and tightened the muscles of her body, trying to scissor her legs until the chains reminded her that she was splayed on the bed.

"Let's see what's underneath those slacks. Would you believe it? I've never seen a lady part up close before. Always wondered what it'd be like, ever since I was a high school girl. I tugged at the zipper. Can I tell you a story, Minodora?"

She shook her head no.

"In high school, I would lie in my bed at night thinking

about this girl in my gym class—Donna-Lynn Deneen—who had jet black hair, just like you. And milky-white skin, just like yours. I saw her naked once, after volleyball. Her locker was next to mine. One foot on the floor, the other raised and planted on the bench. She was bent in half, painting her toenails pink. I saw her from behind. I sat next to her on the bench, pretending to tie my shoes as I looked up and stole glances, shuddering, unable to avert my eyes. She must have heard me panting—just the way you are now—and turned around. Warm smile, those big eyes zooming in on me. She asked if I was okay. Maybe she thought I caught some sort of chill. So, you know what she did? She unwrapped her towel and laid it over my shoulders. She stood before me, naked, giving me comfort. Every night of that semester, I laid in bed at night, visualizing what I wished would have happened next—if only I had had the courage. And now—in all places, the bottom of a Portuguese castle—I finally get my chance. I can't wait to discover all the treasure you're hiding from me. Who are you selling Augusta to? What's his name? Where does he live?"

She screamed something through the funnel.

I leaned forward and massaged her inner thighs. I unzipped her trousers and inched them down to her knees, then tugged at the elastic band of her thong, snapping it against her skin. "Are you going to share your treasure with me, Minodora?"

She howled and jerked like someone possessed with the devil.

"Sounds like you don't want me to have a look." I took my hand away and hoisted myself off her. "Well, that's okay, I guess. I'll just sit over there."

I stood up and walked over to the chair and sat, pretending to be studying the manicure I got for the Masked Oracle Ball.

Minodora's pleading eyes darted as she bounced frantically on the bed, gasping, the plastic funnel in her mouth whistling like a teakettle.

I yawned. "Maybe I'll just go upstairs and take a little nap."

She shook her head frantically.

"Oh? You want me to come back?"

"Yes, yes, yes!" she nodded.

"You sure?"

She shook again, this time even more violently.

"Tell me who your client is."

I walked over and removed the funnel from her mouth.

She panted. When the breathing leveled out, she swallowed. A malicious grin swept over her face. "I sent him pictures of Augusta. He can't wait to have her."

I wanted to punch her in the mouth. "Now where were we?"

Her eyes widened as I went to the bottom of the bed, climbed up, and squatted over her. "Time for me to make my discovery." I unrolled the thong to her splayed knees. "Oh my, it was worth the wait. I finally get my chance to see one of these up close."

I had never been with a woman before. Nor had I thought about it. It was not that I was against it. How consenting persons above the legal age had their goes was no concern of mine. But being with another woman: It simply had not occurred to me. Since I was young, I fancied men. And they fancied me. And there were plenty of them to choose from.

I looked down at that which was presented before me. I was not looking forward to what had to be done next, but the mission was the mission.

I closed my eyes and lowered my head. In my mind's eye,

I imagined it was me on that bed instead of Minodora. That a gentlemen friend was directing his fondest attentions to me and my private area. As I forced my mind into action, the image of one man's face dominated my imagination: that of my former husband, Colonel Cletus Bland III.

As the seconds turned to minutes, Minodora, already under the spell of the herbs, got hotter than a bonfire.

I paused on occasion to further interrogate her, but, despite her animal grunts and groans, she continued to hold out.

I resumed the mission. Though I adored my deceased husband, I was running out of stimulating memories. So I began to visualize others who had over the course of my lifetime pleasured me similarly: that lanky fella in Afghanistan from the motor pool, the supply chain logistics officer in Iraq, that translator from the French news agency, that public affairs officer who came to base with General Loehr, that telecom engineer with red hair, Private Second Class McKim, that optics technician from Texas, General Loehr's budget analyst, that radio systems engineer I met in Cairo, that blue-eyed man from the dental corps, that cyber operations specialist with the eagles tattooed on his shoulders, that C-12 pilot who wore his baseball cap backwards during our session, Command Sergeant Major Moellering, that food safety officer, that biomedical equipment specialist who talked to me in Italian, and the Crabtree brothers. To distract me from the task at hand, I summoned memories of them all, this parade of past pleasure-givers.

Thirty minutes in, my neck was sore. I was running out of memories to summon. There was a brief temptation to visualize Jack, but the situation in which I had seen him nude was not a sensual one. Further, it would have been wrong to take advantage of my sighting, to exploit his exposure in that unwholesome way while he had been doing his duty to his country. Instead, my mind's eye took me as far back as it would go, back to my youth, in West Virginia. I visualized myself perched on that muddy knoll, after Ricky Ray Jeeter, Scooter Skinner and I went skinny-dipping in Beryl's Hole, when . . .

"—*Ahhhhhhhhhhhhhhhh!*"

Chains rattled as Minodora's arms and legs flailed. Her abdomen shuddered. Fingers and toes curled. She was like a five-foot marlin tossed on dry land.

I leapt up, yanked the funnel out of her mouth, and threw it against the wall. "Who'd you sell Augusta to?"

She panted. "I'm peaking. More!"

"I'll give you five more. Who did you sell Augusta to?"

"Kalan Ali. More! More!"

"Where does he live?"

"MORE!"

"WHERE DOES HE LIVE?"

"Yemen!"

"When is he expecting her?"

"I'm coming down."

I went back to her privates and applied the technique I was saving as my very last resort—a technique deployed on me in a Humvee by a small arms technician from the U.N. Peacekeeping Force.

"DA! DA! DA!" she shrieked in Romanian. YES! YES! YES!

I stopped suddenly. "When is he expecting her?"

She looked up at me, pleadingly, her face wet with sweat, mascara streaking her eyelids. "One week."

"Where?"

"Port of Aden. MORE! MORE!"

I gave her ten minutes' more, during which time I captured

the basic intel needed: drop-off and pickup coordinates, contact names, wire transfers, and so on.

I pulled my head back, shook the knots out of my neck, and crawled off the bed, winded.

While a woman's mysteries are beautiful in every way, I never needed to do that again. I'm a man's woman through and through. Born that way.

I went over to the chair and sat down. I scrolled through the contacts list on Minodora's phone in search of Kalan Ali.

"NO! NO! *Curvă!* Stinking whore!"

"I don't appreciate swear words," I said before picking the funnel up off the floor and stuffing it back in her mouth.

I returned to the side chair and logged into the U.S. Special Operations Command's secure web portal, in search of further intel on Kalan Ali. Minodora hissed and cursed through the funnel.

The cell door burst open, revealing Jack and Augusta. My daughter shrieked when she saw me in the natural, except for my boots, and saw Minodora, bound, also naked, but with no boots, and tied up on the bed.

"I heard Minodora screaming through five feet of concrete flooring."

"I got the intel."

Drop-jawed Augusta fixed her gaze on Minodora, who looked like a panicked raccoon trapped in the middle of a flash-flooded river.

"What did you *do* to her?" said Augusta.

"I got the mission done. Now go wait outside, Augusta."

For once, she listened to me. The cell door slammed, and Augusta waited in the corridor.

"You okay?" whispered Jack.

"Fine," I said, setting Minodora's phone aside. I walked over to the bed and yanked the sheet out from under Minodora and covered her, then reached for my bra. Jack, ever the officer and gentleman, removed his shirt and gave it to me to put on. "The client is in Yemen," I told Jack. "A billionaire playboy who sponsors Al-Qaeda terrorist-training camps. He's been on General Loehr's radar for a while."

Jack said, "Nice work, master sergeant."

I recalled Augusta. Jack looked over at barking, red-faced Minodora. "What do we do with her?"

"Turn her over to General Loehr."

"No fucking way," snarled Augusta. "I'm killing that bitch." Minodora's darting eyes doubled in size, and frankly so did mine. Augusta approached Minodora. I'd never seen her like that before. Not only was she angry – for the way she'd been tricked into thinking she'd been chosen as the Queen of Chastity and Charity on her own merit, then kidnapped and nearly sold into sexual slavery – she was filled with righteous indignation.

Jack and I locked eyes. "I'm sure she has some pretty powerful friends—those guys she works for in the Portuguese mafia," he said.

"*Rapazes Infero,* they're called," I said.

"Even if we whisked her off to Guantanamo or some CIA black site, there's still no guarantee she wouldn't walk," Jack lamented.

"That slave-trading bitch dies!" Augusta roared, sounding once again like the sassy teenage female I was ready to strangle before the Masked Oracle Ball but now wanted only to squeeze so tight she burst.

Minodora blinked nervously as she heard her fate discussed.

"I'm going to text the general and request a kill authorization."

Minodora's chains rattled.

General Loehr replied almost instantly. "Good news for you, Augusta," I said. "Bad news for you, Minodora."

Minodora's face went white.

I buttoned the last button on Jack's shirt.

"I don't think the two of you have been formally introduced. Minodora Grigorescu, I'd like you to meet my daughter, Augusta Theodosia Bland."

Minodora eyes bugged out like a horsefly's.

"Let's do it!" shouted Augusta.

"No. Not yet," I said.

Jack and Augusta looked at me, curiously. "Before we do *anything*, I first need to go upstairs and find some mouthwash."

25.

When I returned, Minodora, still manacled, was propped up with pillows. The funnel was gone from her mouth.

"She says she wants to talk," Jack said.

"We got the intel we need. We know the target in Yemen. Her castle is closed. Her kill is authorized. What's there to talk about?"

"She'll give us her entire client list in exchange for not killing her."

"This is a trick. She's buying time. Our job is to get the man with terror ties, per the general's orders. His capture is just a detail at this point. Tomorrow morning I'll dye my hair to match Augusta's, change into her ball gown, get in the container, then go to Yemen and take him out."

"You can't just let her other clients go!" Augusta screamed.

"Yes, we can, Augusta. And must. We can't chase down every sleazeball in Europe who wants a mail-order bride."

"They have terror ties," Minodora interjected.

"Like who, other than Kalan Ali?"

"Get the kill order lifted and I talk. And a guarantee that I am handed over to European law enforcement—not the U.S. military."

I texted the general. Five seconds later: "The general agrees to your terms."

"Let me see the message. Yours to him and his reply."

I showed it to her. After trying to change the terms five times, and failing to make us budge, Minodora finally started naming names: a Somali warlord who traded arms with Iran, a Taliban leader who sourced redheads from Britain and Ireland, a Japanese whiskey-distiller with dubious connections in North Korea who wanted blondes from the East Bloc, and a Norwegian wind-farming entrepreneur backed by a Russian chemical weapons manufacturer who installed Greek and African girls in a brothel near Øvre Årdal.

"It's the same everywhere," Minodora said. "They all want the girls they can't get at home: blondes go to Japan, black girls to Scandinavians bored with blondes, and so on."

I captured names, exact locations, and cell phone numbers and shared them with the general's aide so intercepts could be arranged. "Now tell me everything I need to know about Kalan Ali—and I mean everything—not just the basics you shared during interrogation."

"Someone give me a cigarette."

"No. Not until you start talking."

"He is my best client, of course. Exotic tastes justify exorbitant prices. Demands virgins, insists they're American."

"I know that already. Tell me something I don't know."

"Playboy. Lightweight. Little *pula*. These men who buy, they always have the little ones. But handsome. *Really* good looking. Thin, elegant eyebrows. Wide set lime-green eyes. Spooky, like an animal's. I don't think he's seen his thirty-fifth birthday yet. His father is a telecoms billionaire. The father's plan was to make him president of Yemen."

"Go on," said Jack.

"Young Kalan Ali was put on the path: boarding school in England ... scholarship to Oxford. His humanitarian credentials were to be bolstered with a medical degree from Duke University. Top grades. No discipline problems. Popular among students and faculty at all his schools. But everything fell apart in America, where the stupid boy lost his mind over some piece of *ass,*" she hissed. Her harsh facial expression softened as she reconsidered her assessment. "Actually, she was *fine* ass. *Spectacular* ass. Rich girl. Good family, from Georgia. Smart, too. A medical student. She taught him—a devout Muslim!—to drink bourbon. Made him wear bowties. Taught him to become some sort of—what do you call it?—'Southern Gentleman.' Made him watch every movie ever made about the South and read books. 'Southern Gothic' books, he called them. Some man named O'Connor."

"Some *woman* named O'Connor. Flannery O'Connor," said Jack.

"When he hired me, at a restaurant in Riyadh, he made me look at a dozen pictures of the girl—all of them taken at something called the 'Peachtree Ball' in Atlanta, where her parents lived. Pictures of him in white-tie-and-tails, the girl in a ball gown. I was so bored with his love story I wanted to throw up. He wouldn't stop talking about some stupid movie, *Gone with the Wind*. He and the girl watched it dozen times, he told me. He quoted lines of dialogue from the movie the whole time we were at the restaurant."

"Go on."

"No. I must go to toilet. I don't say 'restroom' like you

Americans. I don't go there to rest. I want people to know exactly what I'm doing there. I go to toilet!"

"Where are the keys to those manacles?" asked Jack.

"Under the mattress, where they'll stay," I said. "This is the trick I warned you about. Augusta, you wait outside. Jack, there's a bedpan over there in the corner. If you'll bring it to me, I'll take care of her 'toilet' while you two wait outside.'

Augusta and Jack left.

"Nice try, Minodora," I said as I slid the pan beneath her. "Now piss. If you even have to."

She did not piss.

Jack and Augusta returned.

Minodora continued with her story: "They were together years, Kalan Ali and his American girlfriend. After they were awarded their medical degrees, they moved to Atlanta, where they intended to establish practices, marry, and start a family. The girl's parents supported the union. Kalan Ali's father—who had already hand-selected his son's teenage Muslim bride—did not. For the first time in his life, the boy disobeyed. On a thirtieth birthday visit back to Yemen, veiled fiancé from Atlanta in tow, the boy nearly broke free of his father. He was prepared to renounce an inheritance, estimated at more than $4.4 billion, when the girl, or her family, or perhaps both, had a change of heart. Within a month of their breakup, she was engaged. To a Jew! Heir to a textile fortune. Old Atlanta family. Kalan Ali had some sort of nervous breakdown and returned to Yemen. Married the girl he was ordered to. He became virulently anti-American. He spoke at rallies and mosques. He supported jihadists, offering funds for weapons. Eventually, he funded the establishment of training camps for Al-Qaeda in Yemen—which you already know about. All the while, the girl from

Georgia who humiliated him dominated his imagination. He stalked her on social media; he hired private investigators to photograph her (and her husband and young family). I told him it would be no problem to snatch her—after yoga class, at the grocery store, wherever. But his honor would not allow him to make so pathetic and unmanly a statement. And to what end? What would really become of him and the girl if he brought her, against her will, to Yemen? So, instead, he searched for a replacement: a Southern girl who would admire and honor him. I was to look for an exact match."

"What about the girls you sent before Augusta?" Augusta asked.

"I'm talking now," Minodora said. "Give me my cigarette."

Jack lit it, transferring it to her mouth and holding it while she sucked. "I could have found one like the girl in the pictures Kalan Ali showed me," she continued after a deep inhale. "Pepper Boyell found a half dozen perfect matches. But I always chose girls with one wrong detail. Too tall, too fat, wrong color eyes. That way, he had to buy more."

"Where are they?" Augusta demanded.

"I sent them to his villa."

"How?"

"In that shipping container that's all decked out to look like a room from that movie he's obsessed with—about the Georgia mansion that burnt down. I'd have preferred to send the girls in a plain crate—waste of money to put a drugged girl in a floating five-star hotel room—but he insisted that the girls, his 'Southern belles,' travel in comfort. For some people, the red Cartier box lined with silk is as glamourous as the ring inside. But not to me. Give it to me in a fucking cardboard box for all I care; I just want the ring. Give me another puff of cigarette."

"Where's the villa?"

"North of Sana'a, just below Luluwah. Built especially for what he called his 'Southern belles.' Modeled after the house from that stupid southern movie he kept talking about, the one about the wind. A 'plantation,' Kalan Ali called it. In the middle of nowhere. Scrubland, desert."

Jack texted the details to our superiors.

"The girls are there now?" I asked.

"Maybe. I don't know?" she said.

Augusta slapped her. "Yes, you do!"

Minodora moistened her lips and leered at Augusta. "Feisty one, you are." She turned to me: "Tell your general I want him to send a text to my lawyer that outlines the terms of our agreement. I am to be turned over to Interpol, Lisbon branch. Have him copy you on the text message so I can see it."

She dictated the number, then reviewed the text and verified it was sent.

My phone pinged.

"What's your general say?"

The general replied with a thumbs-up emoji, which I showed her.

"That's not enough. I want words."

I zapped off a text and the general replied: "THE UNITED STATES GOVERNMENT AGREES TO MINODORA GRIGORESCU'S TERMS. PETER D. LOEHR." I showed her the thread. She nodded approvingly when she saw her lawyer's name in the thread.

"Now give us the truth—the whole truth—or he'll get Interpol to turn you back over to us if we find out you're lying," I said.

"More cigarette." After a long pull, she blew another cloud

of smoke. "Kalan Ali, when he is done with a girl, sends her to the Al-Qaeda training camp he set up in Al-Bayda Governorate. An 'amusement' for the men. Before the brainwashed boys meet their seventy-two virgins in heaven, the gang gets to enjoy one last American slut while they're still on earth."

I looked over and Jack, then back at Minodora. "The girls are still at the camp?"

"The girls are dead. Beheaded when the replacement girl arrives; I've seen the videos, which they will post in social media . . . when the time is right."

Augusta burst into tears and ran out of the cell.

Jack darted over to the corner of the cell, where he vomited.

Minodora looked disdainfully at Jack. "Do you wear a tutu into battle?"

I was careful not to let my face reveal my emotions. "So, no girls are at the compound—this 'plantation'—at the moment?"

"No. Kalan Ali's there, with servants, preparing for Augusta's arrival."

She gave me the once-over. "You will really dress up as Augusta?" she asked. "You look alike, this is true. And you fit my client's profile. But a man can tell the difference between a teenage virgin and an over-thirty *curvă*."

Jack looked curiously at me.

"Whore," I translated.

My phone pinged.

"What's your general say now?"

"He's showing me a satellite image of Kalan Ali's compound in Yemen." I closed out the screen. Time for a PSYOPs maneuver, to see if I could catch Minodora in a lie. "There's a red Rolls-Royce in the driveway. Tell me, Minodora, is that his?"

Minodora laughed. "No one under forty in the Arab world will be caught dead in one. The rich boys, they all drive Ferrari. But Kalan Ali never drives to his house in the desert. He flies his Russian helicopter up from Sana'a."

I showed the image to Jack. Neither a Rolls nor Ferrari appeared in the General's satellite photo—only a Kamov Ka-60 chopper.

I texted the general. "LOCATION CONFIRMED BY ASSET."

"When does my lawyer come to collect me?" Minodora asked.

My phone pinged. "Soon. But take a look at this first, Minodora." I urged Augusta and Jack to gather around the bed. The video feed was fuzzy at first, then the image of Kalan Ali's compound in the desert came into sharp relief.

"Even if your ground troops get over the wall alive, which they won't, the few remaining troops still standing will have an even bigger surprise in store for them when they find out what awaits them inside the house," said Minodora.

The audio transmission began: "Brimstone 8 this is Scorpion 3, I'm eyes on target."

"I don't recall saying anything about ground troops," I said to Minodora.

"Roger that, Scorpion 3."

"Brimstone 8, request you pass coordinates to CrossBow 37."

"Roger that, Scorpion 3."

"Location locked," said CrossBow 37.

"Sweet!"

"Uh, so, whenever you're ready . . ."

We glared at the static image of Kalan Ali's compound. In

the span of one-tenth of a second, it ceased to be: a flash of light, a puff of smoke, a blank screen.

"Thank you for saving me the trip to Yemen," I said. "I wasn't keen to get decked out in that debutante's crown. Would've looked unnatural on me."

"You were marvelous in the Versace boots. Perhaps he'd have fallen for it."

"You just lost your best customer, Minodora," Jack said.

"There's always more," she shrugged.

Jack grinned, flashing his gold star. "Ah, but not for you, Minodora."

"Our business is done. Take me to my holding cell in Lisbon."

"This just in: I'm afraid there's been a change of plan, Minodora," continued Jack, still grinning. "A text from the general." He positioned his phone's screen in front of Minodora's eyes.

"Kill Reauthorized."

"I have friends inside Interpol. High, high up. The best criminal lawyer in Europe. All of you, your fat general included—I've never seen him but can only assume he's fat because he's American—will be dragged in front of a war crimes tribunal at The Hague."

"I don't think so, Minodora. If you look closer," Jack said as he pried the gold star from his front tooth and flung it at the wall, "you'll notice that your lawyer's name seems mysteriously to have disappeared from the thread."

26.

We stripped her naked and stuffed all of Minodora's belongings into a burlap vegetable sack: her red suit, undergarments, jewelry, hair clip, black lizard-skin belt, cigarettes and gold lighter, and Cartier watch. "Hold on to these, Augusta."

I re-manacled Minodora at the wrists and ankles. Augusta wrapped Minodora's black lizard belt around Minodora's neck and tugged the strap tight, transforming it into a leash. Augusta dragged Minodora up the stairs like a stubborn dog you drag out into the rain.

"I know where to take her," Jack said.

The four of us went outdoors, into the orchard behind the castle. The moon was shrouded by clouds. Wind howled, rustling the leaves on the fruit trees.

We walked along a meandering pea-graveled path that snaked its way through the trees. "Salty air never smelled so good," Augusta said, inhaling deeply. "Especially after being drugged and trapped in a shipping container for a week, then locked in a fucking dungeon."

"Mind your language, Augusta!" I told her.

She kicked Minodora in the ankles.

"You kill me and you'll all be dead before sunrise. In

a manner so grotesque you will wish you killed yourselves instead."

"Do you know the slaveship *Temperança?*" Jack asked Minodora as he pressed his palm against her shoulder and guided her along the path.

"Go fuck yourself, *negru.*"

"I see your curiosity is piqued. The night your 'patient intake coordinator' and her husband snatched Augusta in Charleston, Stallings Boyle was giving one of his lectures about the slaveship. Of course, what he was *really* doing was telegraphing to his co-conspiring dinner companions Augusta's destination: Cascais. Anyway, the *Temperança* set off from Lisbon in 1571, for Ghana. At dinner, Stallings explained how just below the castle where we're standing right now, there's a quarter-mile deep chasm, which creates a high-speed whirlpool. Apparently the *Temperança* —which had only left port an hour before— was sucked into the chasm and thrashed into the cliffs, which within minutes turned it into a pile of floating matchsticks. The captain and crew were sucked into the mouth of the gigantic cave right below us—the aptly named *Boca do Inferno,* or Hell's Mouth."

"Do I really have to listen to this horseshit?"

"Here's the part that's salient for you: almost five hundred years later, Stallings told us, the waters below are still littered with skulls and human bones. No treasure hunters or divers will go near the place, still, he said, for fear that they'll get smashed to pieces, too. So, like those sailors who perished in 1571, no one will ever look for you or find you. What do you think of that?"

"I think *Rapazes Infero* will do things to your little Augusta that will make Kalan Ali's boys blush."

"If there's a silver lining in all of this for you, after you go over the cliff, you'll be able to take comfort in knowing that, in your eternal resting place, you will be among 'your people:' fellow slave-traders."

"As the crow is made for stewing, the dog is made for kicking," Minodora hissed.

"What the fuck's *that* supposed to mean?" snapped Augusta.

"Watch your language. I'll translate it later," I said.

We arrived at the cliff's edge. "End of the road, Minodora," Jack said.

We tilted our heads over the side and looked down. Two hundred feet below us the swirling waters of *Boca do Inferno* crashed into the jagged rock.

Augusta, who was afraid of heights, gasped, and stepped back. She stood behind Minodora and made the leash taut, jerking Minodora backwards. Jack and I held Minodora tight, each of us hooking forearms below her armpits.

"Final request? We can't offer a chaplain," Jack said, "but something tells me you're not a believer."

"Yes, one," Minodora said in a voice that betrayed neither regret nor apology, but was as close to gentle as I had heard. Waves pounded into the cliffs below as she stood silent.

"What?"

"Let me see the girl one last time."

Augusta moved around front, cautiously, keeping her distance from Minodora, although the Romanian slave trader was still manacled at wrists and ankles, and in no position to kick or push her off the cliff.

Minodora scanned Augusta from head to toe. The words dripped slowly from her mouth, like droplets of venom from a cobra's fangs, as she hissed at my daughter in Romanian:

"*Eu bluestem Tu, palid piele curvă. Tu voi veșteji și suferi la mele mână!*"Minodora spat in Augusta's eye. "*I curse you, slut!*"

Augusta, shaking, dropped the leash.

"It's okay, honey," I lied.

Augusta reddened. She took her position behind Minodora's back, then lunged forward, planting her palms on Minodora's shoulder blades she pushed with all her might.

The Gypsy slave-trader issued no cry as she plunged into the eager, greedy, gaping mouth of hell.

27.

After Minodora was gone, Augusta, whose stoicism until then impressed me, fell apart. The three of us formed a circle and hugged. "It's over, Augusta," I said, stroking her hair.

We were walking back to the castle as General Loehr's troops arrived. They freed the other girls and secured the perimeter.

"News from the general's aide," said Jack as he looked at his phone. "They booked us in at the best hotel in town. Presidential suite."

"You're going to sleep in a fluffy bed with a soft comforter," I told Augusta as we climbed into a military transport back to town.

"I want to sleep with you," Augusta whispered.

"Of course."

At the hotel, we all realized we were starving, and ordered a feast from room service.

"Tomorrow I'll take you shopping and get you some fresh clothes," I promised Augusta as she demolished the double bacon cheeseburger in front of her.

"I don't care if I ever go shopping again," she said.

"You love shopping! There are boutiques along the beach.

Linen dresses, knitwear, tunics, skirts, shoes, bags, and cute scarves."

"I need a pair of jeans, a t-shirt, and some underwear."

Jack pulled me aside and said he thought it might be best if he gave Augusta and me some alone time. He made a plate of food, grabbed a bottle of beer, and retired to his room.

"I know this has been traumatic. But you'll be back to your old self in no time."

"No, I won't and you know it. Besides, I don't want to be my old self—ever again. My 'old self' was a joke. Clothes and makeup and mean girls and silly boys and stupid Masked Oracle balls."

"I have an uncomfortable question I need to ask you . . ."

Augusta looked up at me, fearful, as though she was in trouble, which, in the past, she usually was when I told her I had an important question to ask her.

"Eww, gross!" she replied when I asked if Minodora had "taken liberties" with her . . . or any of the other girls.

We ate in embarrassed silence. Augusta unwrapped her second burger. "Jack kept calling you 'master sergeant.'"

I told her about my time in the West Virginia National Guard and my work with JSOC in the United States Army.

"I thought you were some sort of jet-setter from the UK who grew up in embassies."

"That's a lie. Cover story."

"You're in the military again?"

"Temporarily."

Her brow furrowed.

"It's time I tell you the story of how I became your stepmother. You're old enough to learn the truth. But Cleet IV is not, so you'll have to promise you won't share what I'm about to tell you with him."

Augusta promised.

I told her how I had served under her father, how her father and I "got involved," how I came to Virginia, pregnant, to share what I thought was news the colonel—whom I was lead to believe was a bachelor—would welcome, how, to my surprise and disappointment, I discovered Colonel Bland was married and a father already, how we ultimately got married, and the heartbreak and heroics surrounding Cleet III's death.

"I've never told you this—and before tonight I'd have *died* before I'd ever tell you this—but we were not a happy family," Augusta confessed. "The house I grew up in was a morgue. Cold, dead, silent. My mom and dad couldn't *stand* each other. The three of us went to Worthington every Sunday for brunch, always dressed up, to prove we were a perfect family. But they lived totally separate lives. It was like there was an invisible line running down the center of Derbyshire Farm: his side and her side. He golfed and drank whiskey with his buddies between tours. But my dad couldn't wait to re-up for service. Mom was obsessed with yoga, tennis, saying malicious things behind the backs of her so-called best girlfriends, social-climbing, staying skinny—and training me to follow in her footsteps."

"I would never deliberately set about to break up a marriage, but I knew after our first night together that your dad and I were destined to be together. He knew too."

"After my mom had her meltdown and left, I hated you most."

"I don't blame you. It had to be somebody's fault and might as well have been mine."

"Until you did what you did for me this week. I would have killed myself before admitting this to you, but in the short time you were with my dad, I saw him smile more than I had his whole life."

I hugged her.

"But he's gone and now you're with Jack."

I was taken aback. "I most certainly am not with Jack. He is a fellow solider, that's all. We were just assigned to a mission together."

Augusta makes a face. "Yeah, right. I see how you look at each other. I know what a crush looks like. And you two have *serious* hots for each other."

"What makes you say that?" I said, pretending not to know what she was talking about.

"I noticed the way he looks at you—and you at him. I thought he was an illiterate Gullah. When we were in my cell, he was asking me about my college plans and I found out he was an Ivy Leaguer. He's a good catch."

"Where a man went to school—or *if* he did—isn't how I evaluate the worthiness of a man."

"And it turns out he went to Princeton and Yale—even better schools than dad went to. Go figure. Not that I care about that, either. Though there was definitely a time when I would have—like, a week ago. All I care about is that he's what a real man is supposed to be: somebody who keeps women safe. Not that you need any help in that department, based on what I saw you do this week." She asked me if I planned to date Jack when we got back to Charleston.

"I don't really date men. Or, historically, they're not so keen to date me, is more like it."

"You intimidate them. You're more man than most men."

"I'm not so sure about that."

We talked all night and into the early morning. In the main room of the suite, on the balcony, and eventually—like two teenage besties—in my bed. We didn't sleep a wink.

She was telling me about the boys at her school, how boring they were to talk to, as we watched a sailboat glide out to sea when freshly-showered Jack—who smelled of expensive soaps and lotions—waltzed out to the balcony. After he knotted the belt on his fluffy white bathrobe, he grabbed a pastry off the cart. "The general is sending us a plane. It's leaving Lajes Field now. Wheels up Portela Airport at ten fifty-one hours."

We should have been overjoyed at the prospect of returning home. Yet, curiously, a mist of collective melancholy hung in the air. The three of us, I reckoned, could have hid out in this coastal town and swam, drank in the sunshine, and eaten Portuguese stew for weeks. It'd have been perfect—if only Cleet IV had been there with us, too.

28.

The C130 was empty, except for the three of us and the two pilots.

Jack nodded his head at Augusta, who was glued to her iPhone. "You sure you want her watching *Rambo* after what she's just been through?"

"She said she wanted to watch a war movie on the flight home. It's the only war movie I know. That's not true. I saw the first few minutes of that *Apocalypse Now* picture, but I thought it dishonored our servicemen and stopped watching. Went to the movies a couple of times in high school, on dates, too, now that I think about it. A war movie played once at that drive-in theater we used to have in Thurmond. But I can't say I saw much of what was happening up on the screen."

"I suppose you'll leave Charleston?" Jack inquired once we were at cruising altitude.

"I suppose. Though I don't know where I'm going to go. Back to Thurmond, I guess. My business is there, though the thing runs itself. Kandi, my front-register girl, has her associate's in retail management. Besides, it's a franchise. You just do what corporate orders you to do and it prints money. Not much different than the Army, if you think about it. Keep your head down and your mouth shut, do what they tell you to do, and pocket the pay. What's next for you?"

"I go where the Bureau sends me," he shrugged.

"You don't want to go and relax for a spell on Gatuh Island?"

"Sure. But the problem is, every time I go back there, I can't relax. All I do is work. Maintaining the land is a full-time job. All the crap and litter that lands at the beaches. The bugs. Then there's managing all those damned alligators—keeping them on their side of the island. I love the place. It's my ancestral home and I will die on that land. At least that's my hope—assuming I don't get tagged on a mission. But, to be honest, I'm alone out there and there's not much to do."

"You know Pepper and Stallings Boyell schemed to pressure you into selling, so they could develop it."

"Of course I knew. Yeah, right. For one hundred and fifty million dollars. It's worth three times that much."

"You were never tempted by the money?"

"No. I was raised to live simply. Eat simply. I'm single. I'm paid well enough by Uncle Sam. And I banked a fortune when I worked in New York. That land stays protected. Those grubby real estate hucksters in Charleston will never get their hands on it. *Ever.*"

He asked me about my talks with Augusta.

"She thinks I should go on a date with you."

He laughed. "Forgive me if I don't see you and me at a chic café on King Street nibbling on charcuterie plates and sipping chardonnay. Instead, I see you in camo and face paint, eating snakes for breakfast."

"I'm not much of a drinker. And I prefer fried bologna on

white bread with mayonnaise to fancy foods. What's that dish you just talked about?"

"Charcuterie. It's a cold meat plate. Cured meats, usually pork products. Bacon, ham, sausage, confit, stuff like that."

"I'd eat that. As for more combat duty, I don't thrill over killing. Between missions—and sometimes on missions—I enjoy the company of men. Been looking for the right one for many years now. But as you learned in Cascais, women in my line of work don't have luck keeping men around."

"I was worried about you in Cascais, Madam Rue."

"'Madam Rue'?"

"'*You know that Gypsy with the gold-capped tooth,*'" he sang. "'*She's got a pad down on Thirty-Fourth and Vine. Sellin' little bottles of . . . Love Potion Number Nine.*'"

"I don't get it."

"It's a song about a Gypsy who whips up a batch of Spanish Fly in her kitchen sink. Portuguese Fly in your case."

I never heard that song. "What was it, exactly, you were worried about?"

"When you 'advance-interrogated' Minodora."

"What worried you?"

"Pretty . . . *extreme,* don't you think? What you had to . . . *do* . . . to get the intel?"

"I've been in far more extreme situations. You do what needs to be done to advance the mission. It's that simple. But if what you're really asking is did I enjoy it, the answer is no. Nor did I hate it. I just *did* it—because that was the job in front of me. In high school, my friend Scooter Skinner tried to get me to come to bed with him and his girlfriend at the time, Donna-Lynn Deneen. I told him I did not fancy women. I still don't."

He grinned.

"Back to men. Your fortunes and misfortunes with the un-fairer sex. You don't really believe that nonsense you told me about the women in your family—that five-hundred-year-old curse."

"I do believe it. And have dedicated my life to breaking it. As have scores of Vaduva women before me. Yet the spell remains unbroken. I came close to breaking it with my husband. I will not lie: I had been with my share of men before Cleet, hoping one might stick. But to no avail. Yet, from the moment me and Cleet were first 'together' I knew he was uniquely qualified to break the spell. And he did. We had true love. Until the wasps got him."

"You weren't specific about how he died when we were on the cargo ship."

I told Jack about the swarm of yellowjackets that descended upon Cleet IV, then a toddler, at the Wounded Warriors fundraiser I hosted in Charlottesville. How Cleet III spread himself across the boy, wrapping his forearms and hands over Cleet IV's head as he sustained what must easily have been a thousand stings. His death by anaphylactic shock.

"A true warrior's death," Jack said. In silence we unwrapped our sandwiches. He was picking specks of oregano off the bun of his ham and cheese sandwich when he asked, "What was it that made Colonel Bland 'uniquely qualified' to bring you true love?"

"Normally I would not dare explain, for fear of being laughed at. But given as how we both applied spells from our various traditions on Minodora—you with the juju, me with my gypsy love spells, I suspect you will not." I told him about the fortune-telling skills my mother taught me—and her mother before her, and her mother before her. "You can tell if a man is destined to bring true love—or unhappiness—by the way his beans hang."

"His *what?*" he said, nearly spitting a potato crisp out of his mouth.

"I know how crazy it sounds. But bear with me: on most men, one bean always hangs lower than the other. And which one hang lower—be it on the right side or left side—has meaning."

"Really?"

"If the left one hangs lower than the right one, that's a man who has never known true love. And is unlikely ever to get it."

"And if the right ball hangs lower?" He bit into his sandwich and shook his head. "I can't believe we're having this conversation."

"It means a woman broke his heart something terrible. And his heart will never truly mend."

A philosophical look swept over his face as he took a swig of orange soda. "This is not a question I ever thought I'd hear myself ask, but . . . which way did the colonel's hang?"

"Even. Which is a one-in-a-million occurrence. That's when you know a man is your destined true love. When people are in love, there is a sort of balance, a harmony—call it what you will—that occurs."

"Plenty of men's balls hang even."

"That's what the colonel said. And he was wrong. Just as you are. I've been with a lot more men than you."

"That assertion can be made without fear of contradiction."

"Sure, they hang even when men get out of cold oceans or after exercise. But most times of the day, and definitely at night, when sleeping, men hang uneven. One is *always* a low-hanger, with rare exception. "

"And the colonel, he was that 'rare exception'?"

"He was indeed, Special Agent Capers. When they hang even in the sac, a man's heart belongs to a woman's completely—and hers belongs to his."

"Did you get a look at mine when we were aboard ship?"

"No. But not for want of trying. The way you scooted around in that bathroom before your shower, hopping every which way like a waterbug."

He laughed. "I guess I'd better start paying closer attention to my balls. I figured until now that my lackluster love life had something to do with the fact that I have never found a woman . . ." He stared hard at me. ". . . until you, that is, who sustained my interest. Turns out my balls must have been hanging the wrong way the whole time. Who knew?"

"Now you do."

"I wonder how they're hanging now?"

"Want that I should take a look?"

We glanced over at Augusta, who, after what she'd been through, was as knocked-out asleep as a hibernating woodchuck.

"If you think it might break a curse, it would be selfish of me not to honor your request."

"It's not a request. Just an idea."

"And a good one."

"Stand up."

He stood.

"Unfasten your belt."

He obliged.

I tugged the trousers and skivvies to his knees. I was silent and unsentimental as I conducted my visual inspection, like an Army doctor giving a physical. I was careful to inspect with eyes only.

"What's the verdict?"

I looked up and gazed into his apricot-colored eyes, then down again at the orb before me, hard and firm as a ripe peach. "I never expected to see one of these again. Not in this lifetime, anyway."

"One's not hanging just the slightest trace lower, a millimeter?"

"No. Perfectly even."

"So, what happens next? Do we need to re-route the plane to Tiffany's?"

"That's premature. We should probably have a go. And if they're still hanging even when we're done, that means it is our destiny to be together. We will find out, definitively, if, as my mama the fortune-teller likes to say, 'it is in the cards.'"

"But what do we do about my problem?"

"Problem?"

His face slackened. "You will recall that I took an oath: no sex before marriage for me." He pulled up his skivvies and fastened his trousers.

I could feel my shoulders slouching. "I understand."

He excused himself, with some urgency, saying he needed to go to the head.

When he returned, he was carrying pillows and a stack of Army blankets. He swaddled the two of us like mummies and said, "I wish—*oh, Lord, but how I do wish!*—we could do more. The best I can do is offer you the world's most passionate cuddle for the duration of the flight home."

"I'll try anything once, Special Agent Capers."

29.

The C130 dropped us at Hunter Army Airfield, near Savannah.

During the two-hour drive over to Charleston, few words were spoken. Jack spent the whole time texting people from his phone while Augusta and me sat in the back of the sedan, looking out the windows, trying as best we were able to get reacquainted with our "home," which wasn't indeed our home, after our overseas ordeal. The car snaked eastward, through winding roads under canopied oaks and weeping willows, past the tidal creeks, docks, and marshlands.

Charleston was bustling when we arrived early evening. The sun was sinking behind the spire of St. Margaret's Episcopal Church on Calhoun Street, in whose basement the members of the Masked Oracle Society—all of them now incarcerated and awaiting trial—once held their sinister meetings.

My stomach knotted as we turned the corner onto Legare Street. I had no desire to inhabit a seventy-five-hundred-square-foot Italian Renaissance mansion now that the mission was complete. It was just cover, that fancy house. Later in the spring, I'd sell it, after the kids finished out the year at Peckham Hall. I'd send Augusta off to college, then take myself and Cleet IV back to West Virginia.

The sedan rolled up to the house, in front of which was parked an Airstream mini-trailer, which was itself hitched, curiously, to a hot pink Bentley. I didn't like the looks of neither the Bentley nor the vardo behind it. "Velvet," I mumbled.

Jack looked at me curiously.

"My mama," I clarified. I was not keen to see my mother just then, despite the fact that I loved her because she was my mama.

"That's some artwork on the Airstream," Jack said as he inspected the hand-painted trailer. "Peacocks, vines, flora, leaping lions, oxen, griffins—and hitched to a Bentley."

"That car's a Bentley? I've never seen one," Augusta said. "Minodora said Rolls Royces and Bentleys were for old people, and Ferraris for young people."

Given my combat experience, I knew what was to follow, as I had seen more soldiers in PTSD situations than I cared to remember. Augusta's face went white. A look of panic swept over her as she recalled the final hours with her captor. She grabbed my hand. "Is he here for me, that man from Yemen?"

I pulled her in tight and hugged her. "He's dead. They're all gone, baby. The Boyells, the Masked Oracle Society, Minodora Grigorescu, Kalan Ali: they're not coming back. They can't get you. Ever. You're safe now. And always will be as long as Special Agent Gullah Jack and I are alive."

Augusta sobbed and squeezed me even tighter.

"Let's go inside. You'll go upstairs and take a hot bath."

I opened the latch on the iron gate.

"I'd like that," Augusta said as I heard the rattle of a chain drag across the yard. From behind a tree leapt my mother's dog, Bitch. She ran straight for Jack and lunged at him, but was short by a foot. Her neck snapped backwards, infuriating her further as she ran in circles barking incessantly.

"Good God," Jack said, grabbing his heart.

"Usually, you say a dog is all bark and no bite. But Bitch is as mean as they come. And she'll gladly bite if you let her. Steer clear."

On the porch a sandwich board displayed an illustrated hand, surrounded by moon crescents and stars: PALM AND TAROT CARD READER: PASTS EXPLAINED, FUTURES TOLD. INQUIRE WITHIN. "Looks like Mama's already set up shop," I grumbled.

"Bet business is slow with that dog in the yard," Jack said.

I glanced over at the carriage house on the way up the pathway. The Crabtree boys' truck was parked, but there was no sign of them. Probably out P.T.-ing.

I opened the front door of the Jeffrey Drane Kimbrell house—my so-called home—out of which wafted a cloud of cigarette smoke.

We waded through the haze, Augusta hacked and wheezed as our feet crunched the cans, cups, bags and wrappers strewn about the floor: Popeye's chicken bags, empty Flamin' Hot Nacho Cheese Doritos bags, opened pizza boxes containing cold, hardened slices, empty beer cans and 7-Up bottles, Little Debbie snack cake wrappers, Chips Ahoy! and Oreo wrappers, empty tins of sardines, CHEEZ-IT boxes, Cherry Coke cans, McDonald's bags, Nilla wafers boxes, a dozen empty Cracker Jack boxes, and 7-Eleven cups sticky at the brim with red liquid.

"Mama? Where you hiding?"

I looked into the parlor, where on one of the antique embroidered sofas that came with the house, sat Mama, Grandmama, and Great-grandmama, all three of them lined up, smoking and watching the news, which was blasting, since Great-grandmama Charlene was now one-hundred-percent deaf. Cleet IV sat Indian-style on the floor in front of them, shoveling chocolate pudding into his mouth. When he saw me, my son leapt up and greeted me and Augusta.

Augusta and I burst into tears; Cleet IV burst out laughing when he saw us cry.

After our reunion was complete, I approached Mama, who was not yet in a reunion frame of mind. "Too smart for her own good," she said, pointing to the broadcaster on TV. "Always rolling her eyes and making them sniffing noises after she says something nasty about the president, like she's Miss Smarty Pants or something."

"Not alluring to men, that's why she's so mad all the time," Grandmama Marlene lamented. "Them chunky black glasses and man's hairdo. Something off with that gal, if you ask me."

Velvet pointed at Great-grandmama Charlene. "Wake up your great-grandmama, girl," she instructed me. "And take that cigarette out of her hand before she burns down another house."

I snatched the cigarette out of her numb fingers. She blinked. "It's me, Great-grandmama Charlene. How you doing?"

Great-grandmama Charlene lit up. "My baby's home."

"She's *my* baby," Mama huffed.

After our reunion, I turned to my mama. "Great-grandmama Charlene burned down a house?"

Mama waved the question away like it was a mosquito. "Tell me about these two?" She pointed at Augusta and Jack.

I told Velvet my connection to each.

"Go get your grandmama another beer," Mama said to Cleet IV.

"I'll clean up that mess on the floor at the entrance," offered Jack.

"What's this about a fire?" I repeated.

"Cleet IV called us from that school of his," Velvet said changing the subject a second time. "Terrible lonesome. And who can blame him? You ship him off to some snooty boarding school and disappear to God-knows-where. That's why we come."

"Grandmama Velvet's home-schoolin' me, mama," Cleet IV said, swabbing globs of pudding from the corners of his mouth with his tongue as he rose to his feet to fetch his grandmother's beer.

"You took him out of Peckham Hall?!"

"Ain't nobody ever got rich speaking Latin."

"I'm paying forty-eight thousand dollars a year to educate him at the best school in the state!"

"Waste of money if you ask me."

Cleet IV returned with Velvet's beer. "Now go upstairs and fetch me another pack of cigarettes, boy. Mine is the Eve Menthol Ultra Lights 120s. If you can't find none, bring me a pack of them Pall Malls in Great-grandmama Charlene's room. There's a carton on the table, next to the gnomes."

"So you came from Thurmond, West Virginia, is that right?" asked Jack, who, because he was well-mannered, attempted to make small talk.

Mama eyed him suspicious. "You ain't from there."

"No," he chuckled. "I'm local."

Wondering what to say next, Jack said, "So did I hear you had a fire at your home?"

She scowled at Jack, then at me. "He's a nosey one, ain't he?"

"Beg your pardon, ma'am."

"Tell me about the fire," I pressed.

"The trailer's fine," mama said as she polished off the Bud Light Lime in front of her and cracked the tab on a fresh one. "No fires. Just roaches. Roaches and bureaucrats. We always had them; roaches, I mean. Bureaucrats, too, now I come to think of it. And we never paid them no never mind—either of them. Got into everything, the roaches. You just sweep them away and say, 'shoo!' and they scatter. They didn't eat none of my stuff. I eat pork and beans, mostly, and they come in cans. But they love them powered donuts your great-grandmama fancies, I can tell you that. She eats them out of the box. Leaves them on the counter for five days, lid open all the time. Bugs get in there at night. Them damned powdered donuts cost me my home."

"It weren't the doughnuts, Velvet, it was the doctor cost us our home," Grandmama Marlene insisted.

Jack returned, munching on Cracker Jacks. "Want some?"

"I have always hated those."

"I told her not to go," Velvet continued. "Nothing good ever comes out of a doctor's visit. She went in anyway—got Scooter Skinner to drive her. Diarrhea, which she couldn't shake. Six days straight. Doctor said she had food poison. Lab tests showed cockroach saliva and waste in her poo. Next thing we know, health officials from Fayette County are banging on our door. Ninety minutes later, they're wrapping the trailer up in yellow tape, like it's a crime scene, condemning the property and telling us we got to find a new place to live. So, we come here."

Jack, who was half-listening as he replied to a text message, mumbled, "I think you'll like Charleston, ladies." When he looked up to see the look on my face, I could tell he regretted saying it. "Though I'm told West Virginia is really beautiful. At least that's what your daughter says."

"How would you know?" hissed Mama, who, I am ashamed to say, had little affinity for black- and brown-skinned people.

"For the last time, Mama. What's all this talk about fire?"

"Cleet, fetch your grandmama some Fig Newtons," barked Velvet in yet another attempt to stall.

"*She* started the fire," Grandmama Marlene said, pointing an accusing finger at Great-grandmama Charlene, whose drooped head was resting on the shoulder of her dingy Middlebury College sweatshirt, which she had worn for twenty years, despite having no affiliation with the institution.

"Which fire?"

"The log cabin."

"You burned down my cabin?"

"We needed a place to go, so we went to your house."

"The house is a fortress. Nobody can get in," I said.

"A Gypsy always gets in," mama said proudly.

"Smoking in bed," grand-mama Marlene said disapprovingly.

"Where's my gear? Did anything survive?"

"Charlene's junk is what set the house ablaze. Any restaurant that put a paper placemat on the table, she saved it so she could put it on her TV tray while she ate. Same with toilet paper. Hundreds of rolls she stole from ladies' rooms over the years. But that's not what caused the trouble. It was when her cigarette ember fell on that stack of *National Enquirers, Stars,* and *Globes* she keeps next to the bed. That really done it. Saving them since the 1960s. Thousands of copies, all of them stacked floor to ceiling. I told her when we was leaving the trailer to throw them out. Weren't like she was ever going to re-read news stories about O.J. Simpson's glove or that Charlie's Angel's gal who had anus-cancer. But she would hear none of it. Cabin went up like a tinderbox. There's good news, though: the insurance men never traced it to smoking. Ricky Ray Jeeter swapped out your stove with one he had at his trailer; his had bad electrical and started fires at his place all the time. The insurance men bought it. Gave us a handsome settlement. Velvet managed all the paperwork since nobody knew where you was."

"Let me guess, Mama, you said you'd send the papers to me for my signature?"

Mama, master forger that she was, grinned proud.

"We bought a new vardo to get here," Grandmama Marlene continued.

"And a Bentley to pull it."

"Feeding Cleet IV costs money," said Mama, keen as always to talk about how my money never went to her but was spent in the service of others. "But don't you worry, girl, there's some left. And before you go scolding me for buying the Bentley, we got it cheap. Belonged to some girl pop star who went to rehab. They was selling it for pennies on the dollar. Bought it sight unseen off the internet and they shipped it direct from Beverly Hills. Besides, you got plenty of money. You can buy your mama a car."

Mama pointed at the TV again. The news-lady was talking about immigration. "Them people think they can just saunter over the border into this country."

"The way your ancestors did in 1823, Mama?"

"The girl's right, Velvet. We was undocumented too," Grandmama Marlene said, disagreeing with her daughter just to be disagreeable, as neither my mama nor hers were particularly interested in public policy matters.

"Ain't no Vaduva woman ever asked permission to cross a

border—not nowhere, not in five hundred years," Mama said proudly.

I looked over at Jack. "Your phone hasn't stopped pinging since we got in the car in Atlanta?"

Jack looked at his watch. "I'm going to have to leave soon. Can we find someplace quiet to talk?"

"Is it serious?"

"We're about to find out. Walk with me. To the porch."

30.

Bitch came barreling across the yard. She ran out of chain at the steps and lunged at Jack, barking something ferocious.

"Can you put the dog inside?" he pleaded.

When I came out, he told me to sit on the porch swing. "What is it? Is *Rapazes Infero* sending someone here? What did the general tell you?"

"It's not *Rapazes Infero*."

"Then what?"

"I have to tell you, that ride over from Lisbon to Savannah is the hands-down weirdest airplane ride I've ever been on."

I had been on weirder flights—most notably that chopper ride in Cairo with General Loehr several years prior—but saw no benefit in raising that topic.

"I've had my share of medics demanding I turn my head and cough during physicals," he continued, "but no one has ever, um, 'evaluated my fitness,' quite the way you did."

"I hope I didn't offend you. But I believe in fate, in destiny, in what's in the cards. I had to find out. I'm sorry if I made you uncomfortable."

"*Comfortably* uncomfortable."

"The first time I had a hunch about you was when we

sailed across the Atlantic on the container ship, when we sat up all night and talked and ate Gullah Grub, then P.T.-ed. I experienced a stirring I had only known once before, with my deceased husband. I tried to spy a glimpse of your front parts when you went into the shower, as I reckoned my hunch was correct. But, as I told you on the flight, you protected yourself from my prying eyes."

He fumbled with his phone, checked the screen, and put it in his pocket. Then he took it out of his pocket and checked it again. "I can't get our time in that airplane out of my mind. I have never been so aroused. And I don't mean in a sexual way—though to be sure the experience was unrivaled in terms of sheer titillation. Actually, what I experienced transcended lust. Going through what we went through together, the way we worked so well together, and then to be exposed before you—in such a literal, but also a figurative way —I felt somehow *elevated.*" He sipped his beer. "Yet when I think about the lives we've chosen, the paths we're on . . ." His voice trailed off. He looked out at my mama's vardo. "I'm sorry, I know I'm not making any sense. For a guy with all my education—"

"*Eddycashun.*"

He laughed. "Yes, for a guy with all my *'eddycashun,'* I'm woefully inarticulate when it comes to matters of the heart."

"If you're saying you fancy me, but that the mission is over and we both have lives to lead, and I'm a great gal and all that, but we just don't have a future together and so on, you will not be the first one to have told me that. I assure you I can take that news and will be A-OK."

"That's not what I'm saying at all."

"Then what are you saying?"

"I have a question."

"Fire away."

Jack dug his phone out of his pocket and texted someone again. He sat there looking at me, and me at him, and we said nothing. It was turning into a crisp night. The absence of buzzing insects and beeping traffic only heightened the silence.

"Cat got your tongue?"

"Yes."

In the distance, I heard the faint sound of a flute. "That's nice," I said to the Jack. "Some girl practicing."

Then I heard the rich tones of clarinets. Then the snare drum: tum-tum, tum-tum, ta-ta-ta-ta-ta-ta-tum-tum. The sound of the music grew louder. By the time the explosion of brass begins—trombones, saxophones, and tubas—I recognized the melody, which made me smile. It was when the cymbals starting clanging in earnest that I saw the marchers turn onto Legare Street. About two dozen uniformed members of the U.S. Army Field Band were belting out a strain of "The Army Goes Rolling Along."

My mama, grandmamas, Cleet IV, and Augusta came out to the porch to find out what all the commotion was about.

Gullah Jack rose from the porch swing and sung to me, which no man had ever done. He sung in the softest, sweetest voice:

> "March along, sing our song, with the Army of the free
> Count the brave, count the true, who have fought to victory
> We're the Army and proud of our name
> We're the Army and proudly proclaim
>
> First to fight for the right,
> And to build the Nation's might,
> And the army goes rolling along

*Proud of all we have done
Fighting till the battle's won
And the army goes rolling along.*

*Then it's Hi! Hi! Hey!
The Army's on its way
Count off the cadence loud and strong (TWO! THREE!)
For where e'er we go
The bad guys always know
That Jack and Tami go rolling along*

*Off to Portugal and Yemen
Solider man and solider woman
And the Army went rolling along."*

Jack bent down on one knee, looked up at me and continued:

*"Deploying wits plus gun and knife
To safeguard sweet Augusta's life
Master Sergeant Vaduva, will you be my wife?"*

The cymbals clashed a final time. Everyone in the band froze. My family stood, huddled around the front door. All eyes were on me as everyone awaited my reply to Jack's question.

I rose from the swing, stood before Jack, and shouted: "YES! YES, I WILL!"

Jack reached into his pocket and pulled out a plastic ring he found in one of the Cracker Jack boxes. "This'll have to do until we get to Tiffany's," he said as he slid it on my finger.

"I don't care about Tiffany's."

My mama and her mamas swooned, as marriage proposals were indeed a rare occurrence in our family.

The band, prepared in the event I said yes, struck up a chord, which summoned the catering vans. Beer and barbeque were unloaded and everyone went into the house to celebrate our engagement.

Earl Scruggs, Bob Wills & His Texas Playboys, and Ernest Tubb blasted, putting all in a festive mood.

"How'd they know to play this?"

"I took notes when we were killing time on that ship, making small talk. I catalogued all your favorite things."

As food was served and beers are chugged, Cleet IV grilled the band members about their instruments, boasting that he too was a musician since his Great-grandmama Charlene passed down to him an "heirloom" guitar (code in Mama's house for stolen) that once belonged to a musical Vaduva ancestor; Augusta made sure plates were piled high, insisting it was her duty to serve the people who serve; Great-grandmama Charlene slept through most of party; Grandmama Marlene asked a clarinetist for advice on how to apply for death pension benefits if your husband dies in combat, despite the fact she had not in her lifetime ever had a husband; and Mama, who in addition to enjoying another half dozen Bud Light Limes downed several shots of cinnamon schnapps, shocked the xylophone player—a young man barely out of high school by all appearances—when she conducted a lewd demonstration with one of his mallets.

The party lasted all evening. After everyone left and the kids went to bed and the grandmamas went to the parlor to watch more news and fall asleep, Jack and I cleaned up. We were hauling Hefty bags out to the curb when I said to Jack, "I didn't want to embarrass you by making my acceptance of your proposal conditional, but there is a condition to marrying you."

"What's that?"

"That we do it as soon as possible? I don't want no six-month engagement. I mean *any* six-month engagement. These women—my mama, grandmama and great-grandmama—are a terrible influence on my grammar. I talk like I'm sixteen the minute I'm around them."

"I find it endearing. And the sooner the better as far as I'm concerned."

I directed his attention to the parlor, where, from behind a cloud of thick smoke the blue hue of the television glowed. "I've got to get away from those crazy women. I love them; they're my kin. But I cannot live under the same roof with them. They can stay here for all I care; the house is paid for free and clear. But you and I have to get out of here. Can we get hitched A.S.A.P. and find a place to live? We can buy something down the street. You can come to Thurmond. I can come with the kids to Gatuh Island. It makes zero difference to me. I just want to get married fast."

Jack rubbed his chin as he deliberated. Finally, he looked at me all serious. "I didn't want to embarrass you either by making the proposal conditional, either, but I'm turning thirty in four days and if I'm still a virgin on my thirtieth birthday, I'm going to shoot myself. So as long as you're prepared to have what you so euphemistically like to call 'a go' five minutes after the ceremony is complete—or more like several hundred 'goes,' as I've got about a decade's worth of goes to catch up on—I accept your terms, master sergeant."

He leaned in and we kissed something fierce, all hot breath and tongues twisted like snakes. Presently, hands began moving over shoulders, chests, breasts, onto buttocks, eventually grazing groin areas. Finally, he stepped away, took a deep breath, and said, "Keep your hands off me until our wedding night, master sergeant. That's an order."

"Yes, major."
"Special Agent Capers; I'm not in the military anymore."

31.

The next day we chartered a boat over to Gatuh Island. Actually, it wasn't so much a charter as a "government-requisitioned vessel": we commandeered Pepper Boyell's sixty-five-foot yacht, the *Hissy Fit*, now U.S. Government property, for the day.

"You're not really brining her to my wedding, Mama?"

"Bitch is a member of this family," she said as the dog barked and leapt and yanked my mama in every which direction. Getting her loaded on the boat was something of an ordeal, but mama swore she'd mind her on the journey.

Everyone was dressed to the nines: a white wedding gown for me, and a peach-colored bridesmaid's dress for Augusta. The elder Vaduva women were sporting new formalwear for the occasion, too: matching velour sweat suits and wrist corsages. Their age earned them the right to dress for comfort, Grandmama Marlene, who picked out the outfits, insisted. Cleet IV looked dashing in his little tuxedo. As did the Crabtree boys, both of them decked out in their formal service uniforms: black berets and dark coats above light blue pants with gold stripe running down the seam. Though they were coated in sweat: Mama had the Crabtrees loading boxes on the boat, lording over them, scolding them at every turn, warning them that the contents were fragile.

The waters were choppy on the ride out to the island. Velvet and Grandmama Marlene threw up over the side, albeit for different reasons. Grandmama Marlene had never been on a boat before, whereas Velvet was suffering from a cinnamon schnapps hangover. Bitch barked at the swooping seagulls. Great-grandmama Charlene slept the whole time, the waves rocking her like a baby in a cradle, though Mama was convinced her grandmama was making "stroke-face." (Great-grandmama Charlene had already had one.)

"Hammerhead!" shouted Cleet IV when we were a mile offshore.

Jack, dressed in a black wedding suit, greeted us when the boat docked at Gatuh Island. The winds were fierce, kicking up dust along the beach as we disembarked.

"Where are all the alligators I've been hearing about?" Augusta asked Jack.

"Opposite side of the island. If you don't bother them, they won't bother you."

Bitch was hysterical, intermittently sniffing and barking. She lunged forward, yanking Mama behind her. She must have smelt the gators on the east side of the island.

"You're welcome to let her off leash and let her go make new friends with the gators," quipped Jack.

"Stop that!" I said and slapped him on the shoulder.

We trod Jack's well-worn footpath, across the beach, over the dunes, and on through the partially-flooded marshlands. Mama complained the whole time, contending walking was bad for us, as it wore out the hips.

In the center of the island, I saw Jack's simple cottage, what was to become our new home. General Loehr's chopper was parked some five hundred yards away from it.

After the general congratulated us on a job well done, and Bitch—who was still making a racket—was chained to a leg on the picnic table, the general said, "Let's get this show on the road!"

Jack assembled the group under a canopy of palm trees.

The general commenced the service. We did not burden ourselves with poem-readings. Nor did the general deliver long-winded sermons, which would have been impossible given Bitch's incessant barking.

Augusta and Cleet IV presented the rings.

"The vows and promises that you make to one another are at the center of the wedding service," the general said. "It is by your promises that . . ." The general looked up from his notes, red-faced. "Goddammit, will somebody do something about that dog!"

"Shut up, Bitch!" shouted Mama. The dog whimpered and lay on its stomach, paws stretched out in front of it.

"It is by your promises that you bind yourselves together husband and wife," the general continued. After the rings were exchanged, he clinched it: "By the authority vested in me as an ordained minister of the Evangelical Lutheran Church— as well as your commanding officer—I, Peter D. Loehr, now pronounce you husband and wife. The bride and groom may kiss."

The whole ceremony was done in under three minutes, with great military efficiency. It was only the second time I ever saw the general smile.

After the ceremony, Jack made a toast to me, I toasted him, then we toasted fallen comrades. "To fallen comrades," the group shouted. We raised our paper cups again and drank lemonade in silence.

Soon thereafter, everyone was gathered round the picnic table for the feast. Velvet sliced up the "mistake" sheetcake she bought at Publix for fifty percent off. "I knew Cleet IV would scrape all the icing off before anyone got to it," she shrugged. "So whether it said 'Congratulations to Tami & Jack' or 'Happy Retirement, Vernon,' I knew it wouldn't make a lick of difference."

Grandmama Marlene and Great-grandmama Charlene both praised the cake, saying it was moist.

One of the Crabtree boys tuned his phone to a country music station and we all milled about and visited.

"It's an honor to finally meet you, young lady. It's my understanding that you're tough as nails," the general said to Augusta. When they were finished with their conversation about Portugal, which the general led with great sensitivity and tact, he pivoted to a new topic, trained diplomat and conversationalist that he was. "So, you're graduating in a few months, I'm told. Then off to college, yes?"

"Probably not, sir."

The general, perplexed, looked at me before returning his penetrating gaze at Augusta. "Tell me about your test scores."

"Augusta got a 1580 on her SATs, a 34 on her A.C.T.," I said proudly.

"But my grades suck."

"Patton was a lousy student. He turned out okay," the general said. "So where to? Let me guess: the University of Virginia, like your father? Or are you looking at one of the Ivies?"

"I've decided to enlist in the United States Army, sir."

"Huh?" I said.

The general was taken aback.

"You're still in shock, Augusta," Jack said, gently placing his hand on her shoulder. "You ought to take the summer off. Chill. Swim. Bum around Europe."

"I'm done 'bumming around.'" She looked at Jack. "I feel the call to serve. Like you, like the general here, like my daddy, and his daddy before him and his before him. And like . . ." she paused and stared sharply at me. ". . . my mom."

"You're talking nonsense," the general said. "Take your wise elders' advice. Take some time off. Re-collect yourself."

"I'm as collected as I've ever been in my life."

The general sighed. "At the very least, stay in school. If you're really serious about the military—which by summer I suspect you won't be—go to UVA, they have an excellent ROTC program."

"I will enlist. In the infantry. There are more Minodora Grigorescus and Kalan Alis out there. And jihadists. Thousands more. And they need to be stopped."

"You're brave, poised and well-educated. A born leader. Like your father. We need you in the officer's ranks Stay in school."

"I'm done being a snob."

"Rubbish. Being an officer doesn't make you a snob; it makes you a leader. And you have the intelligence, moxie and bravery to lead. You're stayin' in school—and that's an order." The general pulled his phone out of his pocket. "When's spring break at your school?" The question sounded less like a question and more like a command.

She furnished the dates.

The general scrolled through his phone and clicked on a contact. "Lieutenant General Schoenberger, please. Major

General Peter Loehr calling." The general's eyebrows furrowed as he waited; the general was unaccustomed to being put on hold. Then he broke into a great big smile. "Look who's talking. The man was awarded a Purple Heart because he didn't have enough good sense to leave a building he was forewarned would be shelled."

The men's banter went back and forth until General Loehr finally said, "I have a candidate for you, Dale. She's coming in mid-March. She's the real deal." After he finished raving about Augusta, the general terminated the call and directed his piercing blue eyes at Augusta. "General Schoenberger is Superintendent of the United States Military Academy at West Point. You're going to see him during your spring break for a personal tour."

"Yes, sir."

Cleet IV approached, icing smeared all over his face and hands—just as Mama predicted. He shoved a present into Jack's hands. "Open it! Open it!"

Jack unwrapped the box: an oyster-shucking knife set and oyster grill pan. "You thought of this?" Jack asked Cleet IV, who looked over at me for a rescue.

"He got a little help from me. We figured if we're moving out to the Sea Islands, and we don't want to starve to death, we'd better learn to shuck oysters."

Jack raised his eyebrow at me. "I should probably down a couple dozen of those now. After all, our honeymoon starts in an hour."

"I've got something better than oysters in store for you, Jack," I teased.

More gifts were opened. The Crabtree boys presented us his-and-hers fishing rods. Grandmama Marlene and

Great-grandmama Charlene went in on a Bob Evans gift certificate. Mama, who wanted to give us her own gift, rose from the picnic table to make a speech. She was not a speech-maker, my mama. I worried that she might say something inappropriate in front of the general, which shamed me, as a person should never be embarrassed by his or her parents.

"When the health people come and evicted us from our home in Thurmond, I told 'em they could keep everything inside. A Gypsy don't get attached to her possessions. She moves on. But I lied. There was one thing they weren't getting. The only gift I ever got. The only one with any sentimental meaning for me. And today I pass it on to you, Tami and Jack."

Velvet signaled the Crabtree boys, who, both of them, brought gigantic boxes over to the picnic table. Velvet assigned Cleet IV the task of opening them with the new oyster-shucking knife.

Inside were gifts, each one wrapped in sheets of the *Crime Times* newspaper. I hadn't a clue what mama had in store for us. I handed my new husband the first gift. He unwrapped it. Beneath the paper was a Kraft marshmallow cream jar labeled "MONTANA." It was filled not with marshmallow cream but a black substance.

"What is it, Velvet?" asked Jack.

"Just you wait," Mama replied.

I unwrapped the second gift, a jar once home to pickled beets, now filled with a similar substance, though of a lighter hue. The words "RHODE ISLAND" were scrawled across a piece of masking tape.

The jars keep being passed to us, and the unwrapping continued—MISSOURI, OREGON, NEW MEXICO.

Everyone was baffled, 'cept for mama, who was relishing all

the suspense she was creating. Finally, as we were unwrapping ARKANSAS, mama explained. "I had a gentleman friend in the 1970s, with whom I done a bit of traveling."

"Ran away with is more like it," Grandmama Marlene sniffed.

"He was a dirt-collector," mama continued, ignoring her mother's quip. "Gathered dirt from forty-three of the fifty United States. 'A memory of the place,' Burnett always said. He collected samples from the same place in every state: interstate highway rest stops. He got black dirt from the mountain states, red clay dirt from Georgia, dirt from North Dakota with broken arrowheads in it, and so on. Personalized gifts for me from the only man I ever loved—the one true love I ever had, the one I thought would break the Vaduva single-woman curse."

Mama's voice trailed off as she struggled to maintain her composure. She swallowed hard. "I want you two to have them, as you have done this family proud by marrying and starting this union."

"Velvet tried for years to sell that dirt on eBay," Grandmama Marlene added, unnecessarily. "There weren't no buyers for dirt then, of course, just as there ain't now."

Mama ignored her mama's second put-down. "Now it's yours, baby. To display in your new home."

Jack and I both thanked Mama.

The general, the last to gift-give, cleared his throat. "I've known you both for a long time. And you are, without a doubt, two of the finest soldiers ever to serve under my command. Or *any* command. So, we'll start with ladies first. Master Sergeant Vaduva—or should I say, Master Sergeant Capers—you have served your country honorably and well. But, as you know, you abandoned your combat post to pursue your previous husband. Though you were never formally charged with desertion, in light of your recent service to your country, the stain of even the threat of a dishonorable discharge from the United States Armed Forces is, in my view—and the view of the Secretary of Defense—a stain wholly unwarranted. To that end, you are today hereby fully reinstated in the Army. Your record is blemish-free. Your pay, pension, and all other benefits—which were suspended when you abandoned your post in Afghanistan—are fully reinstated."

I could feel my eyes widening. I was barely able to contain my joy. I leaned in towards the general, preparing either to hug him, kiss him, or both.

"How much back pay she gets?" Mama asked.

"None of your business, Mama."

"I'm not finished, master sergeant. Now stand at attention."

"Yes, sir!"

"The Secretary of the Army has reposed special trust and confidence in the patriotism, valor, fidelity, and professional excellence of Tamara Vaduva Bland Capers. In view of these qualities and her demonstrated leadership potential and dedicated service to the United States Army, it is my honor, therefore, to promote you to the rank of Sergeant Major."

The general and I exchanged salutes.

"Congratulations, soldier."

My husband was glowing. I was shaking. My mama was weeping. "They gonna give Tami her back pay," she kept repeating to the elder Vaduva women.

The general turned next to my husband. "Special Agent Jackson Edgar Capers, I thought long and hard about a gift that was appropriate for one of the strongest, bravest, and inexplicably, only celibate soldiers to serve under my command. On this, your wedding day, I present to you this gift."

Mama cast a suspicious eye on my new husband. "You ain't never been with a woman?" Mama blurted as Jack unwrapped the package.

"I took an oath, Velvet."

She started laughing. "Wait till you see what my baby's got in store for you!"

"Stop that trash talk, Velvet!" Grandmama Marlene scolded.

Jack flipped through the pages of the *Kama Sutra*, turning the book sideways or upside down every few pages to better study its illustrations. "Thank you, general. This will indeed be helpful."

"And now, if you all will excuse my rushed departure, I am wanted back at the Pentagon." The general chopped his hand through the air three times, a signal to the pilot to fire up the engine. We said our goodbyes as the general walked briskly toward the aircraft.

"Now it's my turn," Jack said, smiling to the remaining guests. "If all of you would kindly excuse the bride and groom. I've got a honeymoon that I'm very, very anxious to begin."

"We'll sit out here and smoke while you two go to the shed," Mama said. "Then we can all ride back together and go to Bob Evans for dinner. We can use that gift card."

"Country fried steak for me," said Grandmama Marlene.

"It ain't gonna work that way, mama," I said. "You're leaving. All of you. Kids included. The Crabtree boys will see all of you back to the house on Legare Street. After you are gone, my new husband and me will have our honeymoon go. So, without further delay, adieu, or whatever it's called, all you now need to git!"

32.

Inside the cottage, the setting sun was barely visible through the palm trees. "Have you ever heard of Walter Benton?" he asked.

I indicated I had not.

"He was a poet. American. In 1943 he wrote a book of poetry called *This Is My Beloved*. An extended love letter to this woman he was obsessed with during the war years. The most passionate love affair of all time. Makes *Casablanca* look like a nursery rhyme. He tells her in the poems he needs her love 'more than hope or money, wisdom, or a drink.' He tells her he consumes her body and soul 'like a glass of sweet milk at bedtime.' When she's not at his side, he puts his arm around the emptiness beside him. He *really* dug this woman, Tami." Jack loaded a compact disc into the stereo. "So, as it turns out, my grandparents bought an LP in the 1960s from a saloon singer, guy named Arthur Prysock. He was from Spartanburg, not far from here. My parents used to see him in the jazz clubs, in the fifties, when things were segregated, and a few times in the late sixties, in Charleston, where they saw him perform live the CD I'm about to play you. Prysock reads verses from Benton's book against a jazz instrumental backdrop. The whole album is spoken word, in Prysock's silky, Southern growl. My grandfather played the record for me years later, when I was a teenager. I didn't get it then. Thought it was stupid and corny. It was only after they were long dead, both my grandparents, as well as my parents, that I gave the album another listen. When I was well into my twenties. It was the most erotic music I'd ever heard. I swore I'd play it on my wedding night."

"And now it's your wedding night."

"As you are about to find out."

He hit the button. Cymbals clanged gently to start the record, which unraveled at a slow, sensual rhythm. The electric bass strutted in. Then the voice of a baritone black man, the voice of a hundred-cigarettes-a-day smoker purred, *"I memorize you. Walking, as if to music. Your dress lies against the cheeks and hollows of your thighs like running water . . ."*

It is music for a go like I ain't never heard before. I felt the acceleration of my heartbeat. "I'm honored you saved this for me, Jack."

"I saved all of this for you," he said, sweeping his hands across the room, bathed in a pale golden late afternoon light, many of its objects in shadow. "Since I was in high school—when all my buddies starting getting regular sex—I've been collecting things for tonight." He pointed at the snack tray and mimicked Arthur Prysock's voice. "'Shellfish, watercress, black olives, wine, smoked cheese, currants in port, and preserved wild cherries.'" He laughed.

"What's so funny about the snacks?"

"That's all the food the love-struck guy in the poem puts out on a spread for his girlfriend—he even pawns his watch to buy her wine—you'll hear about it on track seven."

He pointed to the candles, easily fifty of them, scattered about the one-room cottage. "The antique zinc Latika lanterns I bought in Morocco—after passing on similar—but never exactly right—lanterns in India, Japan, Egypt, and elsewhere."

He pointed to the bedspread, a patchwork quilt made out of animal fur. "Sent fifty dollars a month to a Gullah woman down on Sapelo Island to find old secondhand fur coats nobody wanted—torn, stained, whatever—and chop them up. Saw it in a movie. Should we go test its softness?"

He grabbed me by the hand and ushered me to the bed.

"What is it I'm smelling on you?"

"It's called 'Creed Aventus.' Took me a decade to find. Almost as long to save up for: four hundred and fifty dollars a bottle. Saved it just for tonight."

I sniffed Jack the way animals do. "That stuff is amazing. My knees are getting wobbly."

He pushed me onto the bed. "You're smelling blackcurrant leaves, apple, pineapple, and 'bergamot.'"

"I smell oranges."

"That's the bergamot, I think."

"Nice." I inhaled again, more deeply this time. "I have a wedding present for you," I said.

"Give it to me when we're done."

"You waited this long. A few seconds' delay won't kill you."

"Yes, it will. I'm ready to explode."

"It'll take two seconds." I jumped out of bed and walk over to my backpack.

"A purse?" he asked when I returned. "That's my wedding present?"

"A souvenir from the mission. It's what's inside the purse that counts."

He frowned. "I recognize that purse." He ran his fingers

over the beaded faded burgundy bag with the embroidery and frayed tassels. "Was it Minodora's?"

"No."

"It's not one of Pepper's stupid 'Wine O'clock Somewhere' bags."

"No, but you're getting closer."

"Where have I seen that?"

"All the ladies in the Masked Oracle Society had them the night you and I were at Pepper and Stallings Boyell's house. Your gift is inside."

Jack fished through the bag. He burst out laughing when he pulled the piece of bark out of the bag. "You took this off the Pausinystalia yohimbe tree at Minodora's estate?"

"Just before the general's boys shuttled us back to the hotel. Nature's original date-rape drug."

"To use on me."

"If not you, someone. That's a save-it-for-a-rainy item if ever there was one." I winked at Jack.

"God, please, don't do that again. Pepper Boyell was always winking at me." He studied the bark. "I'm insulted you think I'm going to need it."

"Yes, you will, my husband, when you find out what I've got in store for you."

Jack chewed on the bark. He handed it to me. "Want a bite?"

"Why not? It's our honeymoon."

After we choked on the foul-tasting bark, he climbed out of the bed. "I need a beer to chase this down."

When he came back from the kitchen, he said, "Take off your clothes, Mrs. Capers."

When we were both fully disrobed, he lowered me

backward, onto the bed. He got into plank position, above me, and lowered himself slowly, like someone doing a push-up. Belly-to-belly, we lied flat, like two planks of two-by-four stacked in a lumber yard. Long passionate kisses to my mouth and neck. Nibbles at earlobes. Feet-rubbing. The kissing moved downward. When he entered me, I gasped. "Welcome to your first go."

"The first of many I have planned for this evening," Jack said as a bead of sweat dripped from his forehead onto mine.

For the next five hours, we had our goes—in all the ways Jack dreamed about since he was fifteen, as well as some new ways he learned about in the picture book the general gave him: we had goes in the bed, standing up at the snack table while refueling, and on the kitchen floor. We had goes from the front, from the back, right side up, and upside down. Panting Jack was so soaked with sweat we moved to the shower, where we had yet another go.

"Ready to call it a night?" I said as we stood next to the kitchen table.

"Re-charging with a little silat." My husband performed his slow-motion martial arts dance. "Then I'll have at least one more round in me."

As I nibbled on smoked cheese, currants in port, and preserved wild cherries, he said, "Two things."

"Shoot."

"Minodora said, 'as the crow is made for stewing, the dog is made for kicking.' What did she mean?"

"It's just an old Gypsy proverb. It's about human nature. Some people are saints, others slave-traders, and that's just the way it is."

"Harmless stuff, then?"

"Yes."

"And what about that incantation or whatever she hissed at Augusta. What did she say in Romanian?"

"I won't repeat it."

"Not harmless, stuff."

"No.

"Is there anything we can do about it?"

"Yes. Not talk about it and go back to bed—before the bark wears off."

He hoisted me over his shoulder like a caveman and brought me back to bed.

The bark's effects seemed to be wearing off. "No man can have seven goes, Jack. You need to regenerate your supply for the morning."

"This man can." For more than forty minutes he had me in the 'dragon position' we saw in the *Kama Sutra*. There was much wheezing and moaning and "summoning" on my new husband's part. But to my surprise and delight, he delivered. When we finally finished, I rolled over and massaged his jaw, "I have to get accustomed to an entirely new kind of combat fatigue. Not that I'm complaining," he said between breaths. "Sure as hell beats getting shot at."

"Glad you waited?"

"Am I ever, Mrs. Capers," he huffed as we slid under the mink quilt.

I spooned my new husband. "No chastity oaths were taken in my house when I was growing up, that's for certain. I admire you for that, Jack. That you waited for the right person. Mama actually encouraged me to have sex once I became a ninth grader. What mother does that? 'Men aren't attracted to women because we're interesting,' she used to say. 'It's only cuz we got the honey pot. Just as we're equally uninterested in them, 'cept for their wallets.'"

"That Velvet, she's a piece of work."

"One day I'll show you my zipper tattoo, which is at present all covered up discrete with hair. She put on me when I was fifteen. For now, I think I'll keep it covered. Maintain my mystery in your eyes. She was actually a skilled tattoo artist in her day, mama was. The tradition of Gypsies and tattoos goes back centuries. It's associated with sailors, low class people, rednecks, and criminals, tattooing is—at least here in the U.S. But where we're from, in Romania, it was a high art form. Tattoos were worn proudly—and almost exclusively—by fancy upper-class people, even royalty. Mama was famous across our county for one tattoo she used to do in particular, a beautiful fortune-teller, hair covered in a purple headscarf. A cluster of red roses at the ears. Big hoop earrings. People raved about the Gypsy's eyes: oversized, round, black eyes with long eyelashes. There's people all over Thurmond, Beckley, Lester, Mabscott—all across Raleigh County—who sport her artwork on their bodies. On their calves, backs, biceps, thighs, and buttocks. Of course, she hasn't done the work in years. After that rattler bit her and she lost her index finger, she couldn't grip the needles no more. *Any*more. Which is probably just as well. The world would be better off if there were fewer tattoo artists. It's always young people who put them on. And they're too dumb to look ahead to the time when young people turn into old people. And old people become fat people. There's nothing sadder than seeing one of my mama's former clients coming out of the payday loan store or the Hardee's and you see once-beautiful artwork all smeary now that their thighs or biceps have tripled in size. There was a second tattoo mama put on me when I was in high school, on my bottom. She tattooed the letter 'W' on my bottom, on each butt cheek. But I had it taken off. You had a good look at my bottom tonight, a close-up or two on several occasions. Did you notice any scarring from its removal? I went to a very reputable man in Charlottesville to have it taken off. He assured me it was invisible to the naked eye, the scars. Of course, it's not like I can get back there and see it up close, now can I? So, like Ronald Reagan said when he was negotiating nuclear arms agreements with the Russians, the best approach is to 'trust, but verify.' And there's no one I trust more than you to verify. Could I trouble you to take an up-close look and tell me if you see any scarring or not? Jack? I asked could you take an up-close look at my bottom. Jack? Jack? Why are you so cold?"

33.

"Stop beating yourself up, sergeant major," the general said as we walked behind the horse-drawn cart that carried Major Jack Capers' coffin to a burial plot at Arlington National Cemetery. There's no way you could have known Jack had myocardial ischemia."

"People with it display symptoms. He displayed them all— neck pain, jaw pain, shoulder pain, accelerated heartrates, shortness of breath, profuse sweating, nausea and vomiting, and fatigue. I should have been paying attention."

"We've been over this, sergeant major. He displayed the symptoms during P.T., during high-stress military situations, like when he was ordered at gunpoint to rape a teenage Greek girl, on your honeymoon, when he was exerting himself. Every member of the armed forces—and the human race—displays those symptoms under similar conditions. Every day. He was a soldier in peak physical condition. Pure muscle with no body fat—not some pack-a-day smoker who devoured Big Macs and fries and chocolate shakes all day. How were you to know it was genetic?"

"On the container ship he told me his parents died while he was still a boy. I should have asked what killed them."

"This stops now!" the general said. "Let's go say a prayer."

Around the burial site were clustered some two hundred

people: the elder Vaduva women, my children, Jack's Gullah friends from South Carolina and Georgia, classmates from Princeton and Yale, many of them now bigshots in New York and Washington, dozens of soldiers who had either served above, below, or alongside him. As planes descended on Reagan National Airport, General Loehr read from the holy book:

"When we were baptized in Christ Jesus, we were baptized into His death. We were buried therefore with Him. By baptism into death, so that as Christ was raised from the dead by the glory of the Father, we too might live a new life. For if we have been united with Him in a death like His, we shall certainly be united with Him in a resurrection like His."

After we declared our faith and asked the Lord to hear our prayers, the general continued, "Let us commend Jackson Capers to the mercy of God, our Maker and Redeemer. Into Your hands, o merciful Savior, we commend your servant, Jackson Capers. We humbly beseech you, a sheep of your own fold, a lamb of your own flock, a sinner of your own redeeming. Receive Jack into the arms of your mercy, into the blessed rest of everlasting peace, and into the glorious company of the saints in light. Amen."

"Amen," the congregants repeated.

Cleet IV and Augusta dropped bouquets of orchids onto their stepfather's coffin.

Nobody said much at the after-affair, held at the general's home in Manassas.

Mama sat alone, on the general's front porch, in a rocking chair. Her searing black eyes were locked in on me as she sucked on her Eve 120 cigarette.

I approached. "What is it, Mama?"

"The curse stands."

"Please, Mama. Not now. Not today."

"Two husbands buried. I told you the fate of our women, but you wouldn't listen."

"And I still won't. Not to you. Never."

"You got too big for your britches, girl. Joining the Army, marrying that country club man in Charlottesville, marring a man you barely knew and now living all alone, on your very own private island. If—"

"My children are with me."

"If you'd stayed home in Thurmond and done what I told you to do, had obeyed what was in the cards, you'd not have any of this heartbreak. It's time to go home, all of us, back where we belong."

"You go home. I'm staying in Charleston. On the island I swore to my husband I'd preserve. So, pack up your junk and put Grandmama Marlene and Great-grandmama Charlene in the vardo and head back to West Virginia if that's what you want to do. I'll sell the house on Legare Street and buy someplace nice to live in Thurmond. Me and the kids will visit. But I'm not going back there."

"And do what in Charleston? Find a third man to bury?"

"And live my life, Mama," I said as I walked away.

I went inside the general's house, upstairs to his daughter's room, where I sat on the bed and cried. Mama was right about the curse, of course. I reached into my purse and pulled out the bottle of Jack's expensive cologne. I sprayed a few drops on the back of my hand and sniffed. I had been doing this every few hours since his death to be reminded of his smell.

A ringed knuckle trapped on the door. Without waiting for permission to enter, the general appeared. "That sounded like a hot exchange with your mother."

"Mother-daughter conflict. Happens in every family."

"What are you going to do?"

"Go home?"

"'Home?' You're not really going back to South Carolina to live on a deserted island. Augusta's graduating and will go to West Point. She doesn't know it yet, but she is. Cleet IV will tire of the Robinson Crusoe arrangement in a month, and you know it. Stay here in D.C. I'll find you something at the Pentagon. You can put Cleet in a good local school."

"Gatuh Island is my home now."

"And if your country needs you, sergeant major?"

"I served my country with honor, general."

General Loehr unwrapped a cigar, then scowled when he realized that his wife permitted cigar-smoking only on the front porch rocker. "That you did, sergeant major," he said as he put the cutter back in his pocket. "But don't try to fool either yourself or me that life on a desert island is your calling. You're a soldier. You are called to serve."

"I will keep my mind occupied."

"Doing what? Raking sand, like some Zen priest in Okinawa? Then starting all over from scratch the next morning, after the wind upends everything?"

The general sucked on his unlit cigar. "If you're determined to stay there, maybe you'd consider writing a book? The most highly decorated female soldier ever to serve in the United States Army shares her thoughts on leadership, valor, and combat strategy. You could tell your war stories: Your surveillance work in Al-Karkh, which led you to those two fellas in Fallujah, which got you your Distinguished Service Cross. How you and Colonel Bland captured Corned Beef Hash, the covert ops, PSYOPs and advanced-interrogation techniques that got us

Abdul Kaziz Fazl, Farzaad Shah, Ibad ur Rehman–Ullah and Pepper Boyle, Minodora Grigorescu, and Kalan Ali. It'd be required reading at the Army War College—especially for female soldiers, among whom you are already a legend. Surely you already know this, Tami."

I thought—for a nanosecond—about the prospect of writing a book. It nauseated me. Not the writing part, though to be perfectly honest I dreaded that prospect, as I was no A-student in English. It was the prospect of bragging about my successes that did not sit well with me. Especially since, for every terrorist incident I may have thwarted, or soldier I fought with who survived, too many were carried off battlefields in stretchers. Too many innocent people, noncombatants each and every one of them, were murdered in restaurants or in subways and hotels—from Paris to Madrid to Jakarta to Mumbai to New York City. As the general sat there, waiting patiently for my response—which was not his custom—I wondered if perhaps he was right, that I might indeed get antsy on that island alone. But I wasn't going to share with him my doubts, certainly not today, as he'd have had me on a plane headed to a desert somewhere by sundown. I took the general's hand in mine. "Thank you for your concern and advice, sir. But I ain't no book-writer. We both know that." I stood. "I just want some rest, sir."

We walked down the stairway together, to the foyer. I signaled Augusta to round up Cleet IV. It was time to head back to South Carolina.

"Besides," I said to the general after all of us said our good-byes, "It's too soon for me to write my memories. People write their memories when they've got no history left to make. And I got more history-making in me, general. I can just feel it."

A Humble Request

V.J. Fitz-Howard would be grateful if you'd publish an honest review of *Shrimp & Grit*—even if it's just a sentence or two—on one or more of your favorite platforms.

Tami's Next Stop: PALM BEACH!

After conquering Charlottesville and Charleston, one would think Tami Vaduva—now sitting on a $500 million fortune—would be installed under a palm tree in the Caribbean sipping piña coladas. But in The Lost Cause, duty calls yet again.

Her mission: Infiltrate hermetically-sealed Palm Beach high society, inside which a mysterious expat known only as "El Obelisco" is conspiring to stage a coup d'état in his native country, Argentina.

Will Tami successfully apply her unrivaled military and seductive powers to "capture" the heart of El Obelisco and thwart his diabolical plans? Or will he capture hers instead, and test her loyalty to Uncle Sam?

To find out, join Tami on her romp through sun-drenched Florida, fancy Parisian restaurants and the grand boulevards of Buenos Aires in this crazy, bawdy, campy, action-packed comedy.

Order your copy of *The Lost Cause* today!

Made in the USA
Columbia, SC
10 September 2023